MARK ME

A REVERSE HAREM DARK COLLEGE
ROMANCE

ROYALS OF KNIGHTSGATE (DUET 1)
BOOK 1

SE TRAYNOR

SE Traynor

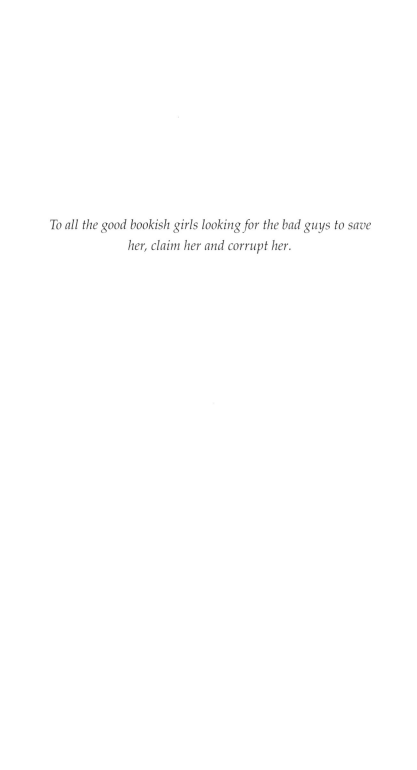

To all the good bookish girls looking for the bad guys to save her, claim her and corrupt her.

PREFACE

This is a contemporary Reverse Harem Dark College Age Romance. All main characters are 21. This is Duet 1 of a planned 3 Duet Series under the Royal Academy of KnightsGate Series.

The Royals of KnightsGate are essentially villains. If you are looking for a soft and cuddly read, you will not find it in these pages.

Mark Me contains adult and graphic content, and reader discretion is advised.

A full list of TWs for this book/duet can be found exclusively at my website: https://evenewton.com/se-traynor

Join my facebook group for real time updates on future reads: https://facebook.com/groups/evenewton

1

ALISTAIR

"**S**outh?"

One.

The lash hits my back, the iron beads on the tendrils breaking my skin. I smile.

"Present."

"West?"

Two.

"Present."

"East?"

Three.

"Present."

"North? Present."

The whip hits my back for the fourth time. I don't flinch, nor do I feel the pain.

Raising my hand, I let the cat whip fly over my shoulder to strike myself for the fifth time.

Five more.

The act of self-flagellation is a ritual the Cardinals have taken part in for centuries. It grounds us.

Focuses us. Keeps us from straying off the path laid out in ancient times.

Feeling the blood trickle down my back as I increase the pressure of the strike, I close my eyes and smile.

The sound of the other three whips is music to my ears. The sounds of the hushed rasps of horror and fear of the inter-Cardinals fill my black soul with something akin to joy.

Ten.

"Rise."

The other three Cardinals, in order, Benedict, Damien, and Charles, rise from kneeling on the cold stone floor of the underground chamber in the old townhouse in the middle of KnightsGate, one of the oldest cities in England and the founding town of our Order.

"Inter-Cardinals. Have you completed the tasks given to you?"

"Yes, Duke."

"Yes, Duke."

"Yes, sir."

"Yes."

Narrowing my eyes at South-West, I tilt my head. "Yes, what?"

"Sir. Duke. Your Grace. Sir?" His nervous tension makes my blood sing. He is the outlier here. He has been brought in as a test. The other three know their place and know it is here, learning at the feet of the masters.

"Pick one."

At my tone, he pales further. "Your Grace-Sir."

Snorting with cold mirth, I nod. "That'll do."

I fucking hate my title. Duke of KnightsGate. My father died last year, and the title landed on me as his only son. I'm twenty-fucking-one and a *Duke*.

Fuck. That.

The contempt is strong, but it isn't something I get to choose.

So I live with it.

Much like I live with the scars I bear from being my father's son. Both inside and out.

"Show me."

North-West is quick to move forward to show me the display laid out on the far side of the chamber.

Nodding, I place my hands behind my back, flexing my shoulders, relishing the burn. "And you went far and wide from each other to get these?"

"Yes, Duke. We have the receipts."

"Good," I murmur, taking in the objects with a critical eye. "Good."

Meeting North-West's eyes, I slap my hand on his shoulder. He is my little protégé. The one who will take my place when we leave here at the end of the year. "How are you getting on in Project True North?"

"She trusts me."

"Are you sure?"

"Yes."

"Enough that you can isolate her?"

"I believe so."

"Do you need more time?" I inquire, almost daring him to ask for more.

His eyes tighten. "No. I do not. I can isolate her."

"That's better." I move away from him,

Benedict steps forward, offering a sealed envelope. The wax crest of our order is prominent against the white paper, a sign that what lies within is meant for my eyes alone. I don't reach out immediately. Instead, I let the moment hang, stretching the silence until it's almost too tight to bear.

Even as my gaze lingers on Benedict, whose face betrays no emotion, I sense South-West's anxiety like a living thing. He shifts his weight from one foot to the other, careful not to look directly at me. He's weak —or at least he appears to be. In this room, in our world, appearances can be deceiving, and weakness can be a ruse as easily as it can be truth.

Finally, I accept the envelope. My thumb brushes over the seal as I break it, noting the meticulous way it had been affixed.

I scan the contents quickly. "The time has come." My voice echoes flatly around the stone walls of our sanctum.

"Yes, North," Benedict replies.

"And security?"

Charles offers his report with a crisp confidence that pleases me. "Exterior, and interior."

My mind races, plotting and planning steps ahead as I've been trained since childhood. "Good." I fold the letter and slip it back into the envelope.

It's time to remind them why they are here—why we all are here.

Charles's eyes burn with that unshakable loyalty

of his. "We're ready for whatever the Order demands, North." His voice is steady, but I catch the flicker of something dark in his gaze. Hunger maybe. Or ambition. Maybe both.

I look around at them, my fellow Cardinals, young men with old souls, bound by secrets and blood oaths and ancient lineages that date back as far as the mid-1300s. "Remember, we must be seamless in our execution. The Order's plans must advance without faltering."

"Yes, North," the three Cardinals say.

The inter-Cardinals remain quiet. They are here to observe now, not participate.

My eyes linger on South-West a moment longer than necessary. He is a freshman, whereas the others are second-years, and it shows. One day, he may move around the compass and end up at North, but he has a long way to go.

But that is why he is here.

"If any of you have doubts or fears," I say with a slight edge, "now is the time to address them." It's a test and a threat all rolled into one.

Silence meets my challenge. Good.

"Very well." I turn toward the exit, conscious of the stinging on my back with every movement—it's a reminder of who I am and what I must do. "You all have your tasks."

As I ascend from the depths of the room beneath the house into the deceptive brightness of day, I can feel the weight of responsibility settling over me. Alistair Gaight, Duke of KnightsGate and leader of an

Order that deals in shades of grey that often tend to be black.

It's a weight that's simultaneously invigorating and suffocating. But I don't let it show as we pull our shirts on, ignoring the lashes as if they weren't even there. Instead, I stride across the ground floor of the multi-million-pound townhouse on the edge of the main campus of the Royal Academy of KnightsGate with the confidence of someone who knows exactly where he's going and why. After all, that's precisely what they expect from me—assurance in the face of chaos.

From the window, I can see students lounging on the grass near the verge, the ancient KG building looming behind them like a fearsome watcher as their laughter pitches through the air. But it's all superficial to me. These are pawns in a much larger game—unaware of the currents moving beneath them.

Benedict Harrington, Earl of Cumberfold, falls into place beside me, silent, observant, my right-hand man. He doesn't need to speak; his presence is enough of a statement. We're partners in this inherited darkness, bound by blood, loyalty and ambition.

"Do you think he'll cave?" Benedict finally asks as Charles and Damien join us in the living room.

"He's close," I reply without hesitation. "But we'll push him right to the edge first."

Benedict nods, understanding without needing an explanation.

"What about Project True North?" Charles St.

James, officially Viscount Beaumont, asks crisply, his face unreadable.

I glance at him sideways. "North-West is sure he can isolate her soon."

"So he says, but if he fails?"

"He won't."

"You have a weird-ass trust in that kid," Damien Wraith, Baron of Mere, mutters as he slumps onto the couch.

Snorting as the façade of North Cardinal drops away, I turn to him. "I see myself in that asshole. What can I say? He's going to be a killer."

"You'd better hope so. You've got a lot riding on him. If he turns out to be useless, the Order won't be happy."

"If he turns out to be useless, I will burn him myself, and North-East will take his place. And if *he* turns out to be just as useless, then little South-West gets to shoot his shot."

"You're fucking mean," Charlie remarks with a laugh. "That kid practically wets himself every time you speak to him, Your-Grace-Sir."

Smirking, I breathe in deeply before I release it. "Call me that again, and I will kick your ass across campus so fast, you won't know what hit you."

"His presence here is of note," Benedict says, turning away from the window to study me intently. "Freshmen almost never get into the Inner Circle."

"Baptism by fire."

Ben shakes his head. "There's more to it that you're not telling us."

Fixing him with a death stare, I take satisfaction in seeing him back down. "If you needed to know, you'd know."

"Noted."

With narrowed eyes, I leave them to it, crossing through the marble-floored entrance hall and taking the stairs two at a time to push open the door to the last room on the first floor.

"True North," I murmur, taking in the light pastels and flowery prints. "Soon, angel. Soon."

2

EVER

Gothic spires claw at a sky so fiercely blue it looks like a promise. This is the moment I step onto the cobblestones of KnightsGate University, and my breath catches. It always does. This place is spectacularly beautiful. Beneath them, ivy creeps over ancient stones, whispering secrets of the past to anyone who dares listen. I adjust the strap of my backpack, feeling the weight of books against my back—my chosen armour in a world that demands more than I sometimes feel capable of giving.

Knight. Ever Knight.

My name is supposed to mean something around here, but I'm just another face in the crowd—a fact I savour more than my morning cup of coffee. My feet carry me forward, past students lounging on the grass on this lovely autumn afternoon with their laptops and textbooks, their laughter slicing through the warm air.

The library's towering doors beckon me from across the quad, the dark wood stark against the limestone buildings that house centuries of tradition. As I push open the doors, the scent of old paper and ink fills my nostrils, a perfume more intoxicating to me than any floral bouquet.

The hush of the sacred space envelopes me as I step inside. I find solace among the rows of leatherbound books and the quiet click of keyboards. The world outside, with its expectations and whispers, fades away. It's just me and the stories that have stood the test of time.

This is where I belong—in the company of words and wisdom, where the only legacy that matters is the one written on these pages.

Slipping between the stacks, I let my fingers graze the spines of countless books, feeling the weight of history in their pages. Each one is a silent witness to the Knight legacy—a name etched into every corner of KnightsGate University. It's an honour and a burden, a double-edged sword that cuts deep whenever whispers follow me down these hallowed halls.

The anticipation sits heavy on my shoulders, a cloak woven from generations of scholarly excellence and philanthropy, expectations as towering as the university's spires.

But unlike the grand statues commemorating my ancestors, there's no marble pedestal elevating me above the masses. My world has always been one of modest means—a home where love was plentiful but luxury scarce. Our family's dwindled fortune is renowned in elite circles. Our downfall, a scandal and a disgrace.

Sometimes, it was easier to get lost in the pages of my books and my studies because there was no doubt in my mind that this was where I wanted to go. But I'd kind of hoped to fly beneath the radar.

No such luck.

KnightsGate might be my birthright, but it's also my battlefield. Here, I fight for grades against the country's elite and for a chance to redefine what it means to be a Knight. Not the gilded figurehead of a bygone era but a student earning her place through merit, sweat, tears and the occasional caffeine-fuelled all-nighter.

They call me a Legacy. I'm pretty sure it's what got me in these hallowed halls, not my straight As and not a hefty donation. Just my ancestors building this place and educating the offspring of Kings and Queens.

Pompous, old assholes.

Some days, I wish I could go back and kick some sense into them. Everyone deserves a top-rate education if they choose it. Not just those born with a silver spoon in their mouths.

Grabbing the book that I'd reserved weeks ago for English Lit, that some dick has hung onto for far longer than they should have, this now means I have to work well into the night to refine the essay that I've struggled on for days without the right materials. Clutching it as I check out, I stride back out into the afternoon and across the quad to head home so I can get started.

"Hey, Ever! Wait up!" The familiar voice pierces through my thoughts, and I slow my pace just enough to let Lila catch up. She falls into step beside me, her rainbow hair streaks of colour against the fading greenery of autumn around us.

"Thought you could escape without me?" Lila teases,

"I was... waiting. You know, meandering slowly," I joke as we pick our pace over the grass verge and scramble down the shortcut to our student house on the corner. Across the square, there are mansions that rise from the ground, built on the fortunes of the old elite. But even my entire three-year University housing allowance wouldn't cover one month in one of those.

The chatter of students fades behind us as we approach our four-bedroom house, standing unpretentious and a bit scruffy at the edges. Its former semi-grandeur has now faded.

"Looks like we've beaten the others home," Lila observes, unlocking the front door with a key that's seen better days and is slightly bent.

"Or they're holed up in their rooms already," I say, almost hinting that *I* need to hole up. And fucking quickly. This essay won't fix itself.

"Wouldn't be surprised," Lila agrees, tossing her bag onto the sofa that's as much a patchwork of fabrics as we are personalities. "Everyone here needs those results."

"Oh, the joys of being the working class amongst the uber-rich."

"Sure. I wish my dad could buy me a degree, but it looks like this ho has to work for a living."

"Not just you," I remind her, but I see the eye roll when she turns her back. I love her, but she doesn't get it. She thinks I have a free ride when it's anything but.

"Crystal's probably knee-deep in her latest art project," Lila says, changing the subject to her scattered roomie. They have to share the largest room, but I don't think either really resent it too much, except maybe in the notorious month of spot tests that the professors love to give us. "I guess it'll be me and my books down here again tonight."

"Well, maybe hole up in the bathroom instead. Cassidy's likely concocting a new culinary experiment. If I were you, I'd run from another curried cupcake high tea."

"Fuck, nooo," Lila wails. "That was hideous."

"Bitches," Sasha says, coming into the room and making her way to the kitchen, her glasses pushed up her head as she carries a mountain of law books. "I'm here for snacks before I head back for Torts. I do not want to be around when Cass makes scrambled eggs with chocolate sauce."

"Ah, the joys of cohabitation," Lila chuckles, collapsing into an armchair that groans under even her slight frame. "Different as night and day, but somehow it works."

"Fun times," I agree. "I also have to bounce

upstairs. Professor Knobhead won't wait for this essay."

The girls snicker at the student-wide nickname for Professor Noblett. But he brought it on himself because he *is* a knobhead.

I stride into the kitchen, where the scent of burnt toast hangs like a bad omen. Sasha, with her dark curls bouncing, is scraping blackened crumbs into the sink, a scowl on her face that could scare off any first-year.

"Fire hazard again, Sash?" I tease, pulling out a chair at our second-hand table.

"Ha-ha," she retorts without looking up. "If this toaster had a spirit animal, it'd be a dragon."

"Or maybe you just have a unique talent for charring bread," Cass interjects from the fridge, her nose wrinkling as she sniffs a carton of milk. She's the mother hen of our group, always making sure we don't contract food poisoning or worse.

"Deadly talents aside, Ever, how do you handle those Fresher noble babies treating you like some kind of museum exhibit? 'Look, it's an actual Knight,'" she adds with a snort, mimicking a posh accent that earns a laugh from us.

"By reminding myself that I'm here to learn, not to entertain," I say, grabbing a piece of somewhat edible toast from Sasha's pile of carbon. "At least this is the last year of it. Everyone else is used to me by now."

"Easy to forget when they're practically curtsying in the corridors," adds Lila from the doorway.

"True," Cass agrees. "But seriously, don't let them

get to you. You've earned your place here, scholarship and all."

"Let's not forget the part-time jobs, side hustles, and—oh—the small detail of actually being smart," Sasha adds, chuckling as she finally prepares a piece of toast that doesn't resemble charcoal.

"Intelligence: apparently the most surprising Knight trait," I muse, biting into the toast and then cringing. Still, it's better than nothing, which is probably what I would've ended up with once I got stuck into my homework.

Before the conversation can delve deeper into whatever the fuck we randomly talk about, a knock at the door cuts through the comfortable hum of our home.

"I'll get it," I say, making my way to the door. Opening it, I reveal the familiar face of Alexander Kensington, Earl of somewhere in England—I think. I don't remember because it doesn't matter to me.

His blue eyes are alight with mischief. "Ever. Ready to cause chaos?"

"Huh?"

"Party at North House? Remember?"

Blinking, I try to recall. Shaking my head, I frown. "Sorry, no can do. I finally got that bloody text from the library, and I have to sort this essay out. It's a disaster due in tomorrow."

His smile widens. "Figured you'd bail, so... I brought biscuits!" He brandishes a tin triumphantly as he strides inside.

"Your timing's impeccable," I say, heading to the

kitchen to put the kettle on. "Tea?"

"Always," he grins, closing the door behind him as he follows me.

The familiar ritual of making tea, the sound of boiling water and the clink of spoons anchor me amidst the swirling aspirations that often threaten to pull me under.

"Your essay will be brilliant," Alex says, his tone turning serious for a fleeting moment. "You always manage to see things differently, Ever. That's your power."

"Thanks, Alex." His words lift me, a life raft thrown in the waves of doubt. "I'll hold onto that thought when I'm wading through edits at 2 AM."

Laughter dances around us, light and unburdened. In this small house with its cracked ceilings and mismatched furniture, I find strength in the echoes of shared dreams and whispered victories. My friends see beyond the name Knight; they see me.

Grinning at Alex, feeling a bit shy as he gives me a wink, that half smirk on his too-handsome face, I wish with everything that I could go to that party with him and maybe get tipsy enough to see past the books and make a move. I'm pretty sure he has friend-zoned me, but sometimes I can't be sure. I'm not that experienced in this area, and while no one knows quite how innocent I am, as that is no one's business but mine, I can't pretend to be something I'm not.

And something tells me I'm not Alex's type, which disappoints me more than I'd like.

3

BENEDICT

Clicking open a hidden folder, the glow from my laptop casts shadows across my room. Ever's room fills the screen. I lean in closer, like a spider watching a fly buzz into its web.

She's there, just as I knew she would be.

Ever, with her waves of golden hair spilling onto her shoulders, doesn't know about my prying eyes that watch her without her consent. It arouses me beyond anything I've ever felt before.

She's busy, hunched over her textbooks, scribbling notes. Her resolve to conquer academia is almost admirable despite everything stacked against her that she isn't even aware of yet. Almost.

Her brow furrows, her lips moving silently as she reads a dense-looking old book propped up before her. The fallen-from-grace scholarship girl, the part-time worker, the outsider in this place of privilege – Ever's all these things, and yet here she is, outworking everyone who's had it handed to them on a silver platter.

It's a game of chess, really, and I'm fixated on her next move. She's the queen on the board, powerful and yet blissfully unaware of the eyes locked on her every night. She doesn't see me, but I see all of her, caught in my digital net. In this twisted game, knowledge is power. Power I intend to keep.

Each tick of the clock stretches longer than the last. My fingers drum an impatient rhythm on the desk. Finally, Ever stirs from her scholarly trance.

She stands, stretches, the lines of exhaustion etched into her posture. The room's silence is profound, her chair whispering over the carpet as she moves. I'm perched on the edge of my seat, staring at my laptop, hungry for what's next. This isn't unusual, but it is different. There is something different about how she walks across the room. Expecting her to go to bed, I tilt my head as she flicks on the light to the tiny en-suite shower room. My gaze moves to the left of the screen, to the cam feed installed in the overhead light fitting. This invasion of her most intimate privacy makes my dick go hard.

With a simple motion that has her shirt slipping off her shoulders, falling away like autumn leaves, my breath catches in my throat as fabric pools at her feet, her skin bathed in the soft glow of the overhead light.

I lean closer, my focus narrowing to the figure on the screen. She doesn't hesitate, her movements natural, unguarded. Each piece of clothing she discards peels back a layer of mystery.

No one but us sees this side of her, this unvarnished truth.

Her luscious tits fall free from the plain cotton bra, and I lick my lips, eyes narrowed further to focus on her slipping her panties off to reveal her shaven pussy. It makes my blood spike. There are rumours about her experience. Rumours I'm desperate to prove one way or the other, but if they're true, then she does this for herself, which makes it even hotter, in my humble opinion. She isn't trying to impress anyone, she just wants to feel good. It is a fragile confidence that will soon be smashed until there is nothing left but a broken little girl begging to be loved.

I will be there.

We all will—the four of us.

The steam rises as she turns on the shower, a mist that veils yet reveals as she stands beneath the showerhead, unaware of me stalking her, spying on her every move. Her hands glide over her skin, slick with soap, and I groan.

"Fuck," I hiss under my breath as I slip my hand into the waistband of my joggers. With a tight grasp, I stroke my stiff cock in rhythm with Ever's languid movements.

She tilts her head back, eyes closed, lost in the soothing warmth of the water. Rivulets run along the curves of her body, over those ripe nipples on her gorgeous tits that are definitely more than a handful. I imagine my fingers tracing the same path. I'm mesmerised by the sight, the craving for her deep inside me grows insatiable with each passing second.

Tugging harder on my cock, the pressure builds, a lust-fuelled tension tight in my gut. My imagination runs wild with the thought of her soft moans filling my ears as I ram my dick into her soft, wet pussy. I lean into the pleasure, into the darkness that cloaks me, allowing myself to drown in the delicious sin of watching her unseen.

"Ever..." The hoarse whisper escapes me as I reach the edge of release; my grip tightens, and my breath comes in ragged gasps. I'm lost to the thrill, the power of knowing her secret moments, the intoxication of this stolen intimacy.

When she runs her hands between her legs, lingering for just a moment longer than necessary, the tension snaps. My orgasm crashes over me like the waves on a stormy shore. Placing my hand over the tip of my cock, I pulse out a stream of cum into my hand with a low groan, leaning back in the chair as I drain my balls, needing so much more than this.

But it isn't time yet. The sect has an order, and seducing Ever Knight so I can taste her skin, her lips, her pussy, isn't on that agenda. Yet.

The time will come.

"Quite the show," Damien drawls from the doorway.

Closing my eyes, I reach for a towel nearby and wipe my hand before shoving my cock back into my pants.

"You don't knock?"

"Oh, I knocked. You groaned your answer. I figured I'd better see if you were injured or whatevs. Seems you're just tossing your cock like a desperate loser."

"Says you," I snarl. "When was the last time *you* got laid?"

His eyes narrow and I know I've hit my mark. It's low and a bit mean, but fuck him and his lousy timing.

He comes closer, leaning in to stare at Ever climbing out of the shower. "Damn, I missed her. Lucky you, catching her at night. She's a morning shower girl, usually."

"Oh?" As much as I'd love to spy on her twenty-four-seven, it's not practical, not possible. We take turns, and it seems Damien has her all to himself in the dawn hours, being the fucking early bird he is, or rather the all-time bird. Asshole insomniac.

But Damien understands the rush, the hunger that drives us. We all do.

I lean back in my chair with a smirk. The sense of victory is sweet, a rich taste that lingers on my tongue. There she is, unaware and so beautifully oblivious that I've jerked off while watching her shower. It's a triumph that warms me more than the post-climax haze.

Ever steps out of the shower, droplets cascading down her skin like liquid diamonds, and I drink in the sight greedily. She wraps a towel around herself, and I lean closer to the screen as if I could breach the distance that separates us. My heart doesn't race; it prowls, a predator sated for now but eager for the next hunt.

She moves gracefully, the elegance of her movements never lost, even in the simplicity of drying off and getting dressed. We both watch, rapt, as she slips into pale pink pyjamas, the soft fabric hugging her form in all the right places. They're modest but somehow accentuate her understated beauty, her classic allure that doesn't scream for attention yet commands it all the same.

She truly is a goddess among women.

The light from her desk lamp casts a halo around her as she settles back into her studying, the golden strands of her wet hair spilling over her shoulders. The way she tucks a loose curl behind her ear with such focus, you'd think she holds the secrets of the universe between those textbook pages.

A sinister smile crosses my face at the dedication that makes Ever who she is—brilliant, independent, untouchable. But here she is, unknowingly touched by our gaze, by our desire. The game is deliciously dark, every move calculated, and the anticipation of what's in her future has me hooked.

A sharp breath fills my lungs, cold and bracing from the cool night air drifting in through the open window. I straighten up, my spine rigid against the leather of the chair. The Four Cardinals are bound by more than friendship. We're bound by a game that's twisted and dangerous, where the stakes are always high.

The shadows know the game as well as I do. They know there's no backing down, not when you're playing with fire

Ever might be my flame, but I'm learning how to control the burn.

4

DAMIEN

The pre-dawn darkness is the worst time. It's when the demons that haunt my soul come out to play. Ignoring them by trying to sleep is pointless, so I embrace them with an intensity that borders on physically painful. The marks left by the cat whip on my back from the ritual yesterday are not enough. My hand itches for the blade in the drawer next to my bed. Closing my eyes, I reach for it, knowing exactly where it is. Pulling it out of the drawer, I lean my elbows on my knees and plant my feet on the floor. The soft, plush bedroom carpet, too big for my liking, is warm and cosy. Everything that is an antonym to the cold harshness that fills my soul like an icicle slowly melting. My room is a cave of deep shadows and secrets. The handle of the knife bites into my flesh as I grip it tightly before slicing the blade over the inside of my arm. Clenching my fist so the blood will well up and spill out down my skin, sticky and warm, I smile softly and open my eyes to see the crimson stain my feet as it drips down. The pain is a whisper of a burn. Nothing more, nothing less. But it takes the edge off the demons, and that's all I need to move out of this room and not wrap a noose around my neck to end it all.

Alistair would fucking kill me if I did that. Even if I were already dead, he'd bring me back just to kill me again. He doesn't believe in failure or giving up. It's probably why I'm still here.

Rising, I drop the knife on the desk near the windows and pick up the laptop. Watching Ever last night after Ben had jerked off watching her in the shower was uneventful. But then it usually is.

And that's the way we like it. No drama. No assholes getting in the way. Just Ever being the good girl we know she is.

Flipping the top open, it's instinct now, this need to check, to watch. The screen blinks to life as I crawl back onto the bed.

The cams flicker to life, revealing Ever's room, and there she is—my obsession, my fixation. Not that she knows. The cameras are our silent witness, tucked away where she can't see, can't suspect. She trusts too easily; that's her weakness. She doesn't know the monsters who are watching her every move, who have integrated themselves into her life to keep her close. But that's the icing on the cake, isn't it? We will strike, and she won't even see us coming.

Watching her, this isn't about safety. This is control. Power. The thrill comes sharp and sweet as I invade her privacy without remorse. Ever is ours to watch, ours to know, even if she's clueless to our silent guarding. I'm her twisted guardian angel with charcoal wings and more scars than I can count.

Leaning back against the pillows, my gaze fixed on the screen as I watch her fast asleep slumped over her homework. She pulled an all-nighter and passed out. It's not uncommon around this University, especially not to Ever, but she won't touch the myriad of drugs floating around to help stave off the exhaustion. The rest of the house sleeps, but here in my darkened lair, I am god. I am voyeur. I am danger. As dawn creeps closer, painting the sky with streaks of grey, I know one thing for sure: No one touches Ever. No one but us.

My body is suddenly tight with a restless energy that won't let me sit still. Slamming the laptop closed, I rise again and barely notice the chill as I slip into a pair of black joggers after sleeping naked; I feel too warm. The weather is turning from what we in this country cling to as the end of summer and moving fully into autumn now.

The hallway is quiet as I walk towards the stairs, a shadow among shadows. The others are still asleep.

I reach the kitchen, the heart of this grand old townhouse we call home while we play our roles at KnightsGate University. The tiles are cold on my bare feet.

"Fucking hell," I grunt when I see Alex leaning against the counter as if he owns the place. "Bit early for you, isn't it?" My tone is sharp. This is *my* time. I don't battle those fucking demons to walk into the dawn and have company, for fuck's sake. He's got a mug pressed to his lips, steam curling up like whispers into the morning air.

"Haven't been to bed yet," he says with a slight slur.

"You look like shit." There's no concern there, just the blunt observation.

"Thanks," he mutters.

Grabbing a mug for myself, I fill it with black coffee, the dark liquid promising a jolt to my system. "Why are you here at this godforsaken hour? Don't you have your own home to go to?"

"Just got back from North House. There was a party..." He trails off, shaking his head. "Where's Alistair?"

"Asleep." The word cuts through the air like a lance. "Like you should be."

"No can do. Have something to say."

"Then say it and get your drunk ass out of my house."

"I'll wait for Alistair."

"No, you'll say it now and leave." This little shit is pissing me off on a grand level now, and that is never a good thing.

He debates that for a few moments and then takes another sip. "There's a bet."

"So what? There's always a bet."

"Not like this one. Or at least, the bet isn't new, but the target? You're going to lose your shit."

I freeze, the mug halfway to my lips. "Who?"

"Ever Knight and the prize? Her virginity."

27

His words hit me like ice water. A sick, boiling anger starts to simmer inside me.

"Is that so?" My voice is steady, but inside, there's a fucking hurricane whipping up in the destruction of my soul. Ever doesn't belong to them. She's ours.

"Who has the bet?"

"Eric, Robbie and that utter tosser, Stanley."

"Second-years?" I mutter, but it's not really a question. "Who the fuck do they think they are?"

"Entitled shitheads, much like everyone around here, but, like, ten times worse."

I see red. They don't get to fantasise about her, bet on her, like she's some prize to be won. They have made a very serious error in picking this target.

"Planning to send a warning?" Alex says, sipping his coffee as he sways from a raucous night of partying and booze.

"Better than that," I snap. "I'm planning to end them. Permanently."

Alistair strides into the kitchen, his presence like a shadow falling over us. He catches the tail end of our conversation, the tension coiling in the air like wire.

"End who?" His voice is calm but edged with something sharp, something dangerous. It's a tone that commands silence and demands respect.

"Ever's virginity is apparently up for grabs," I say without turning, staring Alex down, daring him to look away first. "The new bet by the asshole second-years who think they have a right to even breathe the same air as her."

Alistair's reaction is immediate when I turn

28

around to face him. His eyes darken like a stormy sky. "They want to steal what's not theirs?" There's a lethal chill to his words, a promise of violence that isn't just talk. He will fuck up anyone who tries to screw her, and the rest of us won't be far behind. One of us has to take her virginity - if the rumours are true, and as much as we'd all like to think it'll be us, we know it'll be Alistair. He won't give us a choice, probably not Ever either.

"If they so much as breathe in Ever's direction, they're dead," he hisses, the threat in his voice cutting through the silence of the kitchen. "Damien. We need to push forward. Now."

"Agreed." The word comes out like gravel, rough and edged with malice. My mind races with dark plans. "Those bastards think they can claim what's not theirs," I spit out, picturing Ever's delicate face, oblivious to the vultures circling.

"We're moving up the timetable."

I nod slowly. This is risky, but if we stop one group of jerks, another will pop up. Ever Knight is a prize in many ways, and if they think she has something they can take, something valuable, it will never stop. In a way, I'm kind of surprised it never happened before.

The shadowy corners of the campus that we keep a watchful eye over, no corner left in the dark, just got a hell of a lot more murky, and Ever's would-be conquerors better watch their backs, because for Ever, we don't play by the rules. We write them.

5

CHARLES

The moment I slam into the kitchen, it's like walking onto a battlefield. The air's thick with tension, an unspoken alarm screaming through the silence. With his body rigid, Damien is propped against the counter like he's trying to hold up the world with his back. Alistair is looming like a dark god, his face of thunder telling me that shit is about to hit the fan.

"What's going on?"

Alistair's gaze pins mine, and I try not to flinch. I'm not scared of him, but he is slightly violent in the unpredictable sense. I'll slice your throat without a second thought and walk away, but Alistair will stick around to mutilate your corpse and probably burn it for shits and giggles.

"It's Ever," he starts, and the way he says her name, like it's something holy, something endangered, makes me straighten up.

"What about her?"

"A bet," he growls, the word like a bullet. "Stanley and those other two idiots are planning to see which one of them will take her virginity "

I feel it then, a red-hot surge of anger, a clawing protectiveness over something that belongs to us. "Are you fucking joking?"

"Does my face look like Jack Whitehall's to you?" he snaps and runs his hand through his hair as he stands rigid, his back straight as a board, eyes blazing with that aristocratic fury only he can muster.

The sound of footsteps breaks the charged silence, and Benedict strolls in, all casual like he's not stepping into a war zone. He leans against the doorframe, his gaze flicking over us, taking in every tense line of our bodies before settling on Alistair, who looks like he's about to break someone's face.

"We need to move faster."

"We were just saying that when you came in," Damien says, eyes on Ben.

I lean against the cold granite of the kitchen island, trying to keep my cool. My hands twitch with the urge to do something, anything.

"We need eyes on Ever. Everywhere she goes, every second." My hands flatten on the marble countertop, the cool surface grounding me as I map out the strategy in my head.

Ben quickly catches on that the players have moved and not in the direction we were anticipating.

"Every corner of campus until we are in a position to play checkmate."

Damien leans against the wall, his arms crossed

over his chest, but I see it—the glint of approval in his steely gaze. He doesn't have to say shit for me to know he's got this covered. We all do.

"In the meantime, any prick who even looks her way answers to us."

Benedict's voice slices the silence, low and even. "Surveillance in shifts. No blind spots."

"I'm taking this directly to the rot of this root," Alistair declares, shoving up the sleeves of his designer shirt. "This isn't something we sit and wait out."

"The sect..." His furious gaze pins lasers onto mine like a deadly weapon.

"*I* am the sect at this University."

"Understood," I murmur, dropping my gaze.

"Fuck watching," Alistair snarls, making us all jump slightly. "We need to be proactive. Distract and divide." His dangerous eyes gleam.

"Agreed," I say and then glare at Alex. "You. She knows you and trusts you. Keep those assholes away."

Alex meets my gaze with something hard in his eyes. My insides twist because I know he's got a soft spot for Ever. Not that he would ever admit it out loud. I don't know if Alistair knows and just doesn't give a shit, but it's there for me to see, if no one else.

He nods once, sharply. "I've got it."

Alistair looks ready to tear someone apart with his bare hands, and I know he's not going to just stick to the shadows. He's too much of a predator for that.

"We need a roster," I say, taking charge before this

32

becomes an all-out brawl about who does what first. "Two on Ever, two on Stanley and his crew. Alistair and Damien are on campus this morning anyway, so you two can deal with the three pricks."

Damien nods, his jaw clenched hard enough to shatter stone. "We'll handle it," he says in that cold, calm way of his that makes you know he means business. He doesn't flinch, doesn't waver, just fixes Alistair with a steady look.

Alistair's eyes, dark and dangerous, flick over to Damien. They understand each other, these two. Predators recognising another's territory.

I watch the silent communication between them, like they're speaking in some sort of code only they understand. It's chilling and effective. Benedict is still leaning against the doorframe, but I see the way his eyes have narrowed, like he's calculating every possible outcome in his head. He's always three moves ahead.

"Ben and I will take the afternoon shift," I say, slipping naturally into the role of organiser in the middle of the shitshow.

Benedict pushes himself off the doorframe and steps into the centre of the room as if to seal our dark pact with his presence alone. "We've got a window before this shit escalates," he says so cold, I shiver. "Let's use it to our advantage."

Tension coils tighter in my gut, but it's mixed with purpose now. It feels good to be moving forward with the plan. I hate sitting idle. Always needing to move, to do something, anything to stop the gnawing desire to hurt people every chance I get. It's a toll that takes a mental hit, but I shove it aside.

"We need to be smart. Clean. No fuck-ups," I add, even though it's not necessary. No one dares fuck up on the sect's watch. We might as well take our own lives and be done with it.

Alistair nods once, sharp and decisive.

Damien's eyes meet mine, and there's an understanding there.

It's settled, then. A plan—rough, frantic, but it's something. A shield thrown up around Ever whether she wants it or not because that's what you do when someone you have everything riding on is thrown into the lion's den—you become the damn beast that protects her.

6

EVER

I'm a heartbeat away from being late, and my breath comes in short bursts as I dodge bodies in the frenzied hallway of KnightsGate University. This fucking paper burns a hole in my laptop. My trainers squeak against the polished floor, begging for traction as I weave through clusters of students who move like glaciers.

"Excuse me," I mutter, side-stepping a backpack someone's dropped in the middle of the chaos.

Finally, I burst into the classroom just as the clock ticks its final warning. I slap my assignment submission slip on the professor's desk, my chest heaving, relief flooding through me. That's one deadline that is not going to kick my butt today.

Glad that I decided to take a break and have a shower last night instead of this morning, I would be sitting here unwashed if not for that. I overslept, which almost never happens.

The spot test is a blur of words I speed through,

acing it with time to spare. When the class ends, I barely register the sighs of relief around me before I shove my notebook into my bag and bolt up. There is no rest for the wicked—or those who fear being on time is being late.

I'm out the door, and the world shifts from the stale air of academia to the crispness of autumn outside. The quad is a battlefield of social hierarchies, which even the elite have within the elite, and frisbee games, but right now, it's just an obstacle course between me and my next class, which is, of course, on the other side of the campus. My feet pound the grassy paths as I join the stream of students, all of us reduced to salmon swimming upstream to whatever waits for us in Lecture Hall A, B or C.

"Hey, Ever!"

A male voice shouts, but I don't turn. I can't afford another distraction. There's only forward, only the push to keep moving, to stay afloat in this sea of ambition and expectation that is KnightsGate University.

I cut across the quad, my thoughts a jumbled mess of due dates and essays. Three guys catch up to me, surrounding me, making my heart leap.

Sighing inwardly, I keep moving, forcing them to move with me. These three second-years are complete tools. Entitled rich kids with low-ranking titles, which gives them a chip on their shoulders the size of the Eiffel Tower, amongst the Dukes and Earls that adorn these hallowed halls. Okay, well, *one* Duke. I don't think there's more than one here.

"Ever!" Eric's voice booms over the crowd. His idiot friends, Robbie and that complete tosser, Stanley, move in closer. Wealth and trouble rolled into one trio, with reputations that cling tighter than shadows at midnight.

"Look what we have here," Stanley smirks, circling me like a shark. My heart kicks up a notch, but I stand my ground. His eyes dance with dark amusement, and I'm suddenly the main act in their twisted show.

"Party at ours tonight," Eric says. "You're coming, right?" The question doesn't sound like a question at all. It's an expectation, a demand wrapped in faux-politeness.

I glance around to see students slowing down to catch a bit of the drama, their whispers like static in the air, that they know something I don't. The second-years' gazes lock on me, predatory and gleeful. I'm a deer in headlights, but I won't let them see me flinch.

"Thanks, but no thanks," I say, my words slicing through the charged atmosphere like a blade. I grip the strap of my backpack a little tighter, an anchor in this chaos. "I've got too much on my plate."

Mentally shaking my head that I had to go and explain when I don't owe them shit, I press forward.

"Come on, Ever," Robbie coaxes, his tone low and smooth like silk. His eyes try to meet mine, but I dodge the look. He's playing a game I don't want any part of.

"Seriously, you need some fun," Stanley insists, stepping closer, his hand brushing over my bum.

"Not tonight."

"Don't be a pussy. We're talking an epic night."

I shake my head, wondering what I have to do to get these guys out of my sphere. "Not interested," I state, louder now, hoping my firmness masks the uneasy tremor I feel inside. They have to take the hint, they just have to. No one is helping me. If anything, they're egging them on.

"You should feel special," Stanley murmurs, close to my ear.

"Pass," I retort, pushing past them, and they let me go, but I should've known better. The air's ripe with the stink of their arrogance, and my gut's doing somersaults as they close in again. A suffocating feeling creeps up my spine, their circling forms boxing me into an invisible pen right smack in the middle of the quad with everyone watching.

"Look, I said no." My voice doesn't sound like mine—it's a whisper shouted over a cliff, lost before it ever really had a chance to be heard.

"Aw, come on, Ever. Don't be such a prude," Eric jeers, his words slapping against my last nerve. They're too close now, too fucking close. Their laughter is the sort that says they're not used to being denied anything—least of all by a girl like me.

I want to scream, but I won't give them the satisfaction. I won't.

"Ever looks scared," Robbie starts, but gets cut off by a snort from Stanley.

"Scared? Nah, she just doesn't know how to have fun."

"Trust me, Ever, you'll love it," Eric adds, leaning in closer than comfort allows.

The panic is ready to claw its way out of my throat, when two more guys join the groups surrounding me.

"Fuck off," one of them snarls, and I take a sudden step back as I recognise the Duke of KnightsGate, Alistair Gaight, stepping up to my defence. I've never even spoken to him before.

The guy beside him is silent but screaming volumes. Damien Wraith, I think. His stance is a wall, unyielding and cold. They don't need to say much; their presence alone speaks a language of power that these second-years clearly understand but are stupid enough to challenge.

"Fuck off, Alistair," Stanley spits out, his voice full of bravado or arrogance, I can't tell which. But even as he says it, his eyes dart nervously between Alistair and Damien, like he's second-guessing his choice to play the tough guy.

"Or what?" Alistair challenges with a smirk that doesn't reach his eyes. Those icy blues are all business, and I realise that beneath the designer clothes and polished exterior lies a predator. He doesn't need to throw a punch; his presence alone is a weapon.

"Or we'll—" Stanley starts, but he's cut off by Damien's quiet, bone-chilling chuckle.

"Try us," Damien says, but it's not a threat; it's a dare.

The air is thick with tension, my earlier fear replaced by a strange sense of security standing behind these two imposing figures. I don't know them, but right now, they're the shield between me and the bullies who have made me their target today.

The first punch flies, swift and brutal, shocking me at the suddenness with which it was thrown. Alistair's fist connects with Stanley's jaw, the sound a sickening crack that ricochets through my bones as my mouth drops open.

He stumbles back, surprise etched on his face before it contorts into rage. "Fucking cunt!" he yells, swinging back wildly.

Damien moves then, a shadow slipping through twilight. His own strike is precise, a coiled spring of pent-up energy releasing in a devastating uppercut. Stanley crumples like a marionette with cut strings.

"I said fuck off," Alistair growls, standing over the downed guy. His voice is ice, his stance unyielding. "I dislike having to repeat myself." He crouches down and grabs Stanley's shirt in his fist. "If I have to say it a third time, your mother won't be able to find all the pieces to bury you in the family vault."

Gulping at the chilling threat, I stumble back.

What the fuck is this?

But I can't tear my eyes away.

"Go find someone else to fuck with," Damien says, his tone so cold it could break ice.

The second-years scramble away, leaving behind a trail of wounded pride and muttered threats.

I'm trying to slow my breathing, trying not to freak out completely, when Lila is beside me, her rainbow hair a blur as she scans me from top to bottom.

"Ever, you okay?" she pants, eyes wide with concern. "I heard Stanley and those other two idiots were harassing you."

"So you heard it, but no one bothered to help me?" I spit out, but my gaze lands on Alistair and Damien, my two knights in dark armour.

My gaze locks with Alistair's, and it's like time stands still.

There's a flicker there, something possessive, something that tells me he's not done with me yet.

But then he breaks away, his back straight, every inch the Duke he is, with Damien gliding silently at his side. They don't say a word, just leave a trail of questions in their wake.

"Whoa," Lila whispers, elbowing me gently. "Did they fight off Stanley?"

"Yeah," I mutter. But why? And what does it mean for me? Probably nothing. They probably just hate Stanley as much as I do.

Before Lila can question me further, Alex races up, his easy smile a welcome relief from the tension. He looks like shit, and the fumes of stale alcohol are all around him. I guess he hit up the party at North House without me.

Not that I should have a problem with that.

But I do.

"Ready for the next round of torture?" he asks, nodding towards the looming building of our next classes.

Lila winks at me before answering for us both, but I know there are more questions lurking in the depths of her overactive brain. "Sure. Let's go."

We fall into step with him, and I try to lock away the image of Alistair's intense gaze, the silent threat of Damien's presence. But they're etched in my mind, darkly fascinating, drawing me in despite my better judgement.

7

EVER

The second the door shuts behind us, my shoulders sag. "God, I'm fucked," I mutter, kicking off my shoes without bothering to aim for the rack.

"Tell me about it," Lila groans right next to me. We shuffle into the house like we're wading through mud.

We trudge up to our rooms, and I chuck my bag somewhere near the desk and collapse onto the bed. The mattress grabs hold of me like it missed me all day. I let out this long sigh, trying to get my head straight.

Again, I think of Alistair and Damien and how they swooped in like some dark lords. It gives me a shiver, not all of it fear.

But the question remains: why? I frown at the ceiling, tracing cracks with my eyes. The Duke and the Baron. What's their side of this game?

I know it has to be a game. Stanley and co were definitely goading me into something, bullying me even to go to this party. It wouldn't surprise me one bit if I showed up and no one else was there. Just me and an empty house, feeling like a prick. It's not the first time I've been bullied, it probably won't be the last. I'm too reserved, too shy. Lila kind of saved me from that when we became friends. She has a mouth on her that would put a blush on a sailor's cheeks, so no one dares to talk back to her. She protects me.

But then in swoop Alistair and Damien, two total strangers, two of the most popular guys on campus, and I feel like theirs is an agenda I'm not familiar with. Alistair's gaze, when it locked onto mine, was... raw. It's the only way I can describe it.

I roll over, pressing my face into the pillow. The fabric smells fresh from the laundry yesterday, and I sigh. I've got half a mind just to pass out and forget the world for ten hours, but there's a knot in my stomach that won't let go.

A sudden sound jolts through the floorboards, followed by a tang of something burnt that scratches at the back of my throat.

"Shit. Sasha? What have you burned now?" She is the world's worst cook. I'm on my feet before the words finish their echo, opening my door to a stronger stench. "Fuck!" Adrenaline kicks my heart into overdrive, and I move fast.

Stumbling downstairs, followed by Lila, my hand skids along the rail, slick with sweat or terror.

"Fire," I gasp as we tear through the living room to the kitchen.

"Ever! Ever!" Lila's voice is a sharp stab of reality. I can't see her, but I know she's close, lost in the smoke like I am.

I launch myself towards the danger, towards the heat that wants to sear the flesh from my bones. "Out! Get out!" It's all I can think, all I can scream.

The kitchen door is open, and holy shit—the flames are a live thing, all teeth and claws, devouring the room. Heat slams into me, so fierce it's like a physical blow, and for a second, I can't breathe, can't think. I can't even see where it's coming from.

"Fuck!" It's all I can manage again, a strangled curse that gets swallowed by the roar of the fire.

It's everywhere, climbing the walls, licking at the ceiling, and turning everything it touches into an inferno. My mind's racing, screaming that this is bad, so fucking bad, and I'm here, right in the middle of it.

I spot the fire extinguisher, its red body a beacon of hope against the chaos. With no time to hesitate, I lunge for it, fingers clumsy as I yank the pin free. My hands shake—I've never done this before—but it can't be that hard, right? I aim the nozzle at the base of the flames and hope for the best.

"Come on, come on," I mutter as I squeeze the handle, and foam bursts out, smothering patches of fire. But it's like attacking a dragon with a toothpick.

"Work, damn you!" Desperation gives strength to my voice, to my grip on the extinguisher. The flames hiss and spit, angry at being challenged. They're not backing down. Neither am I.

"Ever! What the fuck? Get out of there!" Lila's cry barely cuts through the roar, but I can't look back, can't take my eyes off the flames before me. This fire will not win. It can't. It's us or it, and I've got too much riding on 'us.' My whole house cannot burn down.

The canister splutters, empty, useless in my hands. My heart slams against my chest, a drumbeat of dread as the heat wraps around me, a suffocating embrace.

"Ever!" Lila's voice shatters the crackle and pop of the fire. She skids into view, eyes huge and reflecting orange horror, grabbing my arm and yanking me away.

"Fuck," Lila breathes out, her usual calm shattered into a million sharp pieces. She's right there with me now—in the thick of it, where every second counts and the wrong move means game over. "Kitchen's screwed!" she screams. "We need to get out."

"Go!" I shout, my voice hoarse with smoke. There is nothing else we can do. As if breaking from a trance, we turn on our heels, the heavy kitchen door slamming shut behind us, and we sprint for the front door.

I yank my phone from the back pocket of my jeans, almost dropping it in my haste. My fingers, slick with sweat, fumble over the screen as we burst through the door and into the cool evening air. I hammer the numbers 999 into the phone, pressing it against my ear.

"Fire," I gasp out the moment the operator answers. "There's a fire at 55 Gate Close!"

"Hurry," Lila shrieks, her voice trembling next to me. She's never been one to lose her shit—the girl who can recite Shakespeare at the drop of a hat is now struggling to string a sentence together.

"Are you outside the building?" the operator asks all business.

"Yes," I confirm, dragging in lungfuls of fresh air that taste like freedom compared to the smoky prison we've just escaped.

"Good. Stay there. Help is on the way."

"Thank you," I whisper, ending the call. My hands shake, but not from the cold—it's pure, undistilled terror. I clutch the phone like a lifeline as we back away, watching the beast roar and ravage everything we hold dear that used to be our sanctuary.

"Where the fuck is everyone else?" I whisper, glancing around. "We need to go back inside! What if they're sleeping or can't move?"

"No!" Lila says as I take a step forward. "Cass and Sash had later classes and were going to the pub after. Crystal went home for the weekend? Remember?"

Nodding slowly, stiffly as I remember.

"But what if—"

"Don't!" She shakes her head, her eyes wide. "Don't go there."

I can only nod again, gripping her hand tight because I can't find the words. There's nothing to say that can make this right. We're just two broke college students with our house on fire. Where the hell do we go from here?

The squeal of the sirens is deafening, and I guess that's one plus. At least Fire and Rescue is here.

"Is everyone out?" one of the firefighters yells.

"We think so," I manage to say, my gaze scanning the group quickly, counting heads as we now have a growing crowd come to gape at our utter misfortune.

"Fuck, there goes everything," Lila mutters next to me, her voice hollow. It's not just about the material stuff—the clothes, the books, the countless cheap trinkets we've hoarded over the years. It's the loss of safety, the certainty that used to wait for us behind these walls.

We're alone in this, truly alone. The flames dance in the reflection of our eyes—they don't care who you are or where you come from. They just consume and move on, leaving you to pick up the pieces of a life you barely recognise anymore.

Lila's grip on my arm is iron, her nails digging in through the fabric of my jacket, which I forgot to remove. My feet are clad only in socks, cold against the pavement, but I barely feel it, numb from the shock and heat that's still pressing against our faces even as we stand across the street.

"Shit, Ever, what the hell do we do now?" Lila's voice cracks and I turn to look at her. Her eyes— usually so bright with plans and laughter—are dull and scared.

I shake my head, lost for words. My phone is a dead weight in my hand, useless after the call. We've done all we can, and yet it feels like nothing at all. The house continues to burn, our lives turning to ash.

"Fuck!" I hiss, the anguish bubbling up. I fight it down, hard. There's no space for breaking apart, not yet.

8

EVER

Watching as the firefighters shuffle in and out, I'm numb. Sasha and Cass joined us a few minutes ago, having already heard about the fire from the pub. Word travels fast around here; I didn't even get a chance to call them before they barrelled over.

The lead firefighter, a stocky man with soot smeared across his cheek, approaches us.

"Good thing your landlord wasn't skimping on safety," he grunts, nodding towards the charred remains of what used to be our kitchen. "That fire door did its job. Kept it mostly contained."

Lila's fingers twitch beside me. Sasha's brow is furrowed, lips pressed into a thin line. Cass stands a little apart, arms wrapped tight around herself like she could physically hold off the cold reality setting in.

"Unfortunately," the firefighter continues, breaking through the haze of shock, "you can't stay here. Not with all the fire and smoke damage. You're going to have to find somewhere else for now."

"Where, though?" Sasha's voice is a whisper, lost amidst the crackling tension.

The four of us huddle together outside in the growing twilight.

"Shit," Lila mutters. "What do we do now?"

I glance at the faces of my friends, seeing my worry reflected back at me. We're supposed to be smart and resourceful – we're the students who ace exams and tackle complex theories – but none of that matters now. We're just four girls, five, including Crystal, who isn't even here to survey the damage, suddenly homeless.

"We need a place to crash," Cass states, breaking the silence that has enveloped us.

"Yeah, well, that's obvious," Lila snaps, frustration edging her tone before she sighs, regret softening her features. "Sorry, this is just... fucked up."

"Understatement of the century," I mutter.

We fall silent again.

"Let's just think," I suggest, even though my brain feels like it's stuffed with cotton. "There has to be somewhere we can go."

Lila blurts out, her voice bouncing off the cold brick walls of the building that's no longer our safe haven. "Someone must have a sofa free or something."

"Yeah, one sofa. There's four of us," Sasha snaps.

"Three," Cass mutters, her eyes glued to the screen of her phone. A second passes and her expression morphs from hope to resignation. "Okay, Mark says I can crash at his. But..." Her voice trails off, and even in the dim light, I see the guilt flit across her face at her boyfriend's offer.

"But what?" Lila presses, her brow furrowing.

"It's in his bed," Cass explains, biting her lip. "So, just me."

"That's good. Good," I sigh, trying to swallow down the bitter taste of envy. At least someone's got a stroke of luck tonight. We all manage weak smiles, knowing better than to hold it against her. She's got a port in the storm; the rest of us are still adrift.

"Okay, what now?" Sasha's voice pulls me back to reality.

"University housing office," I blurt out, "They have to help, right?"

"Let's hope so," Lila adds, her tone not quite matching her optimistic words.

I fish my phone from my pocket and find the number I saved back in fresher's week—just in case.

"KnightsGate University Housing Office, how can I assist you?" The voice on the other end is crisp, detached. It's the emergency after-hours staff. I don't hold out much hope for this, at all.

"Hi, this is Ever Knight, final year student. We've had a fire at our place off campus. Is there anything you can do?" My voice trembles, and I try not to cry. This isn't my strength. I'm the book girl, not the one who solves real-life problems.

"One moment." He disappears, and I wait, tapping my foot impatiently.

"I'm afraid there are no available first-year dorms," the voice replies with zero sympathy or further help.

"Can you double check, please?"

"There's nothing. Private landlords handle off-campus housing. You'll have to make your own arrangements." The finality in his tone slams into me hard. He doesn't give a flying shit.

"Please, isn't there anything?" I press, my words bordering on begging.

"Try calling back during office hours on Monday. Goodnight." Click.

"Asshole!" I spit out the word as if it might rid me of the sour taste of rejection.

"Guess that's a no?" Sasha asks, eyeing me warily.

"Big fat no."

"Great," Lila mutters. "Just great."

"Ever!" Alex calls from the other side of the road. I don't think twice and run to him, needing something, some*one* who can tell me this is going to be okay.

"Alex!" My voice breaks on his name.

I throw myself at him, wrapping my arms around his broad frame. He holds me, but there's no passion in his embrace, no tightening of his arms. It's a friendly hug, and that's all it is. It just makes me cry harder. Not that I'm in love with him or anything, it only drives home that I'm all alone.

"Shh, don't worry," he murmurs.

Tears sting my eyes, trailing down my cheeks.

"All right, ladies!" A firefighter's voice cuts through the haze of my self-pity, and Alex lets me go, placing his hand on the small of my back as he crosses us back over the road. "You can head in to grab some things, but make it quick. We can't have you staying in there."

"Thanks," Sasha says, tugging her jacket tighter around herself as we turn back toward the house that's no longer a home.

"Keep it to one bag each," another firefighter adds.

"God, what a mess," Lila whispers as we step over the threshold.

Smoke clings to our clothes as we trudge up the stairs, each step heavier than the last. My mind races with where I'll crash tonight, but it's like running in a dream—slow, getting nowhere. One thing at a time. Pack and at least have some stuff to keep me warm if I have to sleep under a bush tonight.

We reach our rooms, and it's a grab-and-dash job. I shove jeans, shirts, and anything I can into my bag— it all feels so trivial now.

"Grab my bookbag and shove whatever you can in, please," I mutter to Alex who has followed me into my room. "Definitely anything that belongs to the Academy."

"Sure," he murmurs, distracted as he checks his phone. "Got somewhere you can crash," he says, looking up with a reassuring smile. It's like he's offering me an umbrella in a hurricane. "A friend's place."

"Really?" A flicker of hope sparks, but it's quick to fade as reality sets in. "And Lila? Sasha?"

"Room for one." His gaze meets mine, and he shrugs.

"Right." The word tastes bitter, like ashes. I nod, trying to stitch together a thank-you, but it gets lost somewhere between my lips and the lump in my throat.

"You okay?" Alex's voice is low, close behind me.

"Sure," I lie, my voice flat. "But what about them?"

Alex steps closer, his presence a towering certainty in the cramped space. "They've got other friends. They'll figure something out." His tone isn't cold but practical, like he's discussing a chess move and not our lives.

"Feels wrong, ditching them," I confess, the guilt gnawing at my insides.

"Sometimes you have to look after number one, Ever." He shrugs as if it's that simple.

I know he's right. Cass did. We all have to. I'm grateful for his help, but it feels like accepting a lifeboat while knowing others are still on the sinking ship.

"Where is this place?" I ask, shouldering my bag. It feels heavier now, laden with more than clothes and books—like each item is soaked in the night's chaos.

"Not far." Alex avoids my gaze, and I sense he's not telling me everything. But I'm too tired to dig deeper.

"Fine." My reply is short, clipped with the edge of my fraying nerves. There's no room for softness right now, not when the world's turned brittle.

"Let's go then." He leads the way downstairs, and I follow, the guilt trailing me like a shadow I can't shake off.

I hit the bottom step and almost collide with Lila. Her phone is glued to her ear, brow furrowed as she nods along to whatever her mum's saying on the other end. Sasha's sitting on the floor, scrolling through her contacts like they might magically conjure up a spare room.

"Any luck?" I ask, my voice hoarse from the smoke and the shouting earlier.

Lila pockets her phone and manages a small smile. "Heading home for the weekend. Mum's freaking out. She thinks I'm about to turn into a fireball or something." She rolls her eyes, but I can tell she's relieved, she's back to her old self, mostly. "I'll sort something once I'm there. If I have to commute, it's not that far. Couple of hours either way."

Sasha looks up from her phone, a resigned sigh escaping her lips. "My cousin's going to let me crash in her dorm. It's tiny as hell, but it beats sleeping out here," she says, gesturing out to the cold, unforgiving street that's become our temporary refuge.

The tight knot of panic in my chest eases a fraction. They're not going to be homeless because of this mess. But the relief is bittersweet. Our lives are scattered now, like the ashes that must be settling in the burned-out kitchen.

"Good," I murmur, trying to infuse some warmth into the word. "That's good you guys have places to go."

"You?"

"Alex has sorted something out for me."

Lila gives me a one armed hug, her body trembling slightly against mine. "Thank fuck. This is not how I thought our last year would start off."

"Me either. Be safe."

She nods, and Sasha rises to also give me a hug. "We'll see you on the other side."

Whatever that means.

"Yeah. We're good," I lie because I'm anything but okay. I'm crashing at a stranger's place with no idea what to do next.

9

ALISTAIR

Smoke curls into the sky, like a signal fire warning me of what's coming. I stand at the window, my hands shoved in my pockets, breathing evenly, slowly. This isn't just another day at KnightsGate; it's a reckoning.

The Gaight name weighs on me, heavy as the stone walls that surround this place. Dad was a cruel bastard who loved power more than his own child. Now that title is mine, and it's a beast I have to tame, or it'll eat me alive just like it did him. But I won't be him. I can't be.

I'm here, stuck in the thick of this ancient university's politics, because of a legacy that's both a curse and a privilege. The expectations are suffocating. Lead, succeed, dominate—those words are etched into my brain, carved there since I was old enough to understand that failure isn't an option for a Gaight.

It was drummed into me since I was old enough to understand words, maybe even before, that one day

I'll be here, with the responsibility of the sect on my shoulders. I was told to lead with the iron will no one will ever see coming, and if anyone dares to cross me, they'll learn quickly that I'm every bit the force to be reckoned with.

It's not that I don't want this responsibility. I want it. I *need* it. I need it more than I need air to breathe because it's my legacy. But it comes with a ton of shit that I sometimes wish would just fuck off.

Like this moment.

It's too early. It's too soon. This plan was several months away, and yet here we are because some fucking worthless pricks think they can take what's ours.

Adapt, pivot and move forward.

Shit happens, it's how you deal with it that matters.

The door opens softly, and I don't need to turn to know it's Benedict. His presence is like something felt more than seen. He's here now, quiet as ever, drifting across the carpet until he stands next to me, his eyes fixed on the same view that has me entranced.

We're watching her world burn, and there is something profoundly beautiful about the plumes of smoke that billow through the twilight.

"What now?" he asks, gaze still fixed on the sight over the square.

"North-West has his orders."

He waits a few seconds and then turns his head to stare at me. "This is too important to lie at the feet of a second-year."

"He's got this."

"He'd better," he grunts.

"Or?" I lay the challenge down, provoking him into saying what is on his mind.

He turns his whole body to face me, but I don't give him the same respect. I don't even look at him.

"Speaking as South Cardinal, if this goes sideways, North, I will be forced to place a vote of no confidence in you to the sect."

A laugh escapes me, humourless and sharp as shattered glass. "But of course. I'd expect nothing less from you, South."

"Good." He's all business, every inch the South Cardinal, the Earl of Cumberfold, ready to play his part. "Just making sure we understand each other."

"Always."

Benedict nods, the action sharp, a silent seal on our grim pact. We turn back to the window, two shadows cast long by the dying light, watching the disorder that grips KnightsGate like a vice.

"As your best friend, I seriously hope the faith you have in that kid isn't going to fuck us over."

"I told you before, he's got this."

"Stanley and the other two knobs," Benedict's voice cuts through the stillness as he suddenly changes the topic. "What's the verdict?"

"Handled," I murmur, my eyes not leaving the view. "Damien and I made sure they're pissed and thus stupid." The taste of violence lingers on my tongue, a bitter reminder of deeds best left in darkness.

"So they'll come back for more?" There's an edge to his question, a hint of steel beneath the calm.

"Yes. Stanley has an ego that won't let this lie, and he doesn't know when to drop shit. And that is exactly what I'm hoping for. If the rumours are true, we need to weed him out and then cut him down."

Benedict exhales sharply, a sound like the hiss of a snake, and I know he's taking in every bit of the chaos outside. "They'll come at you harder now."

"Yeah." The truth is stark and straightforward. We both know it. "Let them come. We're ready, and all I need is an excuse."

We lapse into silence then, the only sound the distant cries that waft up from over the square. Benedict, Charles, Damien and I are four pieces on this chessboard, poised for the coming storm. We've played this game since we were kids, climbing through the ranks and being taught at our father's feet.

This place isn't just an elite University where royalty gain an education, it's the black heart that beats for one purpose and one purpose only.

To further the sect's cause.

An offshoot of the Knights Templar, KnightsGate has been twisted to defend its assets in whatever aspect that may include. As the centuries turn, so does the mission statement. Like sand, it shifts, it's fluid.

Benedict moves next to me, restless. "We should prepare."

"In a minute." I can't move just yet. Not until I

watch every last wisp of smoke disappear into the darkening sky.

"Fair enough," he says after a moment and steps back from the window.

"Careful there, Ben. You sound like you actually think this will work."

His snort of cold mirth pulls my lips up into a half smile.

"There is hope."

Nodding, I remain there for what feels like hours but is only minutes more, lost in thought.

But Ben is right. We need to prepare. The moment we've been waiting for has arrived, and while it is sooner than anticipated, that doesn't make it any less real.

10

EVER

My trainers are silent against the red-bricked road of this fancy square that looks like it's straight out of some old English movie. It's all a bit *too* posh. Our side of the large square is where the faded grandeur sits. An enormous piece of immaculate grass separates us from *them*. The autumn chill nips at my skin in the growing night, and I tighten by hand on the holdall strap that weighs a ton. Alex has my book bag slung over his shoulder like it weighs nothing, even though I know he has at least three monumental tomes in there that belong to the Uni Library.

He doesn't slow down, only a determined stride, as if he has purpose, and I have to pick up my pace to keep up with him.

As we turn right, instead of left off the square, my eyes bug out. We are headed into serious elite territory here. The very air seems to scream its protest at a commoner like me. My mouth goes dry as Alex leads me to the biggest, fanciest townhouse on the square. It's a mansion with three stories, balconies and wrought iron gates that lead onto a short path.

"Erm," I mutter, staring up at it as Alex pushes the gate open and waits impatiently for me to catch up. It's beautiful and imposing, and for a second, I feel like I'm in over my head.

The thought of living in this place, even for a few nights until I sort out something more permanent, sits heavy and uncomfortable in my stomach, like I've swallowed a rock.

"Alex, wait," I call out, and he pauses, turning back with a questioning arch of his eyebrow.

I gesture to the imposing structure before us. "There's no way I can afford to stay here."

He steps closer, bright blue eyes locking onto mine as he runs his hand through his dark hair. There's a reassuring intensity in his gaze that almost makes me believe everything will be okay. "Ever, relax. My friends know the score. They won't ask for more than you can afford. If they ask for anything."

"What?" I baulk at the thought of living rent-free *anywhere*.

He shrugs. "This place is old family property. No rent, no mortgage. They'll probably ask you to buy your own food, but that's it."

My sceptical snort cuts through the tension between us. This whole scene feels like a setup for a joke where I'm the punchline.

Again.

I back up two steps with a shake of my head.

"Seriously, they're fine with you staying here... while your house gets fixed." His hand finds my shoulder, grip firm yet somehow comforting.

The pause in his sentence catches my attention, but I don't have anything to say right now. I feel sick. There is no way these guys are going to let me stay here for free or even my meagre housing allowance. I'll be able to stay one night, and then I'll have to move on.

"You need a place to stay; they're offering one."

Reluctance gnaws at me as I glance from his face to the townhouse and back again. But Alex's words, laced with that charismatic certainty of his, chip away at my resolve. I let out a sigh, knowing deep down that options are slim. "Okay, but only because I'm desperate."

"Trust me," he says with a ghost of a smile. "This is the right move."

"Easy for you to say," I mutter, but my protest dies as I realise I've already started to give in. I'm tired, hungry, and in need of a good cry in private. This place will offer me those things.

Tonight.

"You won't find anything else this close to campus. Not without selling a kidney or something."

A bitter chuckle escapes me, and I shake my head because it's true, painfully so. The hours I pour into work and study leave no room for house hunting, let alone the energy to move again. And yet...

"Ever, you're overthinking this," Alex says as if

reading my mind. His hand hovers near mine, an offer of support I'm not sure I should take.

"Am I?" I snap, sharper than intended. "Because it feels like I'm being realistic."

"Realistic is for the real world. You're still in university, and you need a place to stay."

His words hit hard. The truth is, I *am* out of options right now, backed into a corner by circumstance.

"Fine," I say, the word feeling like surrender, even as it frees me from the limbo I've been trapped in. "I'll stay. But just until I sort something else out."

"Good," he agrees, and there's a glimmer of victory in his eyes but also something like relief.

Gripping my bag tightly with both hands, we stride up to the front door. a fancy crest looms above us, carved into the stone, demanding respect—or maybe fear. It's hard to tell which.

I gulp.

Who the hell lives here?

We stop at the door. It's massive, ancient-looking, imposing as fuck, with the coat of arms staring down at us.

Reaching out, I finally land on the cool metal of the brass lion's head knocker. I give it two sharp raps, louder than I intend, and my pulse races at the sound echoing behind the wood.

"Ready for this?" Alex asks, his voice low.

"Fuck no," I confess, but there's no turning back now.

He chuckles, but it's dark, a little bit terrifying.

The door opens easily, and there stands the owner in front of me, cool blue eyes staring right into mine. My breath hitches, caught somewhere between my throat and the tightness in my chest.

"Ever Knight," Alex says. "This is Alistair Gaight."

"Duke of KnightsGate," I whisper, wondering how in the hell I didn't know he lived across the square from us.

"Ever," Alistair says, and it's like ice and fire all at once. "Welcome home."

11

EVER

For a split second, I'm frozen, caught in the web of his icy blue gaze. The tension is thick with something unspoken as Alistair's hand moves, a silent command to follow him. His face gives nothing away, but I move forward to catch up, urgency gnawing at my insides, and I step through the doorway with Alex close behind. He shuts the door, and I jump, feeling trapped.

My breath comes in ragged gasps as I trail behind Alistair through this house that screams money and power. The kind of ancient wealth that slams into you, leaving you reeling. In the living room, three more men are seated casually, but all eyes are on me as I stumble in, my bag feeling far too heavy for me to carry now. I drop it, and it lands on my foot, but I don't wince and show weakness. I feel that will get me eaten alive in this den of vipers.

"Ever," Alistair says, voice smooth as silk,

dangerous as a blade sliding across skin. "Glad to have you here."

"Thanks for extending the invite. I'll find something else as soon as I can," I murmur, my voice steady despite the chaos of nerves inside me.

"No need. The room is yours as long as you want it," Alistair says easily, but the intensity in his eyes is starting to make me panic.

Their stares are heavy and expectant as if they're waiting for me to crack open and spill secrets I don't even have. I shift my weight, trying to shake off the feeling of being an exhibit under scrutiny.

Alistair clears his throat, and the sound echoes against the high, ornate ceilings. "Gentlemen, this is Ever Knight."

"Ever," the one I know around as Benedict says, his green eyes studying me like I'm some puzzle he's set on solving. "I'm Benedict Harrington, Earl of Cumberfold."

I gulp.

The title thrown casually in there only serves to remind me I'm a nobody. A peasant. They'll probably expect me to be their maid to help pay my way.

The other guy I sort of know from earlier when he came to my rescue, Damien Wraith, lifts his chin in acknowledgement, a slight smirk playing on his lips, his grey eyes brooding and a little bit terrifying. "Damien Wraith, Baron of Mere."

Blinking rapidly to clear my head, I find that I can't. This is strange. Surreal, even.

The fourth guy, who is also just a name and a face,

Charles, gives me a quick, almost conspiratorial wink. "Charles St. James, Viscount Beaumont."

"Hi," I breathe out, my voice sounding small in the vast room. I force myself to meet their stares, even though it feels like I'm on display. "Ever Knight. No title. Just me. A nobody."

Alistair's smile is slow and lazy, almost as if he knows he's got me on the ropes, which was his plan all along. "You are a legacy, Ever. Not a nobody."

I shake my head vehemently. "You have the wrong impression of me if that's what you think."

His eyes flash with something dangerous, and I gulp again, but my mouth has gone dry, and I force down a cough without much luck.

"Welcome to KnightsGate Manor," Benedict says, rising from his seat. He's all casual elegance, his movements fluid as he approaches. "May I show you to your room?"

"Okay," I bleat, the word coming out more as a question than an affirmation. Doubt crowds my mind as Benedict leans down to pick up my bag and takes the bookbag from Alex, who is standing nervously off to the side. With a shaky smile at the Lords of the Manor, like literally, for fuck's sake, Benedict leads the way, and I follow cautiously. The door closes behind us with a soft click, sealing away most of the tension, but it still hums in my veins, electric and alive.

The grand staircase unfolds before us, each step across the marble floor a squeak in the quiet. I'm going to have to buy new shoes or go barefoot at this rate. Benedict's back is straight, his stride sure. I tail him, trying to match the rhythm of his pace, my hand trailing along the polished bannister as we head up the sweeping staircase, overlooked by a plethora of former Dukes and Duchesses and other nobility. It feels cool, solid beneath my fingers, grounding me.

The second-floor hallway stretches out, doors flanking us on either side. Each one is closed, holding its own mystery, its own slice of this enigmatic world I've stumbled into.

Benedict pauses at the final door, a fraction open. It whooshes softly as I push it wider, the sound cutting through the hush that wraps around us. My gaze sweeps the room, and for a moment, I'm rooted to the spot.

Pale colours wash over the walls and fabrics, pastels that catch the light from the bedside lamp in soft whispers. It's a sharp departure from the heavy opulence below—no dark woods, antiques, old portraits or cold marble here. Instead, the space feels gentle, like a sigh in the night.

My feet sink into the plush carpet, a softness that seems to swallow the sound of my hesitant steps. The room breathes tranquillity, the kind I've never known either at my parents' house or the student house that went up in flames.

"Do you like it?" Benedict asks, his tone almost hesitant as if he is waiting to hear me say yes and will be crushed if I say no.

"Yes. It's nice." *Nice?* Understatement of the year. A nook by the window calls to me, its cushions whispering promises of stolen moments with dog-eared books and forgotten cups of tea. It's a corner of peace in a world that seems to be spinning faster than I can keep up.

"Nice," he repeats.

Noticing the way he studies me, eyes intent as if trying to decipher the thoughts I'm scrambling to hide, I squirm under his gaze, feeling exposed without having said much at all.

"Lovely, it's lovely. Really, it's more than I could've expected." I mean it, but my words come out tangled, laced with the uncertainty that dogs my every step in this grand house that reeks of wealth and secrets.

"Good," he says, a shadow of a smile ghosting across his face. "Make yourself at home."

Home. The word feels foreign on my tongue, too heavy to carry around in a place where I don't belong. But the soft glow of the lamp and the gentle embrace of the space chip away at the wall I've built around myself, brick by brick.

"Thank you," I croak before the silence can stretch into awkwardness, into something that demands more answers than I'm ready to give.

He nods once, more to himself than to me, then steps back, hands slipping into the pockets of his casual yet expensive-looking trousers. "I'll leave you to it, then." There's a finality in his tone, a quiet understanding that I need space.

The door clicks shut behind him, leaving me alone in the middle of the pastel sanctuary. Silence floods the room, thick and expectant, and I exhale loudly.

My heart races, a staccato rhythm against the softness around me.

Why do I suddenly feel like I'm a pawn who hasn't figured out the rules of the game yet?

It's not a great feeling, but I'm exhausted, so I kick off my shoes and sink onto the bed. The room's comfort mocks me; it's all too nice, too welcoming. I'm no stranger to mind games—I grew up with whispers and sideways glances—but this? This is a new level.

"Keep it together, Ever," I whisper, my voice sounding foreign in the quiet. My fingers drum anxiously on my thighs as I scan the room. Alistair, Benedict, Charles, and Damien are enigmas wrapped in tailored suits and secretive smiles. They're the kind of guys who own a room just by stepping into it, and now, somehow, I've stepped into theirs.

I force myself to stand, to move. My hands shake a little as I unzip my duffel bag, the sound loud in the silence. I pull out my jeans and well-worn t-shirts, each piece a reminder of the scrimping, saving, and scholarships that got me here.

These men are a puzzle, but I'm good at puzzles.

I place a photo of Mum and Dad on the dresser, their smiles frozen in time. It's a reminder of where I come from, of the legacy teetering on the edge of obscurity. I can't let them down. Not now.

Shoving my clothes into the enormous antique dresser, the wood creaking with age, the action is mechanical, grounding. But my brain's still on overdrive. This seems too much of a coincidence for my liking. First, Alistair and Damien came to my rescue when I didn't know them from Adam, only their names and faces and that they're the most popular and wealthy elite at this Academy, and now I'm living under their roof. If this is some kind of game or whatever they're playing, I need to learn the rules fast. Because one thing's certain: there's no going back now.

12

EVER

It's the crack of dawn, and I've barely slept despite my exhaustion. I need coffee, so I'm going to have to move in the direction of downstairs, which I was trying to avoid for as long as possible. Hopefully, none of the guys will be up already.

No such luck.

The moment I step into the kitchen, I'm like a trapped rat.

Alistair is lounging near the far counter, looking every bit the Duke he is. His posture screams power, even as he laughs at something Damien says. Damien's in the corner, shrouded in shadows that match his dark attire. He's got this intense look on his face like he's calculating his next move in a strategic game, only he knows he's playing. Benedict, perched on a stool at the kitchen island, his eyes thoughtful, probably pondering some deep philosophical theory.

"Ever," Charles greets me, his voice laced with a carefree charm that seems to come naturally to him.

He's sitting on the counter, holding a mug of coffee that smells delicious, a vintage T-shirt clinging to his torso in a way that's both casual and a little showy. His hazel eyes twinkle with mischief. He is the only one in the room who doesn't seem weighed down by some heavy ancestral legacy.

"Oh, hi," I murmur, my voice steadier than I feel. Observing them and their ease with each other, the way their personalities clash and meld, is like watching a play where everyone knows their part except me. I should say something witty and join the banter, but instead, I hover by the door, feeling like an intruder in their polished, privileged world. "I didn't expect anyone else up."

Cringing at the lameness, it doesn't seem like they care.

Benedict's voice cuts through the hum of their debate, "Ever, would you like to sit?" His eyes hold a calm inquiry, yet I sense layers beneath his simple offer.

"Okay," I murmur and edge closer to them. The stool is comfortable and hugs my ass, still feeling every bit the outsider even sitting down.

Around me, the conversation spirals into territories of philosophy and ethics, topics that are galaxies away from my day-to-day worries about term papers and rent. Alistair throws out a point about moral relativism with a confidence that commands attention, while Damien counters with a sharp-edged insight into human behaviour.

My gaze flickers to Charles, who flashes a quick

grin before diving back into the fray, his argument laced with dramatic flair. It's like they're speaking another language—one I can't quite grasp.

Standing abruptly, I blurt out. "I'm going to make some coffee."

There are nods and murmurs but no real pause in their intellectual tennis match. I retreat to the corner where the fancy coffee maker lies in wait, relieved to escape into the normalcy of making coffee.

Only it's so fucking complicated, I need a degree in rocket science.

Staring at it, wondering where I start, Charles comes up behind me and leans over the top of me, his body intimately close to mine as he reaches for a mug.

"Grab a pod," he says.

"Pod?"

He chuckles and gestures to the display in the cupboard under the mugs, which has every flavour of coffee known to man. Aiming for a plain one, I hand it to him, my hand shaking nervously. Our fingers brush, and I stifle my gasp of surprise at how warm his fingers are, but then mentally roll my eyes at myself. He's been holding a hot mug of coffee. Of course his hands are warm.

He grins, and I watch what he does with this pod to make my coffee, hoping I can re-enact that next time.

"See, easy," he says.

"Easy peasey," I murmur.

The smell of fresh coffee fills the air, which is a small comfort.

Feeling as if the other guys are ignoring me, I slip out of the kitchen into the entrance hall to open the front door. Stepping out, I turn my face up to the warm sun briefly and sighing deeply as I take a sip of coffee.

"Hey, Ever! Fancy meeting you here," Alex's voice slices through the silence as he ambles up the path, all easy confidence and a dark smile. "There's a party tonight at Jensen's place. You should come."

"Hey, Alex. You're around bright and early." I blink at him, my pulse quickening. A party sounds like a slice of normal university life, something to drown out the disquieting elegance of this house.

"Came to see how you were settling in."

"It's okay, I guess."

He nods. "So, party?"

"Yeah, okay," I say, grasping the idea like a lifeline. "Sounds fun."

"Good. It's decided then." He claps his hands once with finality. "Figured you need a break after the fire, take your mind off it. Anyway, I'll swing by around seven, meet me on the corner."

"I will," I answer, grateful for the distraction. "Right then, I'll see you later."

Once inside my room, I shut the door behind me, leaning against it with a sigh. The room feels too big, too grand. Who am I kidding? This isn't my world.

Deciding to get ahead with my reading for classes on Monday, it'll hopefully take my mind off this situation. I pull out my textbooks, scattering them across the bed. My fingers trace the spines, landing on 'Modern British Literature.'

As I flip through the pages, my mind wanders. I should be looking for a new place, a normal place, where the walls don't whisper secrets or judge me for my lack of a title. But the thought of house hunting exhausts me before I even begin.

I don't have that many friends. All my real friends lived in that house with me. I don't really have anywhere else to go. Would it be so bad staying here until the landlord gets the kitchen fixed?

Pushing that question aside, for now, I lose myself in the poetic tragedies of Thomas Hardy, where the stakes are high, hearts are broken, and everyone is beautifully doomed. It's strangely comforting.

By the time I glance at the clock, hours have slipped by, and hunger is gnawing at my stomach. Time for food. I skipped breakfast, but I can't go without lunch. Leaving my room, barefoot this time, I pad down the grand staircase to the kitchen.

Charles is in there, raiding the fridge. Before I can escape back to my room to try again later, he looks up, his hazel eyes lighting up with a spark of mischief. "Hey, Ever," he says, closing the fridge door with his elbow. "You hungry?"

"Yeah."

"You skipped breakfast." It's not an accusation, merely an observation, but it unnerves me all the same.

"Had some reading to do."

"Well, make yourself whatever."

"Thanks, Charles. I guess we will have to sit down and work out how that will work."

"Call me Charlie, and how what will work?"

"Food, bills, rent..."

I let that last one hang there, and he shrugs. "There's no rent, and Alistair's trust manager sorts the bills, so I wouldn't know what was what, even if you asked me." He shrugs nonchalantly. "If you want to buy your own food, be my guest, I guess."

I nod slowly, deciding that clearly, Alistair is the one to talk to regarding these matters.

"Okay, Charlie," I say, smiling despite myself. His ease is refreshing to the intensity of the others. "Have you eaten?"

"Was just looking."

"Well, allow me. Sandwiches good?" I ask, opening the fridge and staring at the contents.

"Sandwiches are king," he replies with a loud laugh.

"Good," I giggle and finally feel at ease here, although I doubt that will last.

I cobble together a meal, sharing bits of bread, ham and cheese, laughter mingling with the clink of cutlery. It feels normal.

"So English Lit, huh?" Charlie says through a mouthful of sandwich. "That's some heavy reading."

"How did you know?"

He gives me an eye roll. "Everyone knows who you are, Ever Knight."

"Of course," I murmur. "You?"

"Drama. We're all playing parts, aren't we? Just

depends on the stage. So might as well capitalise on that." He winks, and I laugh.

"Can't argue with that."

Time ticks by, and the comfort of camaraderie lingers as I slip back upstairs, buoyed by this interaction. When I get back to my room, it's time to prep for this party. I need this night out more than I care to admit.

I'm not huge on social gatherings, but the thought of staying here is like a weight pressing down on me. I need to get out and forget about everything for a while.

Steam fills the en-suite bathroom as hot water cascades down. I step in, letting the heat wash away the remnants of the unease that clings like a second skin.

Later, wrapped in a towel, I survey the wardrobe I've yet to fully unpack. The floral dress calls to me. White fabric dotted with soft pastels—it's simple, yet it makes me feel like I belong to something beautiful, if just for an evening. Slipping it on, the fabric falls just right, brushing my thighs with a whisper to just above my knees.

Black ballet flats complete the look, understated but classy.

As I wait for Alex, I catch my reflection in the mirror. The girl staring back seems ready for anything, different from the one who climbed those stairs yesterday, weighed down by the shadows of this house and the flames that engulfed mine.

I'm ready for a night of escape, a respite from the

looming decisions and the unsettling atmosphere in the house. The thought of music and mindless chatter is like a promise of freedom, and I cling to it, hopeful.

Almost tiptoeing so I don't alert anyone to the fact I'm leaving the house, I cross the entrance hall quietly, slip through the front doors and head out down the path to see Alex waiting for me on the corner.

"Why the cloak and dagger?" I ask with a laugh.

"I wasn't sure if we'd face resistance," he says, returning the chuckle darkly. "Not in the mood to fight for my right to party, you know?"

"Yeah," I murmur, getting it totally. Somehow the idea that Alistair would interrogate us on our plans is not all that out there.

We walk briskly down the street, the night air a welcome slap against my skin. The sound of the party grows louder with every step, a siren song promising oblivion. As we approach the big house, its windows pulsing with light and bass thumps against my chest like a second heartbeat.

"Ready to forget everything for a while?" Alex asks, his voice tinged with an edge that tells me he's just as desperate to drown out reality as I am.

"Definitely," I say, and together, we step into the chaos, letting the wave of music and drunken laughter wash over us, sweeping us into the anonymity of the crowd.

13

CHARLES

Something feels off. The jolt of anxiety that shoots through me is like a live wire.

Turning to the laptop on my desk, I bring up the cams in Ever's room. She's not there, nor in her bathroom.

Scanning through every feed in the rest of the house, I eventually see her slipping quietly out of the front door timestamped ten minutes ago.

Rising swiftly, my chair sealing across the room on its wheels, I race from the room. "Guys, we have a problem," I shout into the hallway, bringing them all to me from various rooms around the upper townhouse.

"What is it?" Alistair asks.

"Ever has left the building."

"What? Where?"

"That's what we need to find out. She went out the front door about ten minutes ago."

"Shit! You mean she is under our roof, and we lost her?"

"Seems that way."

We stand there, a bunch of guys, usually so full of bravado, now just four guys standing in the hallway, wondering what in the fuck just happened. Our eyes are glued to the stairs, each wrapped in our own brand of tension.

"Did she seriously just go out there alone?" Damien's voice is a low growl, breaking the silence like a crack of thunder. His stance is stiff, the muscles in his arms twitching like he's ready to punch something—or someone.

"Did *we* seriously just let her?" Alistair growls back. "What the fuck is this?"

"Not a prison," I mutter, but he hears me anyway and gives me *that* glare that could kill a man from fifty feet. Too bad, I'm no ordinary man.

Alistair's face is a mask of fury, his blue eyes burning cold. "Where the fuck did she go?"

Before anyone can answer that, Damien receives a phone call. He growls something unintelligible and then sighs. When he hangs up, his face is grim.

"Sebastian, South-West, just spotted her at a party a few streets down. She arrived with Alex."

"What the fucking fuck?" Alistair snarls. "What the fuck are you waiting for? Move!"

"Party crashers it is then," Damien says, and even though his lips twist into a smirk, there's no humour in his eyes. They're calculating, like he's already running through a thousand scenarios in his mind.

"This has disaster written all over it," I snap. "It's a catch-22. We can't demand she never leave this house, but this... I don't like it."

"Let's get moving, then." The words come out curt, commanding attention as we stride toward the door, each caught up in our turbulent thoughts.

I remember the way Ever laughed earlier when I told her one of my stupid jokes, the sound was like music over the constant buzz of worry in my head. I'm falling for her—hard—and it's more than just obsession. She is sweet, kind and funny, and her questions about paying her way made me melt. She isn't some gold digger, opportunistic or not. She really needs to feel independent and not kept or, worse for her, I think, a charity case.

"Ever is too good, too pure for this crap. Jensen and his mates are pieces of shit. These guys will bully her, and she won't have anywhere to turn."

"No way Alex can handle this on his own. I don't know what possessed me to leave these doors unlocked." Alistair's strides are growing increasingly difficult to keep up with.

"Let's hope we're not too late." Damien's words hang heavy, like a dark cloud before a storm.

My heart thumps erratically, not from fear but from a burning need to shield Ever from the world's filth.

Her purity is ours to cherish, to claim, and any other fucker who thinks they can lay their dirty hands on her will be severely punished.

Fuck, I never thought I'd fall like this. Not just

lust, not just this twisted game, but something deeper. Something real.

The party is close, its pulse throbbing in the distance, a beacon drawing us forward.

"Keep sharp," I mutter, my gaze slicing through the night. "We find Ever; we watch over her, whether she likes it or not."

Damien nods, a ghost of agreement in the dark. Even now, my skin crawls with the anticipation of what awaits at that party. But above all, the drive to protect Ever overshadows everything else.

Tonight, we're the guardians cloaked in the velvet night, and nothing will stop us from keeping her safe.

The house looms ahead, a beast with a thumping heartbeat of bass and shrieks of laughter and chatter. We push through the door, and it's like diving into chaos. People are everywhere, grinding, laughing, spilling their drinks. The air reeks of sweat and booze, and my skin prickles with the pulse of the music that's way too loud.

"Damn," Damien murmurs, his voice nearly lost in the noise. "This is a fucking nightmare."

I spot a guy by the staircase, banknotes rolled tight, white powder dusting his nostrils. My fists itch to wipe the smug look off his face. I hate drugs—their grip on people, the way they wreck lives. It takes everything in me not to beat some sense into him, but there's a bigger mission tonight.

Alistair's gaze is on me, knowing my thoughts, and he nods when I stand down, his eyes cold as ice. Ben's gaze flickers around, taking in the scene with a silent fury. We start moving, cutting through the crowd, too wrapped up in their own world to notice the predators among them.

"Check the corners," Damien says, voice low.

We edge past dancers, our eyes scanning every flushed face, looking for that wave of blonde hair, those green eyes that shift like the sea. But it's like she's a ghost, slipping through our fingers. The longer it takes to find her, the tighter my chest gets, like a vice squeezing all the air out.

"Where is she?" Alistair mutters, his usual composure fraying at the edges. "She has to be here."

"Keep looking," I snap, shoving past a couple locked in a sloppy kiss.

We weave deeper into the crowd, dodging elbows and sloshed drinks. The desperation's a living thing now, clawing up my throat. Ever is in here somewhere, and every second we don't have eyes on her is a second too long.

"This is insanity. Split up," I command, voice raw with urgency. The bass of the music pulses through the floorboards as I shove my way through the swarm of bodies. Sweat and alcohol fog the air, but all I can taste is the fear that Ever is in danger without us.

Damien disappears into the crowd. Alistair moves off without a word, cutting through the chaos like a ship's prow through dark waves. People move for him, and it's not surprising. He's got that whole Duke thing working for him. Big time. Ben gives me a curt nod, already scanning the room with his sharp gaze.

I'm diving through the sea of students now. Every second drags, heavy as chains.

"Fuck!" I spit out when a couple stumbles into me, sloshing their drinks. I don't have time for this.

I push their drunk asses back, heart racing. Each corner I check, every empty space, sends a new spike of panic through me. Where is she? Why can't I find her?

Then I spot Alex, his lips locked with some girl who's definitely not Ever. His hands roam over her like he's got no care in the world. Rage boils in my gut, hot and vicious.

"Alex!" I barrel through the last few feet separating us. He doesn't hear me, too lost in the kiss.

"Where the fuck is Ever?" I grab his shoulder, yanking him back.

His eyes meet mine, confused at first. "Charlie—"

"Ever!" I shout over the noise, my voice cracking with the terror of what might be happening to her right this second. "Where the fuck is she?"

14

EVER

My eyes dart from face to face, searching for that familiar mop of dark hair, those piercing blue eyes – but Alex is a ghost in this crowd. I shove through the swarm of bodies heading for the back garden, where the party is growing more raucous by the second, the beat of the music thumping against my chest like a second heartbeat.

"Ever! Hey!" I jerk around at the sound of my name as I reach the kitchen. It's Jade from English Lit, her red curls bouncing around her. Relief floods me. At least I'm not alone in this chaos. I weave my way over, forcing a smile. "Hey, Jade."

"You came with Alex?" Jade's voice slices through the thumping bass as she leans in.

"Yeah. Have you seen him?"

"He's inside somewhere with Verity. He has his tongue stuck down her throat. Sorry, girl."

My cheeks heat up with annoyance and the sad

feeling of betrayal. It's ridiculous. I don't own him. We aren't even dating.

I shrug, trying to appear nonchalant. "Good for them." My hand tightens around the cool surface of my drink, the condensation slippery against my skin. I take a sip. The bitterness of the tonic laced with vodka burns my throat. This is my second one, and I'm feeling the effects already.

"God, it's so packed in here," Jade complains, scanning the room. "Want to head outside for some air?"

"Yeah, I was on my way out when you called me." The room tilts a fraction, and my stomach lurches.

Shit.

I try to steady myself, my fingers fumbling for the wall.

"Ever? You okay?" Jade's voice seems distant, concern etched into her brows.

"Fine," I lie, gripping the wall like a lifeline. My vision swims, colours and shapes blending together in an abstract painting that refuses to hold still. I blink hard, willing the dizziness to pass. But it clings to me, persistent and growing stronger by the second.

I'm spinning. The room, a blur of laughing faces, feels like a carousel cranked up too high. Panic claws at my throat, raw and suffocating.

"Bathroom," I mutter and shove through bodies that seem to move in slow motion, their laughter distorting into something sinister.

"Excuse me," I slur, but no one hears—or cares.

The staircase looms ahead, a mountain I have to

climb. Each step feels like wading through molasses; my limbs are heavy, detached from my command. I can't shake the fog in my head or clear the mist from my vision.

"Fuck."

My hand skims the wall, searching for stability in this tilting world. I need to make it upstairs, lock myself in the bathroom, and splash cold water on my face. Anything to feel real again.

Someone brushes past, their shoulder knocking into mine. It sends me reeling, but I catch myself before I fall.

"Sorry," I mumble, though I don't know why I'm apologising.

The air thickens in my lungs with every step I take upward. By the time I reach the upstairs hallway, everything's a battle. My breathing is ragged, my heart thuds in a rhythm that's all off.

The bathroom door is in sight.

"Ever Knight," Stanley leers, suddenly blocking my path. His eyes glint with a darkness that chills me more than the sweat on my skin.

"Move," I manage to say, but my voice is just a thread of sound, barely there.

"Why rush? Party's just starting for us." He smirks.

"I'm not interested," I say, trying to sound firm. But my knees are jelly, my head's spinning, and I know I'm not convincing anyone.

"Too damn bad." He leans in, and I can smell the beer on his breath.

I want to scream, run, fight—but I'm locked in place, my body refusing to cooperate.

"Go to hell," I spit out, even as fear coils tight in my gut.

"Already on my way," he says casually. "But first, I'm going to win my bet."

What bet?

He steps even closer, and every alarm bell in my head rings in warning.

"Back off," I warn, pushing against his chest with hands that might as well be made of air.

"Come on, Ever. Don't play hard to get." He grins, and it's all teeth—predatory. "You should feel special. I don't usually work this hard for it."

For what?

I need to get away from him, but my head spins, and I nearly throw up.

"Fuck you," I grunt as my vision tunnels, and the edges of the world grow dark.

"Feisty," he mocks, not even fazed. His hand reaches for me, and I dodge, trying to keep some space between us. But my legs betray me, shaky as a newborn deer, and every movement feels like wading through thick mud.

"Let me go." The words scrape out, desperation edging into my tone despite my attempt to sound commanding. His laugh is a dark rumble that echoes in the tightening space around us.

"Sorry, darling. You're not going anywhere." Stanley's fingers grip my arm; his touch feels like a phantom. There, but not. I jerk away, revolted by the contact. My mind screams for me to run, to fight, to do anything but stand here like a lamb for slaughter.

Panic surges, a tidal wave threatening to sweep me under. I've faced bullies before, stared down sneers and whispered rumours, nasty words and caustic glares. But this is different. This is physical, immediate, and terrifyingly real.

"Stop," I gasp, vision blurring, each word punctuated by a desperate hope that someone, anyone, will hear me over the thumping bass downstairs. But the party goes on, oblivious to my fear.

Darkness creeps further in at the edges of my sight, and I can't hold it back much longer.

"Please," I whisper, the fight draining out of me. It's a plea, a crack in my armour, and I hate myself for it. But I'm drowning, and I don't know how to swim in these shark-infested waters.

Stanley's grip tightens, and I know I'm losing. My body sags against him, strength seeping out like sand through my fingers. I always thought I'd be braver, stronger, and would somehow rise above the rest when push came to shove. But here, now, I'm just another girl, trapped and fading fast.

"Shh," he coos, a twisted lullaby for the darkness claiming me. "Just relax. It'll all be over soon."

My knees buckle, and I realise the truth—I can't fight any longer.

Stanley's fingers dig into my arm like iron claws as he hauls me through the crowd of oblivious party-goers. I stumble over something wet. The music thumps in time with the pulsing fear in my veins, a sinister soundtrack to this nightmare.

Stanley pushes open a door to an empty room and shoves me inside. The slam of the door behind us echoes like a gunshot. My back hits the mattress as he tosses me onto the bed, my dress bunching up around my thighs, skin exposed and vulnerable. A scream claws at my throat, but it's muffled by the thick air, heavy with my dread.

"Please," I try again, the word dissolving into a whimper. My hands clutch at the sheets, looking for something, anything, to ground me in this spinning world.

"Shut up," Stanley growls, looming over me. His eyes are dark pits of malice, and I know pleading is useless. But I can't help it; it's all I have left.

The room shrinks around us, walls closing in, trapping me with him. My heart races, a frantic drum-beat against the silence that has fallen. I push at his chest, my movements weak and sluggish. My mind screams at me to fight, to kick, to claw, but my limbs don't obey.

"Get off!" It's a yell, a command, but it lacks strength. Stanley just smirks, a predator savouring his prey.

"Make me," he taunts, and I feel the last vestiges of control slip away as darkness creeps into the edges of my vision, muddying my thoughts and dragging me under. I'm drowning in shadows, and Stanley is the lead weight pulling me down. The idea of giving in terrifies me, but it's getting harder to hold on to consciousness.

My eyelids flutter, heavy with dread, and the last thing I see is Stanley's face, twisted with cruelty before I'm lost to the darkness.

15

DAMIEN

Sweat mingles with the sticky residue of spilt booze as I shove through the heaving mass of bodies, but all I can think about is Ever. Where the fuck is she?

"Move," I grunt, nudging past a couple too wrapped up in each other to notice the desperation clawing at my throat. Their laughter rings hollow in my ears.

I scan the swarm of students in the house's kitchen frantically.

"Shit," I mutter, ducking as a cup arcs over the crowd, its contents raining down like a boozy meteor shower.

Turning back, I head for the stairs. "Screw this."

I take them two at a time, my boots thumping loudly to my ears. Each step ramps up the tension, a coiled spring ready to snap.

"Damien!" A voice cuts through the noise behind

me, sharp like a blade. I don't have to look back to know it's Alistair. His tone commands attention, always has, but right now, it's just background noise.

Not breaking stride, I hit the hallway, eyes snapping to each door as I pass. They're all closed, secrets tucked away behind flimsy barriers. I shove open the first one and see a couple making out. Not Ever. I slam it shut and move on.

Alistair's footsteps thunder up behind me, his presence like an approaching storm and he kicks the next door open. He is taking no prisoners. He blames himself for this, for not locking her up and laying down the law.

The sounds of the party fade into a dull buzz behind the doors we kick open, searching. My demons are out and ready to play. It's been too long since they tasted someone's blood other than mine. They're craving it, and I'm more than willing to give it to them.

One by one, we clear them. An empty study, a bathroom with a line of coke forgotten on the counter, another bedroom with a passed-out guy snoring on the bed.

"Ever," I whisper a silent plea that she's anywhere but behind this last door.

I grip the doorknob and twist, pushing the door open with a force that nearly snaps the hinges.

The scene hits me, and it's like a red flag to a bull.

Ever is motionless on the bed, her golden hair fanned out like a halo on the pillow. Her dress is bunched at her waist, and Stanley's fingers are hooked into the side of her underwear.

He looms over her, pants around his ankles. "Fuck off, will you? Trying to win a bet here."

His head turns slightly as if he senses the sudden danger, but he doesn't stop, doesn't even pause. Anger—cold, brutal, and vicious—whips through me like a gale. I want to tear him apart.

"Stanley." His name comes out as a growl, and I'm moving before I think, my body coiled and ready to strike.

Heat surges through the usual ice in my veins, a wildfire of fury that can't be quenched. I launch at Stanley and rip him away from her. Ever is vulnerable and defenceless.

Stanley's sneer is revolting. The bastard actually thinks he's got control here, like he's the king of this sordid castle. "Jealous?"

His words are a match to the powder keg in me. But instead of exploding, something colder settles over my rage.

"If you've touched her, I'm going to slice your guts open and burn them," I snarl, ripping off my black tee and throwing it over Ever to cover her up as best I can. I should be kicking his fucking head in, but I need to know first if he's violated her. If he has, his death will be slow and painful instead of quick and over too soon. Every line of my body is coiled, tensed for the moment he makes the wrong move.

"Back the fuck off, Stanley," Alistair growls. The words slice through the thick air, every syllable a razor-sharp warning. Ben and Charlie have joined us and flank him, our presence a united front against the vile scene before us.

Stanley just smirks, his eyes gleaming with sick satisfaction. "Too late. I've already claimed my prize," he taunts, clearly underestimating the fury he's ignited.

I don't hesitate. My body moves on its own accord, driven by a primal urge to protect, to destroy anything that threatens her. My fist flies, connecting with the side of Stanley's face with a satisfying crunch. The room tilts into mayhem, the sounds of the party outside muffled by the crescendo of chaos within these four walls.

We're a tangle of limbs and rage, my every hit driven by the image of Ever lying there, helpless. Stanley tries to fight back, but I'm relentless, every punch another message that he messed with the wrong girl. There's no holding back—not now, not when it comes to her; I'm a storm of violence, every cell screaming for justice. My knuckles collide with his face again and again, my mind blazing.

Hearing the sounds of fighting behind me, I look up to see Robbie and Eric have joined their buddy. Robbie lunges at me, his bulky frame a blur of motion, but Alistair is faster, gripping him by the collar and practically garrotting him with his own shirt. I ignore the newcomers, throwing a sharp elbow out, catching Stanley in the ribs. Pain explodes across his face; satisfaction surges through me.

"Fuck you!" Eric screams, diving into the fray

with wild, swinging fists aiming for Ben. Ben, ever the calm strategist, ducks and weaves like a shadow, his movements precise, each strike calculated. Charlie, with that manic gleam in his eyes, joins the chaos, tackling Eric from the side. They crash into a desk, splintering wood under the force.

And then it's a free-for-all brawl. Party-goers stream in, some joining in with their fists, others placing bets or recording it on their phones. It's a fucking shitshow.

And no place for a murder.

Catching Alistair's eyes as he slams his fist into Eric's face, he knows it as well as I do.

The room is full of grunts and curses, bodies slamming against plaster and furniture with sickening thuds. We're a whirlwind of fury.

"Stay down, asshole!" I snarl at Stanley, who's scrambling to recover, blood streaming from his bust face. My boot connects with his stomach, and he doubles over, gasping, but that's when I knee him in his dick. His pants are open, but his cock is stashed and he'd better hope to fuck, he's a lying cunt and didn't get as far as sticking his dick in our girl.

"Damien!" Alistair calls out, and I sense rather than see Robbie barrelling toward me again. I pivot on my heel, my fist flying out to meet his charge head-on. There's a crunch, and Robbie stumbles back, his nose gushing blood.

Stanley tries to crawl away, but I grab him by the collar, yanking him back into the fight.

"Give up, Stanley," I hiss, my voice cold as steel. "You're done."

His eyes are wide, fear finally seeping into the cracks of his smug facade as he struggles beneath my grip.

"Did you fuck her?" I growl, my fist bunched into his shirt.

"No," he stammers. "I swear, I didn't fuck her."

My fist flies for the last time, connecting with his jaw in a satisfying snap. His body goes limp, and I know he won't be getting up anytime soon.

I shove myself away from him, my breaths coming hard and fast. The room is a wreck; shattered glass, splintered wood, reminders of the violence we've just unleashed. But none of it matters as I turn toward Ever, still lying motionless on the bed as the fight rages on around her. Students are giggling and recording this entire thing, and Ever is lying half-naked on the bed, completely out cold.

"Jesus," I snap and shove a first year in the face with my palm as he holds his phone up to Ever. He stumbles back into a group of guys like fucking dominoes.

"Ever," I say, my voice breaking. Her name is a lifeline, pulling me back from the edge of darkness. I step over to her, gently touching her shoulder. "Can you hear me?"

No response.

"Shit, Ever," I murmur, brushing a strand of golden hair from her face. Her skin is too pale, her lips parted slightly, vulnerable in a way that wrenches at something deep inside me.

"Damien," Alistair's voice cuts through, but I barely hear him. My world has narrowed to the girl before me—to Ever, with her ethereal beauty now marred by this ugly night. "Get her the fuck out of here."

"Ever, I'm sorry we let this happen to you," I whisper, more to myself than to her. "I'll burn the fucking world down before I let anyone hurt you again."

My hands shake as I remove my tee and yank down her dress to cover her. "You're safe," I whisper, unsure if she hears me.

Her head lolls as I scoop her up, cradling her close against my chest. The fight is just noise and blurs now, a background to the weight of her in my arms. She's too light like she's already slipping away from this world.

Alistair's got Alex by the collar out in the hallway, his face pure thunder. I don't envy that kid one bit. But he deserves everything the sect leader is going to throw at him. "Let's move," he barks, and we sweep through the room and down the stairs.

We spill into the cool night, Ever's breath ghosting against my neck. I tighten my hold on her. If anyone so much as looks at her wrong, I'll fucking slaughter them, the consequences be damned.

"I'm going to nail that fucker to the wall by his balls," Alistair growls, tightening his hold on Alex.

"Fucking shame that can't be tonight," I mutter,

but it's too messy. Too many variables. Too many witnesses.

As we stride away from the house, I don't look back. There's nothing for us there, not anymore, only forward, where I can keep her safe. Where I can make sure the darkness of this night never touches Ever again.

16

BENEDICT

Brushing back the tangled strands of Ever's golden hair from her pale face, I shudder as I think about what could have happened. She's out cold, her chest rising and falling in a steady rhythm that is reassuring but no less infuriating.

"Damn it, Alex! What were you thinking?" Alistair's shout from the hallway snaps my attention from Ever's peaceful slumber. "You are fucking done, do you hear me? Fucking done."

I step into the hallway just in time to see Alistair's fist connect with Alex's jaw, a sickening crack that echoes off the walls. Driven by rage, he towers over Alex, his muscles coiled for another strike.

"Wait!" Alex exclaims, holding his hands up. "Wait!" Blood trickles from his split lip as he scrambles backwards, his hands up as if to shield himself from the relentless storm that is Alistair's wrath. "Please, Alistair, you have to listen." But the words are lost under the weight of Alistair's next punch, a blow that sends Alex sprawling to the ground.

He kicks Alex, who curls into a ball on the plush carpet of the hallway.

Ever's safety, our shared obsession, has become the fuse that ignited this explosion of rage, and there's no telling how far the fire will spread.

"Listen, Alistair, I wasn't even there!" Alex pleads, his voice cracking under the strain. "I arrived at the same time you did!"

"Fucking liar!" Alistair snarls and leans down to grip Alex's shirt to lunch him again. "You took her from this house and then abandoned her, you absolute cunt!" He kicks Alex in the ribs, then he pauses, nostrils flaring, as he glares down at Alex. The silence is heavy, thick with the tension of a storm yet to pass.

Damien hovers near the doorway, filling up the space with an intensity that's almost tangible. He doesn't move, doesn't speak, but his eyes are locked on Alex. They're like chips of ice, yet there's a fire behind them, a fierce protectiveness that blazes silently. His jaw is set, lips a thin line, betraying nothing of what must be raging inside him.

"Damien," I start as he takes a step towards Alex, but he holds up a hand, silencing me without a word.

"Your clothes," Charlie murmurs, glaring down at Alex, still curled up on the floor. "That isn't what you were wearing when I saw you earlier."

"What?" Alex spits out, wiping blood from his mouth. "I didn't see you earlier."

Charlie grunts and hauls the kid to his feet.

"What do you mean by that?" I ask, arms folded, gaze raking over his black jeans and black tee.

Charlie, his face contorted with rage, grabs Alex by the collar with the kind of force that has 'reckoning' written all over it. "Start explaining what the fuck this is before I let Alistair kill you."

Alex sneers. He knows no one lets Alistair do anything, but then it fades as he remembers that Alistair *will* kill him if this doesn't get explained in two seconds flat.

"Ever texted me a bit ago asking where I was. I was at home. So, I texted her back, asking where she was. I didn't get a reply, so I checked her location on the Find My Friends app and saw she was at that party. I knew there was going to be drugs and the less kosher crowd there, so I moved my ass as fast as I could to get to her. I couldn't find her, and the next thing I knew, there was a massive fight going upstairs. What the fuck is going on? Why the fuck did *you* let her go there?" He rushes it all out, stumbling over his sentences and glancing at Ever in fear.

"Us?" Alistair booms, practically deafening us.

"So, you're saying you didn't invite Ever to a party, and you didn't take her from his house? I ask steadily, the words sounding unbelievable to my own ears.

"No!" he spits out. "This is your baby now. My work is done."

"So, who was it?" Alistair's tone is deathly quiet, sending an icy chill skittering down my spine.

"Good fucking question."

"That's why he looked a bit confused when I ran into him at the party," Charlie mutters. "Like it took him a second to recognise me."

"What?" I turn on him with a questioning glare.

"Alex, or whoever, was with this girl, had his tongue stuck down her throat and his hand up her skirt."

"Who?" Alex baulks as if this news makes *any* difference to anyone.

"Verity someone..." Charlie waves his hand before he grimaces and focuses again.

"Jesus," Alex mutters. "So, someone is impersonating me?"

"You have got to be fucking deluded if you think I'm buying that!" Alistair hisses.

"One way to find out," Damien says. "Give me your phone."

Alex digs in his pocket and hands it over after he unlocks it.

Damien's eyebrow goes up, and he shows me the texts between him and Ever.

"Fuck," I mutter, my eyes shooting up to pin Alex's until he squirms. "You have a twin we don't know about?"

"No!" he says, aghast. "I'm an only child! You know this. You know my family!"

"Do we?" Alistair growls.

He grabs Alex again and stalks off downstairs, followed by Damien. Charlie scampers off and returns shortly with a bowl, which he hands to me.

"She's going to need that when she wakes up."

Nodding, I take it and turn back to Ever, my head pounding with the clusterfuck of the situation. It's a fucking mess, a catastrophe waiting to implode, and she's in the middle of it, silent and unknowing. The Four Cardinals, we call ourselves, but right now, we're just four screwed-up guys losing it over a girl who deserves better than any of us.

Pulling up the desk chair, I sit in it and place the bowl on the floor, watching her, ready for action.

The minutes tick by, and I can hear the shouts from downstairs as Alistair, Damien, and Charlie try to get to the bottom of this, but I'm not leaving Ever. This is our fault.

I'm pretty sure she wasn't sexually assaulted in the sense that Stanley raped her. But it was seconds away from happening. If we hadn't shown up when we did, she would've been violated in the worst way possible, and there would've been no coming back from that. How the fuck this all happened is a mystery that needs solving, but I can't focus on that. I have to leave that in the hands of the other guys. Ever needs me here.

Seconds later, she groans and curls up on her side. Then she sits up suddenly, and I move like lightning, grabbing the bowl and placing it in front of her. Her gaze locks with mine in shock before she sticks her head in the bowl and throws up the entire contents of her stomach. I push her hair back and murmur to her in between heaves until she is completely done and flops back to the bed. Crossing over to the bathroom, I throw the vomit in the toilet, flush and then swill out the bowl, taking it back to her for round two.

She whimpers as I sit next to her, placing the bowl back on the floor, and I take her hand. "Hey."

"Fuck," she groans. "What the fuck?"

"I was kind of hoping you'd tell me that?"

Her eyes flutter open, and she turns her head, going paler but holding onto the retch. "Too much vodka," she murmurs.

"What's the last thing you remember?" I ask carefully.

She frowns. "I was at that party. Alex ditched me, and I got drunk, I guess. I only had two. I think. The last thing I remember, I was heading for the bathroom, and then I woke up here."

Breathing in deeply, I let it out slowly. She doesn't remember. Roofied, without a doubt. That fucking cunt is dead.

She groans and closes her eyes again. I grip her fingers tighter before letting go. "I'll leave you to rest."

She nods, and I stand up to leave, seeing Charlie hovering in the doorway.

When I close the door quietly, he asks, "Why didn't you tell her?"

"She doesn't need to know how close she was to being violated. Not yet. We will tell her, but let her heal first from the effects of the drug."

"And what if she was raped? Shouldn't we call the doctor?"

"I don't think she was."

"How can you be sure?"

Shaking my head, I sigh. "Her legs were still closed, her knickers still on. If Stanley had fucked her, she'd have been more..."

"Yeah," he says, thankfully not needing me to continue. "We'd better be right about this."

"No shit," I murmur and head off down the stairs to see what the hell is going on with Alex and whoever the fuck took Ever from us earlier.

17

ALISTAIR

Pacing back and forth like a caged animal in the living room of my ancestral townhouse, the thick carpet does nothing to muffle the anger in my steps. I stop, glaring at Alex.

"So, you're telling me you've got an evil twin that Sebastian saw with Ever?" My voice is ice, cutting through the bullshit.

Alex backs up until his ass hits the edge of the desk. "I swear, Alistair, I don't know what you're talking about. This is the first time I've heard about some doppelgänger wreaking havoc. All I have to go on is fucking nervous Seb calling you and Charlie running into some guy!"

"Convenient," I snort, not buying it for a second. "You expect me to believe you didn't know? With all that's at stake?"

He shoves his hands through his hair, a mess of frustration. "Hell, I feel guilty enough as it is, okay? If

I had a bloody twin, don't you think I'd know about it?"

"Guilty?" My eyebrow arches. "Why guilty if you're innocent?"

"Because it's my face he's wearing, isn't it?" His voice rises, tinged with desperation. "And now Ever's caught in this mess because of me. I'm as blindsided by this as you are."

Verging on the edge of believing him, I back off, but if this is true, it's a puzzle piece we had no idea about, which is... unnerving. If there's a twin, he's not just a threat to our plans but to Ever, too. The thought alone sets my blood boiling.

Just then, Ben and Charlie barge in, their faces etched with concern.

"What?" I snap as they look pretty shifty, like I've missed something vital.

"We've decided not to tell Ever about being spiked and Stanley nearly violating her. She doesn't need that stress." Ben gives me a hard stare as if daring me to challenge his decision.

Charlie nods in agreement when I shift my steely glare onto him.

"Nearly violating? How can we be so sure?"

"Apart from the way she was laid out when we arrived before Stanley got too arrogant, he said he was *trying* to win the bet," Damien mutters. "It stands to reason that he didn't get to her. We stopped him. This time."

"Yeah," Ben murmurs.

Their words hang heavy in the air. None of us

want to add to Ever's burdens. She's got this fire in her, no doubt, but even fire can be snuffed out if you smother it with too much crap.

"Fine," I say, knowing they're right but hating that we have to keep secrets from her at all. "But we watch her back twice as hard now." My gaze meets Damien's, and I see the same protective fury there. Ever might not know about the danger, but we'll damn well shield her from it.

Ben leans forward, hands flat on the mahogany table that's seen more secrets than a confessional. "She's got her studies, her work... the last thing Ever needs is to worry about Stanley and his fucking mates."

"Work. I'm not loving the idea of her going there," Damien murmurs.

My gaze snaps to Damien's. "I know, but are you going to be the one to tell her she can't go to work?"

"No," he says almost sulkily, which makes me snort despite the gravity of this entire situation.

"All we need to do is up the level of eyes on her." A shield made of flesh and bone because nobody's laying a finger on her. Never again.

Charlie's glance flickers to me and then to Damien, his voice low but fierce. "We keep her safe. Always in sight, always guarded. Even in her room."

Damien's nod is slight, his gaze doesn't waver, steel-grey eyes fixed like he's already scanning for threats in the shadows. "Cams are already up in there. So we just shift surveillance, even in our own home." His icy gaze lands on Alex.

"Nothing touches her," I confirm. It's simple, really. Ever's untouchable, and we're the barrier between her and the world that doesn't know just how damn precious she is.

Following Damien's stare, I turn to Alex, my glare pinning him to the spot.

"I want a list of every single time you've stepped foot in this house over the past month."

Alex stiffens, his eyes narrowing as he takes in that request. He knows I'm not fucking around; the stakes are miles high, and his next move is crucial.

"Fine," he mutters, jaw set. The reluctance is there, thick in his voice, but so is the resignation.

"Make it quick," I command. "Your memory had better match mine, Alex. Because if that imposter has been here more than today's twice, *you* are in deep shit."

He doesn't argue. Instead, he strides over to the bureau—an old piece of furniture that's all dark wood and history—and yanks open a drawer for a pen and paper. He sits, the chair creaking under the sudden weight, and scribbles down dates and times from his phone.

I watch him, every line he draws, every number he writes, a knot tightening in my gut. His presence here, in this room, at that bureau—it's always been benign before. But now, suspicion taints the air, colouring everything with potential betrayal.

"Remember," I say, my voice low, a warning threading through each syllable. "Details, Alex. Exact details."

He nods, not looking up, focused entirely on the task at hand. His hand moves quickly, but there's a tremble there—a slight shake that betrays the nerves he's trying so hard to hide.

I turn away, giving him space to work but not enough to breathe easily. The truth is out there, tangled in lies and shadows, and I'll drag it into the light, no matter what it takes. Nobody fucks with us —nobody fucks with our girl—and gets away with it.

"Another thing," I murmur, my voice cutting through the silence like a blade despite the low tone. "You need to talk to your parents. Now."

He glares at me from the bureau, his pen pausing mid-sentence. "Alistair, I can't—"

"Can't or won't?" I take a step closer, feeling the edges of my self-control fray. "Because if there's some clichéd, evil, long-lost twin out there wearing your fucking face, screwing with us, I need to know. *We* need to know."

He drops the pen, a soft clatter against the polished wood. "It's not that simple. You think I want some stranger claiming part of my life?"

"Fuck what *you* want," I say coldly. "This is bigger than you."

From the corner, Damien moves, a shadow peeling away from the wall. His eyes are hard, watchful. He's been quiet too long, but when he speaks, everyone listens.

"Ever is in danger," he murmurs, his voice low enough that you have to strain to hear. "If you're telling the truth, which remains to be seen, by the way, that means a twin exists; we have to find out for sure. For Ever's sake."

Alex runs a hand through his hair, a mess of frustration and fear. "Fine," he relents, the word sounding bitter. "I'll call them. But this is going to stir up so much shit, Alistair. Real shit. Your mother will be calling on you after my mother gets through with her about whatever pile of manure this is. So don't you fucking dare come at me again telling me I'm lying. You fucking owe me."

"Fuck off, you little cunt. Distant cousins or not, I don't owe you shit."

"sect business means family comes into it. It's always the way it's been, it's always the way it will go. This is enormous, Alex. Don't you get it?" Charlie is way more tactful than I am, and at times like this, I'm glad of his easy presence. I know I'm too intense for people to be comfortable around me, but it's the way I was brought up, the way my childhood played out. The way I was made a Duke at twenty and not just any fucking Duke, but the Duke of goddamm KnightsGate. The stronghold for everything we hold, all that we live by.

Damien nods once, a sharp, decisive movement. "There is no choice, Alex. The longer we wait, the more dangerous it gets for her. You should know by now that I won't stand by and watch that happen."

Silence settles heavy as a shroud. Alex reaches for his phone with hands that aren't quite steady.

"After you've made that list, asshole," I growl, giving him a slight reprieve. The list trumps the twin in this present moment. If an outsider has infiltrated us, shit hitting the fan isn't even going to cover it. We will all have some serious explaining to do, me most of all.

So we wait and watch as our world threatens to unravel thread by thread, but then I move into action and grab my phone and pen. I know by memory every sect meeting we've had in the last month, in the last year, even, but there have been times when Alex has been here alone while we planned his descent into Ever Knight's life as her best buddy and confidant. Those times are hazy.

Compiling my list and snatching Alex's from him, I dismiss him. "Make that phone call as soon as you get back to your house," I instruct.

He nods reluctantly, but I know he will on the knowledge that if he doesn't, he is done for.

"We need a meeting."

The other guys nod.

"I'll tell Ever we'll be out," Damien says. "So she doesn't come down and freak out if we're not here."

Nodding my agreement with that, the thought of her being afraid because we aren't here settles nicely in my gut. It means her dependence on us has grown. But personally, I don't think we are there yet. If anything, it's probably the opposite.

So we will wait, seduce, manipulate until there is nothing left for her but us.

18

EVER

Blinking awake, the taste of the night's mistakes still heavy on my tongue, my head is a jumbled mess like someone tossed my brain in a blender and hit puree. Fucking vodka. I squint at the window; it's darker than it has any right to be. What time is it? How long have I been out? Groaning, I squint at the clock and see it's late Saturday night. Still. I'd been hoping it was Sunday already. Unless a day has passed, but I doubt it the way I still feel like I've been hit by a truck, only for it to reverse and do it again.

A knock shatters the silence, sharp and unexpected.

"Ever? Are you awake?" The voice is low, almost a whisper, but there's no mistaking Damien's cool tone.

"Yeah. Come in," I say, but my voice is hoarse, revealing more of my vulnerability than I'd like. The door inches open, and he sticks his head around the door. His pale skin and dark attire are like a shadow come to life, and those light grey eyes fix on me with an intensity that both unnerves and captivates.

"Hey." He stuffs his hands into his pockets, looking casual, but it's a façade. Even I know it.

"Hey."

He steps inside, a fluid motion that reminds me of a ghost on TV shows. The door shuts with a soft click, sealing us in this space that suddenly feels too small, too intimate. I gulp, pushing up to sit against my headboard.

"Everything okay?" My voice trails off as he lifts a finger to his lips, signalling silence. There's something about the slow, intentional way he moves toward me that makes my heart race, but not from fear. It's anticipation, maybe, or just the weird buzz of seeing him out of his element.

"I should be asking you that," he murmurs, and there's a softness to his voice I'm not used to, not that I've heard him speak all that often while I've been here. He pauses by the dresser.

"I've been better."

"I bet." He takes another step, closing the distance between us. I should be wary, on guard. But as Damien stands there, looking more human than the brooding Baron I've grown accustomed to in such a short amount of time, my defences start to crumble.

Despite the discomfort it brings, I find myself trapped in the pull of those stormy slate eyes, unable to look away.

"Ever," Damien starts, his voice low. "The guys and I have to head out for a bit. A meeting." His eyebrows knit together, a silent show of concern. "Will you be okay here by yourself?"

I blink, processing the question. The house feels too quiet, too large. Being alone doesn't usually bother me, but in this unfamiliar place, with my head still spinning from the vodka and the darkness creeping into the early morning, it's different.

"Meeting? At this time? What are you? Vampires?" I try to make a joke, and he gives me a cursory smile.

"Something like that," he murmurs, but I can't tell if he's joking or not. I mean, I *know* he's joking. Vampires don't exist. Right? I wouldn't put it past this enigmatic man to be something otherworldly. He has that ethereal quality to him, making him stand out from the crowd. Then I shake my head at myself. I've seen him in daylight, so he's definitely not a vampire.

Why are you even still thinking about this, you fucking idiot?

"Uhm yeah, fine," I lie to his question from moments ago, forcing strength into my words, which I hope he doesn't notice in the slight tremor in my voice. "I don't need anyone to watch over me."

"Good," he replies, but his gaze lingers a moment longer as if he's trying to read the truth behind my lie. It's clear that he's torn between leaving and staying, his protective instincts battling with respect for my independence.

In this brief interaction, I've seen more of Damien than I thought I would—the concern etched in his features, the careful consideration of if I'll be okay without them here. It's a side of him that I'll bet is rare and unexpected, leaving me wondering about the layers I've yet to uncover.

My mind races, trying to balance the weight of solitude against the anchor of independence. There's a tangle of unease in my gut, but I can't let that scare me into clinging to someone else's shadow. I've always been the master of my ship, steering through rough waters with a steady hand.

"Yep." My eyes drop to his bare arm sticking out of a black t-shirt, and I press my lips together at the sight of the carefully carved-out cuts in his flesh. Thin, deliberate lines that map out a hidden pain. They're harsh of a story untold, and I wonder what demons he battles in the dark, in the silence. It shocks me to see these scars so openly displayed, as if they're just another part of him he doesn't bother to hide. My throat tightens, but I swallow the words that threaten to spill over.

It's none of my business.

"I'll check on you when we get back."

I nod, and he leaves me. The room feels colder when the door clicks shut behind him. Alone, I sit up, wrapping my arms around myself—not for warmth, but in a self-made promise that I'll be okay. Just me, by myself. In this big old house with creepy portraits and intense men.

Trying to shake the cobwebs from my head, my mind becomes a bit clearer after that interaction with the exquisite Baron, who is under my skin, whether I want him there or not now.

What was in that vodka?

My mind feels like it's been wrapped in gauze, thoughts stumbling over each other in a sluggish dance where clarity is scarce but making its appearance known. I push myself up, using the edge of the bed for support. The room tilts a little, but I steady myself with a deep breath. It's getting easier to think now, to focus.

"Two drinks," I mutter, pressing a hand to my forehead. "Just two, that's all." It doesn't add up, the fogginess, the lost hours. I've always had a good head on my shoulders when it comes to booze. Could someone have spiked it? The idea sends tentacles of fear creeping over my skin. Who would do that? Why?

I sit heavily again, fists pressed against my temples, willing myself to remember. Pieces of the night flit through my memory—laughter, chatter, Alex, talking to Jade, but nothing concrete, nothing I can grab onto. A wave of frustration washes over me. I hate not knowing, hate the vulnerability of it all.

"Never again." I utter the words millions of people across the globe have muttered over the centuries when they wake with the hangover from hell. "Never, ever again."

But right now, I need to focus on getting through tonight and getting back to normal. Whatever 'normal' means in this weird game of privilege and secrets that royals of KnightsGate Academy seemingly love to play.

The longer I'm in this house, the more I'm starting

to feel that I'm missing something, a part of the joke where the punchline makes sense.

Then that tiny paranoid piece of my mind rears up, jeering that I'm the butt of this joke, and I crawl back under the covers, pulling them over my head.

Eyes closed, I let out a slow breath, trying to steady the swirl of thoughts in my head. Damien's face floats behind my lids. Those light grey eyes that seem to see right through the bullshit. Genuine? Maybe. But everything in this house has two faces, maybe more. It's like a fucking Scooby-Doo mansion. Eyes everywhere, watching, waiting.

I want to forget the fire that chewed up my weekend, the taste of vodka sharp on my tongue, and the black holes in my memory.

Sleep—that's what I need.

Tomorrow is another day, another battle. I just hope I end up on the winning side of the next one because right now, I feel like I'm failing, being crushed and beaten.

With a final deep breath, I let go, surrendering to the exhaustion that tugs at my bones, dragging me down into a restless slumber where the only certainty is the rise and fall of my own breath.

19

CHARLES

The sect room waits, a chamber of whispered conspiracies and unbreakable bonds. Alistair moves through the dark, lighting black candles, their pale glow cutting through the gloom, casting long shadows that dance across the walls like spectres of doubt.

This place is as ancient as the secrets it keeps, tucked away beneath the manicured lawns of KnightsGate University and the townhouse above, its corridors meander for miles under the city, ensuring complete secrecy as we come and go.

With one hand on the hem of my white tee, I pull it off and toss it carelessly to the floor. It's an act, all of this, like we're on stage and the world's our audience. Only, there's no applause down here, just the silent understanding of the ritual to come.

Muscles tense, I'm ready for what comes next. It's fucked up how much I look forward to this, how much I need it.

Picking up my cat o' nine tails whip, I move into the compass position between Alistair and Ben. I am East. I am air, new beginnings, new growth.

Kneeling, I close my eyes as Alistair begins roll call. It's ritual, it's protocol, it's comforting.

The first whip cracks against my skin, the sting sharp and immediate. Heat blooms on my back, and I suppress a groan of longing as my cock goes stiff. It's a relief, this pain, something tangible to hold onto, and it arouses me far past any other experience.

"East?"

"Present."

The lash comes quickly, another hit that forces the breath from my lungs. It's a rhythm we all fall into—the sound of leather on flesh, the quiet huffs of exertion.

With each strike, lightning runs through me, electric and raw. My body responds with adrenaline and something darker, something primal. This makes me feel alive, focused, as if every part of me is on fire.

Ten.

It's done. My breathing's heavy, my back tight with pain, but there's a clarity in my mind that's addictive. I've never felt more present than right here, right now, with the echo of the ritual ringing in my ears.

"Rise." Alistair's voice is solid, grounding.

"True North is under this roof now. That changes everything."

He stands still, hands behind his back like he's about to address Parliament rather than us lot. "She can't be left alone. Not for a second. Not again. We watch but not crowd. We fucked up badly here, and each of us will administer a further twenty lashes as punishment for our lack of care to her." His gaze pierces each of ours, lingering just long enough to drive the point home before he starts pacing.

I nod slowly. We all knew it was coming. It's why he wanted us here without the inter-Cardinals.

"Surveillance round the clock." The idea of watching Ever while she is unaware, gives my hard-on a hard-on, and I shift uncomfortably.

"Exactly." Alistair glares at each of us, one-by-one. "We stick to her so close she'll think we're her shadow. She moves, we move. She breathes, we're there."

"Got it."

"It is your responsibility to inform your inter-Cardinal," Alistair snaps, his voice echoing off the chamber walls. "They're in this too. Everyone's on Ever-watch."

I nod, the weight of this reality sinking in. These inter-Cardinals, secondary to our core group but crucial nonetheless, are a network we can't do without. They're our eyes and ears beyond these walls.

"And Stanley?" I ask. "He needs dealing with in a permanent sense."

"We'll keep them swimming until it's time to pull the plug."

Whatever Alistair has in store for Stanley, it's clear he's not sharing yet, which thrills me. It's going to be dark, deviant and utterly devastating.

I can't fucking wait.

"Understood," I reply, meeting his gaze head-on.

"On your knees."

We all drop at the command of North Cardinal and raise our whips again. Throwing it over my shoulder, I close my eyes as it hits my back in a delicate spot that has been worn down already. Smiling, as I feel the blood seep out, I strike harder. This is our penance, our shared sin and salvation, all wrapped into this dark communion.

Each lash is a reminder of our failure to protect True North, to keep her safe from the predators that circle. Alistair's steady count is a mantra that keeps me centred as I take my punishment. The pain is acute, a cleansing fire that sears away any hesitation, any doubt.

The whip cracks against me for the fifteenth time, enduring our purgatory for her sake. I welcome the pain and let it fill every corner of my being until there's nothing else left.

I'm going to need a fucking good wank after this.

Stifling the snort of amusement as my fucked-up brain comes up with that thought, I grip the whip handle tighter.

My knees are weak when we reach twenty, but my intention is ironclad. We rise as one, brothers in arms and darkness, ready to lay our lives on the line for the cause. For her.

Tonight, and every night after that—until death or disgrace do us part—we'll watch over Ever with a vigilance born from obsession and necessity.

"Dismissed," Alistair says curtly, and we move to leave the chamber. But as I walk through these cold, damp corridors towards the world above, the taste of iron in my mouth, I feel a twisted sense of anticipation even as my back screams with pain, flogged to my limit by my own hand.

We're the Cardinals, and we'll stop at nothing to get what we want.

20

EVER

The moment I step down the last stair, their voices hit me like a slap. The entrance hall of the grand townhouse is buzzing with tension, and my friends are at the centre of it. Sasha is flanked by Cass, and they're both talking at Alistair, who stands there, cool as ever, a dark brow arched in silent command.

"Ever!" Sasha calls out, relief flooding her voice as she spots me. She ducks around Alistair, so he turns around to watch her flying towards me. "Alex told us where you were staying."

Cass's expression mirrors Sasha's as they close in on me, their glares sharp enough to cut glass. "How are you feeling?" Cass asks, her voice laced with concern.

Alistair catches my eye for a brief second before he turns away, heading past us up the stairs, as if granting permission for this private huddle.

"Where's your phone?" Sasha's question pulls me back to the present mess.

"I bloody lost it," I admit. "Somewhere at Jensen's party, I guess."

"We've been trying to reach you for hours." Cass's hands are restless, fingers twisting around a lock of her hair.

Sasha steps closer, lowering her voice. "We'll cut to the chase. There's a video." Her words drip with urgency. "From Jensen's party. You're in it, passed out on a bed while some fight is breaking out around you."

"What? What are you talking about?"

I feel the sharp edges of reality slicing through the foggy aftermath of the night before.

"Ever, it looks bad," Cass says, her eyes dark with worry. "The whole campus is buzzing about it. And not in a good way."

"Shit," I curse under my breath.

Sasha grabs my arm, her grip firm. "There's more. It's Stanley." Her voice is a hushed whisper, but it might as well be a scream in my ears. "He had a bet going to take your V-card. He's in the video. Damien is smashing his face in. Look?"

"Stanley?" The name hits like a punch, bile rising in my throat.

Sasha holds her phone up to show me this video, and they're not wrong. Damien is going to town on Stanley's face while I'm just lying there comatose with a t-shirt thrown over me. "And everyone has seen this?"

"Pretty much," Cass murmurs. "Ever, what can we do?"

"Surely, I'd know if he..." I can't even say it. The idea of him touching me without my consent makes my skin crawl.

The silence from Sasha and Cass is deafening. Their eyes dart away, and it's all the answer I need.

"Fuck." My mind races, trying to piece together fragments of last night, but there's nothing. Just darkness and a void where memories should be.

"I'm going to the infirmary," I blurt out, my voice shaky but resolute.

"We'll come with you," Sasha starts, but I cut her off with a raised hand.

"I have to know for sure. I can't just sit here freaking out about what might or might not have happened." The words come out in a rush, and I'm already moving, propelling toward action, toward truth.

"Good idea," Cass says, nodding firmly. "And you should report it to the Academy, too."

"Maybe," I say, not yet ready to think about that part. My mind's a whirlwind, and I need one thing at a time. "But I want to go alone."

Their mouths open, protest on the tip of their tongues, but then they close them again. They get it. This is something I have to face by myself.

"Okay, but find a way to get in touch later, okay? So we know you're okay," Sasha says, her brows knitting together in concern. "Anything you need, we're here."

"Thanks," I mumble, already halfway to the door. I feel their eyes on my back, heavy with worry, but I don't look back. I can't. There's only forward now, to the infirmary, to the answers I dread and need all at once.

With shaky legs, I cross over the square and onto the campus grounds, each step towards the infirmary tightening the knot in my stomach. The campus is quiet, with only a few students milling around, taking advantage of the little sun traps in the autumn sun. I shiver, realising I walked out without my jacket and in my flip-flops, but this is too important to worry about details. My world has shrunk to a single, terrifying point.

Why didn't the guys tell me? Did they know about the bet? What actually happened to me last night? Do they even owe me anything? They barely know me.

The questions and possible scenarios flood my mind, making it difficult to breathe.

Winding my way to the far corner where the University Infirmary is located, I shove open the door, the cool silence greeting me despite it being packed out with students with various ailments. The receptionist looks up with a smile. "Can I help you?" she asks.

"Uhm... Yeah. I... uhm..." I manage, hating how my voice wobbles. "You know what? It's fine. It's fine," I blabber in panic and back away.

"Wait!" the receptionist says, launching out of her chair and approaching me quickly. "Don't go. We can talk in private."

Blinking rapidly, I nod, feeling like this is happening to someone else. She leads me into a private exam room and closes the door.

"I know that look," she murmurs, keeping her distance. "Tell me what's going on."

I swallow hard, choosing my words like they're glass shards. "There's a video from a party last night." I force the details out, feeling sick. "I was passed out. I thought I was drunk, but then maybe I wondered if I'd been spiked? I need to know if something happened. Please, I'm a virgin; it should be easy to check, right?"

"We can do that. We'll take care of you and make sure you know for certain. I'll get Nurse Grace. She will be in shortly. This is a priority. Don't leave before you've seen her, okay, love?"

"Ever. Ever Knight. Okay, I won't."

She nods and slips out while I sit on the edge of the sterile bed, my legs swinging slightly over the side. The paper beneath me crinkles with every jittery movement. I'm alone in a room that smells like disinfectant and anxiety, my stomach doing flips as I wait for the nurse to arrive.

The door opens, and a nurse with kind eyes and a clipboard enters. "Ever Knight? I'm Nurse Grace. Flick told me about your situation. We'll get you some answers, okay, hun?"

"Okay."

She pulls the curtain across and, from the other side, calls out, "Slip your jeans and knickers off and lie back. Put the sheet over your lower half."

"Okay." It's the only word I can manage right now. Everything else seems too complex. I feel exposed under the fluorescent lights, vulnerable in a way that goes beyond the physical. It's as if this examination could lay bare more than just my body— it could unravel all the secrets I've kept even from myself.

"Have you ever had an internal exam before?" she asks, coming through the gap in the curtain.

"No."

"Don't worry, I'll be quick. Try to relax, okay, hun?"

I can only nod as I bend my knees, and she gently pushes my legs apart. I am mortified. This is beyond humiliating. I hate every second, but I need to know.

She works methodically, explaining each step before she takes it, giving me some sense of control in a situation where I feel I have none. Her touch is clinical and impersonal, but I flinch whenever she touches me.

"Deep breaths, Ever. You're doing great," Nurse Grace says, sensing my unease. She offers a small smile before she goes back to work.

I nod, taking her advice and inhaling deeply, attempting to slow the racing of my heart to still the tremor in my limbs. Relief fights with dread inside me, each battling for supremacy. Relief that I'm finally getting answers, dread of what those answers might be.

There is nothing to say right now because what can you say to someone who's peering into the most private corners of your life, searching for evidence of a violation you prayed never happened?

"Your hymen is still intact, so there was no penetration."

"Fuck," I breathe out and then burst into tears, holding my hands up to my face. "I'm sorry, I'm sorry."

"Hey," she says, rising and pulling the sheet over the top of me again. "It's okay. Let it out. What happened is scary and should never happen to anyone. You need to report this to the Chancellor, Ever. Do you think you can do that?"

Shaking my head, I try to stifle the sobs. "I don't know. What if they don't believe me?"

"These cases are always taken with the utmost seriousness, I can assure you. I will be there to make sure of it."

The relief that hits me isn't gentle or soothing; it's a tidal wave crashing over me with such force I almost gasp. For a second, I can't speak, can't move. It's like my body is rebooting after shutting down from sheer terror.

"Thank you," I manage to choke out eventually, my voice hoarse as if I've been screaming for hours. Maybe in my head, I have been. "I'll think about it."

She nods, unclips a form from her board, and holds it out. I take it and fold it, placing it on the bed next to me.

"You can get dressed now."

My legs feel shaky as I slide off the examination table, but they hold. Barely.

"Take care of yourself, Ever," she advises, handing me a leaflet on counselling services.

"Will do." The words are automatic, but gratitude warms them. I turn my back to get dressed while she slips out again, and I pick up the form, shoving it in my back pocket but leaving the leaflet. Trying my best to be invisible, I walk out of the infirmary as fast as I can.

Outside, the world hasn't stopped turning. I let out a long breath, feeling the weight on my shoulders lift that, if nothing else, Stanley, or anyone else for that matter, didn't violate my body while I was unconscious. I will never let myself be put in that situation again, I vow as I walk away from the infirmary, my sanctuary, in this moment of chaos.

Feeling better but wary, I stride across campus, my steps uneven on the cobblestone paths.

"Hey, Ever!" Nick Henderson's voice jabs at my bubble of relief like a needle. He's leaning against an oak tree, smugness oozing from his smirk as if he's the cat that got the cream. "Looking for this?"

My phone dangles from his fingers.

"Yeah. Give it back, Nick," I snap, more out of anxiety than bravado.

"Sure thing, sweet cheeks." His eyes rake over me, leaving a trail of grime. "But it'll cost you. How about a little favour? One blow job, and it's all yours again."

Disgust twists in my gut, thick and bitter. He's nothing more than a bully, using leverage like a weapon.

"Go to hell," I spit out, now pissed off. Who do these entitled assholes think they are?

"Don't play coy, Ever. We know the truth now. The good girl not so good after all!" a voice hurls my way, venom wrapped in laughter.

"Did you enjoy the party, Ever? Looked like you did!" another taunts, their words a sharpened edge against my already raw nerves.

"Little slut!"

"Give him a blow job for your phone back, Ever. You know you want to!"

I don't even know who these people are.

Heat creeps up my neck, setting my face aflame. I'm surrounded, trapped by this circle of mockery. My phone, my privacy, my dignity—held ransom by sneering faces.

The tears that are still so close to the surface from my breakdown only minutes ago sting my eyes, betraying the panic clawing at my insides. I can't cry here; I won't give them the satisfaction.

"You're going to make her cry," Nick taunts, waving my phone in front of me, goading me.

I'm about to run and forget about the phone when a familiar voice cuts through the jeers of the bullies.

"Enough."

The single word slices through the noise, a command that resonates with power. Alistair steps forward, his presence like a shadow overtaking the sun. His blue eyes are ice as they fix on Nick, and his voice is a low rumble laced with danger.

"Hand it over, Henderson. Or I can guarantee she'll get it back with your hand still attached."

The crowd parts like he's Moses and we're the Red Sea. Nick, with all his bravado, suddenly looks like a cornered animal, his eyes darting for an out that doesn't exist. He tosses my phone towards me, a coward's retreat.

"Thought so," Alistair says, his gaze never leaving Nick as my phone arcs through the air, a shiny black rectangle with my name embossed in gold on the cover, a symbol of my recent humiliation.

"Shit," I whisper as it slips through my fumbling fingers, but Alistair's reflexes are lightning-fast. His hand snaps out, catching it before it can smash against the concrete. He doesn't even look at me as he hands it over, his eyes still locked on Nick, who backs away, swallowed up by the dispersing crowd.

"Thanks," I mutter, clutching my phone like a shield. Alistair nods, then turns to me with an unreadable expression.

"Let's get you home," he says.

I nod, eager to escape the jeers that still echo in my mind. We walk in silence for a few minutes, my thoughts swirling chaotically. When I finally speak, my voice is steadier than I feel.

"Now that I've got you, we need to talk about the rent," I blurt out and then cringe inwardly as his curious sapphire gaze lands on me with interest.

"Rent? It's not necessary."

"But I want to," I insist, clinging to this one thing I can control and the one conversation that will distract me enough from this nightmare of a weekend. I never thought I'd say this, but roll on Monday. "I have my housing allowance. I'll give it to you every week now instead of the landlord."

Alistair studies me for a moment longer before nodding once. "If that's what you want."

"It is," I confirm, feeling a tiny measure of power returning to me. At least when it comes to this, I can stand on my own two feet.

"On one condition."

Dread fills my soul. "Oh?"

"You agree to make KnightsGate Manor your home for the rest of the academic year."

As we approach the towering building of Knights-Gate Manor, the gothic structure is an extension of the Royal Academy behind us, I hesitate.

"I'm not sure how that would work with my landlord."

"His house set on fire. He can't expect you to be loyal to him when he fixes it. You need a roof over your head and stability, not flitting around from house to house."

Well, he's not wrong there.

"Fine." I finally exhale the word more than say it. It feels like a pact made with the devil, but I have no idea why. "And thanks for earlier and for letting me stay and for yesterday as well."

A smirk curls his lips as he pushes open the heavy front door with an ease that speaks of power. "We look after our own, Ever, and you're ours."

His words send a trail of ice down the back of my

neck, mingling fear with an undeniable rush. I'm part of 'their' world—protected, but also possessed in some intangible way. As we step into the entrance hall, the sensation only intensifies, the shadows seeming to whisper secrets I'm not sure I want to hear, that I'm not *ready* to hear.

21

EVER

Monday morning arrives with my head throbbing mercilessly as I take two more painkillers, a relentless reminder of Saturday night's spiked drink. There is no doubt in my mind now that is what it was, and that Stanley gave it to me to rape me to win his sick bet. I glare at the form I filled out late last night with loathing. I wasn't sure at first, but then I found anger, and Stanley Richfucker, Lord Asshole, is going down. I glance at the form to make sure I didn't actually write that down.

Stanley Richford, Lord Ashdown.

The morning grey light filtering through my curtains feels like an assault on my gritty eyes, but I force myself off the bed, determined to scrub away the haze clinging to my thoughts.

The shower's hot spray stings my skin—a welcome pain. As the water cascades over me, I try to imagine it washing away the physical and mental toxins.

I dress on autopilot: a pair of high-waisted jeans that hug my legs just right and a loose ivory sweater that falls off one shoulder—a touch of understated elegance. Giving them a sniff, they smell faintly of smoke, but it's going to have to do. The way the breeze is picking up outside, it'll be blown away by the time I reach class. Uncoiling my hair from the shower-bun, I leave it down and glance at the clock before shoving books into my bag and sliding my laptop beside them. There is no time for breakfast; the thought alone churns my stomach.

Still.

Heading down the stairs with my jacket slung over my arm and my bookbag on my shoulder, I grin. Charlie is waiting by the door, his hazel eyes scanning me with interest.

"Looking cute, Ever," he teases.

"Thanks," I murmur, stepping out into the crisp autumn air. "Back at you." Leaves crunch underfoot, and I pull my jacket on as the breeze whacks us in the face. "Fuck, that came out of nowhere."

"Wouldn't be England if it didn't."

"Fact," I reply with a snort of amusement. "You're in this early? Thought the drama students liked a lie-in?"

"What's that?" he jokes, but shakes his head. "Got Art History this morning."

"Heavy shit on a Monday morning."

"No kidding."

We walk side by side, his presence a bizarre comfort despite feeling like I'm being watched.

"You ready for Test Week?" he asks as we leave the square. I'm not sure when it was decided we'd walk in together, but it's nice, I guess.

"Always."

"Hey, you okay? After everything?" Charlie nudges me gently with his elbow.

"Yep. Fine," I lie, not fine at all.

Charlie doesn't press further, but I catch him shooting me a worried glance before going back to staring in front.

Falling into an easy silence, we reach the building of my first class, and he gives me a playful salute. "Knock 'em dead, Professor's pet."

"Ha-ha," I retort, but his laughter follows me inside, along with the invisible eyes I feel lurking around every corner.

I shake it off. It's probably me just freaking out over Stanley drugging me.

An hour later, shuffling into English Lit, my mind clinging to the last threads of Advanced Poetry and Metaphor from the class I just left, I smile and finally feel myself again. I'm in my element, and no one can touch me here.

"Shakespeare's sonnets," the Professor drones as I sit quickly and drag my books out. Feeling eyes on my back, I turn before I can stop myself.

Benedict.

He's a few rows back, his eyes fixed on the front,

pen scribbling across his notebook like he's actually into it. My brain stalls. Has he always been here?

I try to focus on the lecture, but my thoughts keep snagging on Benedict. He's the quiet storm, the deep waters you don't see coming until you're drowning, and I never knew he was in this class with me until now. I guess my head is totally on my work when I'm in here, soaking up the knowledge like a sponge, eager for the words.

When we are dismissed, I practically bolt from the room. The campus cafe promises caffeine and normalcy, two things I'm desperate for.

"Ever!" Lila catches up to me as I push through the door.

"Hey," I breathe out as we fall into the long queue. "How was home? Did you figure something out?"

"Same old." She shrugs, her smile not quite reaching her eyes. "Yeah. I found a new place with Hardy and his mates."

My stomach drops. "Lila, those guys non-stop party central."

She rolls her eyes, hands digging into her pockets. "Needs must. It's cheap, and I won't be there much anyway. I'm going to commute a few times a week and go home on weekends or when there are exams. It's fine."

"Okay, sounds like a plan," I mutter, because what else can I say?

We shuffle forward in line, the scent of roasted coffee beans almost enough to ease the knots growing in my stomach again now that I'm out in the open. I reach for a stir stick, twirling it between my fingers as I peer over at the pastry display.

Something makes me turn around and I see Alistair, lounging at a table across the room, his designer jacket thrown over the chair beside him with careless elegance.

"Alistair the hot Duke," Lila murmurs, following my gaze.

"Hard to miss," I mutter back.

"How goes things at their abode?"

"Weird, but okay," I mutter fixated on his dark hair and blue-eyed intensity, sipping an espresso like it's nectar of the gods. Our eyes lock, and his lips curve into a luscious half-smile. He doesn't drop his gaze, so I'm the one to do it as I turn back to order my coffee.

"Ever, you okay?" Lila asks, nudging me with her elbow as we collect our drinks. "I heard about everything."

"Yep. Fine," I lie again. It's like a thing now.

"You sure? I know you told us what happened at the clinic, but this has got to be freaking you out."

"Honestly, it's fine. I'm good. Just want to forget, you know?"

"Yeah."

Catching Alistair's gaze again as we head out into the late morning, I wonder why I never really noticed these guys before. I knew vaguely who they were, who doesn't? But now they're like ghosts, haunting every corner I turn. Did I just not notice them before?

Or is this a game, creeping closer until I can't ignore them anymore?

Lila chats about her classes, but I'm only half-listening. My mind races, trying to piece together the why behind their sudden omnipresence. It feels like a puzzle I'm not smart enough to solve. Not yet, anyway.

"Ever, seriously, are you sure you're good?" Lila presses, concern etching her features.

"Promise, I'm good," I reassure her.

I take a long gulp of my coffee, wishing it could wash away the unease that's settled in my chest. I meet Alistair's stare one more time through the café window before turning away. He's still there, still watching, and I wonder what move he'll make next.

In my next class, I slide into my seat, my mind a whirlpool of thoughts. Books sprawl across the desk, but the words blur together, indecipherable as my focus fractures, and I try to anchor my attention to the professor's lecture on Gothic literature. But it's no use, my ears catch every hushed whisper, every stare. Everyone knows about what happened, and it's not going away.

Is that why the guys are suddenly surrounding me? To protect me again?

The clock ticks torturously slow, mocking me. Every minute stretches, a marathon to the end of the day. When it's finally over, relief floods me, but it's chased by the dread of walking out into the open, into the crude jokes and cruel laughs.

The crisp autumn breeze whips my hair around

my face, and I curl it back over my ears. I shuffle my bag higher on my shoulder, willing my feet to move faster across the fallen leaves that carpet the walkway.

"Ever, wait."

Damien's voice crashes into my escape. He falls into step beside me, his presence both a shield and a cage. I suck in a deep breath, trying to swallow down the nagging suspicion crawling under my skin.

"Hey," he says, and it's casual, too casual for someone who's part of the group that's suffocating me with their silent surveillance.

"Hi," I reply, my voice tight. "Good day?"

"Usual." He shrugs, tucking his hands into the pockets of his dark jeans.

"So I hear you're pretty great at study stuff. I suck, and I need to ace this year. After this week, would you mind sitting with me, maybe going over how I can focus on the work and not any and everything else?"

"Don't you get a pass anyway?"

The words are out of my mouth before I can stop them, and I wince as his face goes blank.

"What makes you say that?"

"I'm sorry!" I blurt out. "It was rude and unfounded."

"Wow, you don't mince words, do you?" His slight smile puts me at ease that he isn't really offended, probably more shocked at my accusation.

"Sorry."

"Stop apologising. You're right, I do, but I want more than that."

His confirmation of the suspicions that surround the elite at this University hits me square in the chest. It makes me sad that the class divide is still so strong.

"Sure, I can help you."

We round the corner, and the house looms ahead, a sanctuary that's lost its sanctity. I quicken my pace, eager to slip inside and shed the invisible cloak of everyone's attention.

"Thanks. You're the best."

This whole conversation has been weird and almost forced. I don't get it. Why is he trying to have a conversation with me?

"See you later, Ever." Damien's farewell is a whisper against the back of my neck as he follows me inside, a ghost touch that promises I'm never truly alone.

"Later," I echo, and the front door closes behind me with a click that sounds oddly like a lock sealing me in.

I dart up the stairs and down the hallway to my room. The door swings open, and I stumble inside, slamming it shut with a shove of my shoulder. The sound echoes, a resounding declaration of temporary solitude.

Alone. Finally.

I lean back against the wood, letting my head fall back with a thud. My breath comes out in a rush as I try to banish the twisted knot of anxiety in my stomach. I peel off my jacket, tossing it carelessly onto the bed, where it lands in a crumpled heap, mirroring the disarray of my thoughts.

"Safe." The word is a whisper to myself, a feeble attempt to calm the racing of my pulse. I kick off my shoes and toe them aside. There is no need for pretences now, no eyes to judge, no whispers to dissect.

It's another battle, another day to navigate the precarious waters of KnightsGate University. But tonight, I have a reprieve. Tonight, I'm just Ever—no titles, no expectations, no prying eyes, no videos following me around, no whispers behind my back.

And for now, that's enough.

22

BENEDICT

Stalking the aisles, I shadow her every move. She is pensive, strolling through the stacks, wandering as if in deep thought. She has no idea I'm even here, as I'm pretty sure she had no clue I was in her English Lit class, either. Usually, I sit at the back or skip it, knowing I'll ace it regardless. My mind works on a different level. It 'gets' poetry, prose, novels and plays, just like it is easy for me to grasp Philosophy. Okay, it doesn't take a genius to figure out that both my affluent and noble parents are in these fields, so it's a given I would have some of their brains, but still, it takes more than showing up to really understand the subjects.

Ever doesn't even look up as I quietly walk down the same aisle she is standing in and when she reaches for a book without even looking up, showing me how well she knows this section, I reach for it too. Her fingers brush against mine, and I fight back the tingle as sparks fly between us.

"Sorry," she says, still not looking up.

"No worries," I murmur, letting my hand linger just a moment too long.

Ever finally glances up, those emerald eyes of hers shifting like the rolling English hills. They settle into a shade that tells me she's more curious than annoyed.

"Benedict," she breathes, tilting her head slightly, her blonde hair cascading over one shoulder. "Sorry, I'm totally out of it."

"Understandable," I murmur, causing her to give me a sharp glare.

I have to come clean with her about what we know. The longer this goes on, the worse it will be for everyone involved when she finds out we know exactly what happened and could've prevented it had we not been blindsided by her sudden appearance under our roof and how to navigate that. And don't even get started on the fucking evil twin. Jesus. What a shitshow.

Stepping back to give her space, but not before grabbing another book near the one she wants. "Guess we have the same taste."

"Seems like it," she says with a small smile, pulling the book closer. "You're into Brontë?"

"Actually, yeah." I nod, watching the way her eyes light up. 'Wuthering Heights' is a dark labyrinth of the human psyche, don't you think?"

"Exactly!" She lights up, clutching the book to her chest. "It's all twisted love and revenge—makes you wonder about the depth of passion, doesn't it? Wow, I didn't know… so when I saw you in English Lit, you actually read it?"

Snickering, I nod. "Yeah. I'm not a star attendee, but it's my major, like you."

"Why didn't you say?"

"Kinda figured you'd already have seen me. Call me egotistical." I give her a half smile that draws her gaze to my lips.

"Sorry, I'm focused when it comes to classes. Bit of a nerd."

"A hot nerd, though." I cringe at the sheer lameness of that statement.

She giggles, though, to my relief. "Well, the same could be said for you."

"I'll take it." The desire that courses through me that she thinks I'm hot is something I never imagined one syllable would ever do to me. "But passion can drive people to do crazy things." The words tumble out, edged with more truth than I intend. "In the books, you know? Charlotte's work is fascinating, too. Do you prefer her over Emily?"

"Hard to say." Ever purses her lips in thought. "I admire Charlotte for 'Jane Eyre.' There's something raw and real about Jane's character, her resilience."

"Resilience," I echo, thinking how that word fits Ever perfectly. She's always stood apart, her name synonymous with the university itself, yet she doesn't flaunt it. "That's one hell of a trait to write about."

"Right?" She nods eagerly. "And what about you? Who's your literary hero?"

"Orwell," I say without hesitation. "His grip on

dystopian futures is chilling. Makes you look at society differently."

"Dark, but insightful." A knowing look crosses her face as if she sees through me. "I guess we both appreciate a story that digs deep into the darker side of things."

"Something like that," I agree, feeling the weight of my own secrets. The library around us seems to close in, books filled with truths and lies alike. In this moment, with Ever, I'm painfully aware of which ones I'm living.

"Okay, Benedict. Let's see if your taste in literature is as good as you say." There is a spark of challenge that pulls me deeper into her orbit.

"Challenge accepted. And call me Ben, please," I say, my voice steady though my pulse isn't. With her, it's the thrill of the chase, the shared whispers between the lines. It's dangerous, and fuck, I can't seem to get enough. I don't want this interaction to end. "Fancy a coffee?"

Ever looks up from the shelf, her gaze reflecting the lights, giving them a near-mystical glow.

"Sure, I could use a break from all this." She waves a hand at the labyrinth of shelves, and we start walking side by side out of the library.

The brisk air hits us as we step outside and make our way to the Academy café. It's a small place, but it's warm and smells like roasted beans and freshly baked pastries—a sharp difference from the musty scent of the library.

We order our coffees and grab a corner table away

from the late afternoon rush. The steam from the cups blurs the world around us, and for a moment, it's just us and our shared love for words.

"Hit me with your top three books."

"Only three?" I joke. "That's like asking a parent to pick their favourite child."

"Ouch, that sounds like it has backstory."

Snorting and nearly choking on the sip of coffee, I shake my head. "Only child. You?"

I already know. I know most superficial things about her. I'm going to use this time to dig deeper so that when I drive my cock into her pussy and the words, 'I love you' tumble from my lips, I mean them with every part of my soul.

"Yep. Kind of a lonely upbringing. I'm sure you've heard the tales."

Frowning, as I wasn't expecting that dark of an opener, it turns to a warm flutter that she felt she could open up that quickly to me.

"I have, but that is a topic for another time, if you decide you want to speak more on it. Right now, you want my top three books, right?"

The option is laid bare for her to decide which way she wants to swing.

"Right."

"'1984', 'Crime and Punishment', and 'To Kill a Mockingbird'. What about you?"

"Nice choices," she nods approvingly. "And quick on the draw. I like that. For me, it's 'Wuthering Heights', 'The Bell Jar', and 'Pride and Prejudice'."

"Classics with strong characters and even stronger emotions," I observe. "I should have guessed."

"Guilty as charged." She takes a sip from her cup, her gaze fixed somewhere in the middle distance. "I actually want to write something one day. Something real, you know? That speaks to people."

My heart thumps at this piece of her she has shared.

I lean forward, eager to hear more. "What kind of story?"

"Something raw that dives into human struggles and resilience," she confides, her fingers tapping a rhythm on the table.

"Sounds powerful. You've got the unique perspective, I guess," I venture cautiously, dodging artfully back into her upbringing.

"You could say that."

"I have no doubt you'll inspire."

"Thanks, Ben." A blush creeps into her cheeks, and she gives me a shy smile. "And what about you? Any secret aspirations?"

Trying not to choke on the word 'secret', I laugh dryly. "Yeah, I've thought about writing, too. Maybe something philosophical, exploring the nature of choice and freedom."

"Then you're halfway there already." She points at me with a flourish. "Just need to put pen to paper. Or fingers to keyboard." She giggles again, and it's the most adorable thing I've ever heard. A far cry from the frail, unconscious woman we found on the verge of losing her entire being to some fucking prick who needs his dick chopped off.

"Here's to future bestsellers and the fantastic stories we'll tell."

"Cheers to that."

Our laughter mingles with the clatter of the café, and for a moment, the darkness that usually clings to me feels a little lighter, and I want to keep talking to her, picking her brains on what makes her tick and what drives her.

"Have you read 'The Night Circus'?" I ask as our conversation lingers on our favourite reads. "It's like the author paints with words."

"I have," she replies, her eyes lighting up. "The way magic is woven into the narrative—it's stunning." She leans back, animated. "But what really got me was the subtlety of the romance, how it built up slowly."

"Yes." I grin, surprised and thrilled by our shared appreciation. "It wasn't just about the spectacle—it was the nuance, the tension between the characters."

"Character-driven stories always hit harder, don't they? Like in 'Atonement.' The twist there shattered me," she says, a touch of enthusiasm in her voice.

"Briony's realisation and the consequences?" I shake my head in disbelief. "That ending is brutal."

"Right? You think it's one thing, but then—" Ever snaps her fingers, "—it flips on you."

"Perfectly executed." I nod, feeling that buzz you get when someone just gets it. Gets *you*. We're vibing on a level I didn't know was possible with anyone.

"Dark academia novels, though." She shifts, eager to dive into another topic. "There's something about them—the ambience, the intellect, the moral ambiguity."

"Like 'If We Were Villains'?" I suggest, watching her reaction closely. This change in topic has hit me hard in the guts. We are standing on the edge of a cliff, just waiting to fall off and plummet to the ground where secrets and darkness lie in wait.

"God, yes!" Her expression is pure excitement. "The blurred lines between right and wrong, the loyalty among the characters even as everything falls apart."

"Life's not black and white," I muse aloud, our thoughts mirroring each other, as I try to drip-feed her possibilities that she is going to have to accept sooner rather than later. "It's all those shades of grey that make a story resonate."

"Yes! Exactly, Ben. You get it." Her green eyes lock onto mine, and it's like we're the only two people who understand some secret language.

Fuck. I've fallen for her in one afternoon on a level that is intellectual, spiritual and emotional. The obsession with her pales in comparison to this sudden surge of raw intensity; I need to know more. I need to know *everything*.

Ever is finishing her coffee and looking at her phone. "I'd better get moving. These essays won't write themselves," she says lightly.

"True. Can I read them when you're done?"

Her wide, shocked stare makes me curse inwardly.

I've pushed too far, too fast. "Really?"

"Yes, really. I want to be the one to say I read your early work when you're a literary genius claiming your Pulitzer in a few years."

"Oh, my. Now you're talking dirty to me."

My cock springs to attention. "Is that a yes?" My voice is hoarse with desire.

"Sure, I guess. As long as you promise to be kind."

"Always. But I'm sure they will be exceptional, just like the woman who created them."

Our gaze locks and I lean forward, ready to capture her mouth with mine, but she breaks off and stands up, clearing her throat.

Disappointed, I rise as well. "I'll walk back with you."

"Sure," she murmurs, and things have taken a sudden cooler turn. I shot my bolt too soon, and now I've ruined everything.

Walking side by side, our footsteps fall into a comfortable rhythm despite the sudden awkwardness surrounding us.

"This was good," I say, my hands shoved into my pockets, needing to break the silence.

"It was," Ever agrees with a soft smile. "I didn't expect to find someone here who actually shared my taste in books."

"KnightsGate has its surprises."

"That it does."

As we reach the front steps of our shared house, the silence isn't awkward anymore; it's filled with unspoken words, a mutual understanding that we've stumbled upon something rare—a genuine connection in a place where appearances often matter more than reality.

But something is holding her back.

For me, there's a pull, an urge to keep her with me, to spill every thought I've ever had about literature, life, everything. But *I* hold back, respecting the space between us, not wanting to scare her off completely.

There are cameras here, always watching, but my heart's drumming a rhythm that drowns out caution.

"I really enjoyed talking with you, Ben," she murmurs, swinging back to warm as I gaze down into those mesmerising eyes.

"Me too." My hand brushes hers, and I'm lost.

No force on earth can stop me this time. I lean in, close enough to feel her breath mingle with mine. The world narrows down to this moment, to the warmth radiating from her skin. I can't resist—it's like gravity pulling me in—and I brush my lips lightly against hers, a whisper of a kiss that says everything I've left unsaid.

She stiffens, surprise etched on her features. Pulling back, her hand flies to her mouth, and I immediately step away, my chest tight.

My apology tumbles out, rough around the edges. "I'm sorry."

Her eyes are wide, searching mine, and I brace for the fallout. But it's not just the cameras I'm worried about; it's the fear of having crossed a line I can't redraw.

"It's okay," Ever says, her voice steady even as her eyes dart away for a split second. "It's just after the other night, I'm cautious."

I nod, taking in her guarded stance. The way she wraps her arms around herself tells me more than words could. "I get it."

"It's been weird, you know? Feeling like everyone's watching, waiting for me to crack." Her words are a jumble of her thoughts, and again, I'm honoured that she is spilling her soul to me. But the guilt is strong, and I have to tell her we know.

"That's understandable. But you're not alone. We are here for you, Ever. We won't let you be hurt again. I can promise you that."

"Did you guys know? About what happened to me?" Ever's voice cuts through the night, a sharp edge of suspicion beneath her words.

I feel the ground shift under my feet, and my throat tightens. This is it—the moment I dread. "We did. Or we pieced it together. We were going to tell you, but after you woke up and you felt so sick, we didn't think the time was right, and then you found out on your own the next day. Do you hate us?"

She studies me, searching for something in my face, and I wonder if she sees through the thin veneer. All we know is tangled up in silence and secrets, and here I am, feeding her more half-truths.

"No, no, of course not. It's a weird situation, and you barely even know me. I would feel uncomfortable telling someone all that as well while they vomited into a bowl in front of you." She gives me a shaky smile, but it's genuine. She really doesn't hold it against us for keeping this from her before she found out anyway.

"If anything, I owe you all a thanks," Ever murmurs, her voice softening the chill of the evening air. "You've all been really great to me on the worst weekend of my life."

"We're here for you." I don't really know what else to say. I feel like shit she is taking this so well, *thanking* us even. We are utter pieces of shit.

"I appreciate that. It's nice to have someone in my corner."

She turns, disappearing into the shadows of the house as she pushes the door open. My gaze lingers on the space she vacated, feeling the echo of her absence like a physical ache.

I lean against the cold, unforgiving doorframe, my eyes closing as I imagine what it would have been like to press my lips against hers just a little longer, a little harder, to slip my tongue into her mouth. Her scent, her warmth, her nearness—it's maddening.

Ever is under my skin, living in my veins, pulsing with every beat of my heart. I want her—all of her— and this twisted game of half-truths and hidden desires is shredding me from the inside out.

She's more than an obsession; she's a need that gnaws at me, relentless and raw. I open my eyes, staring down the silent hallway. She's so close, but might as well be miles away. I need to possess her, to claim her as mine, but for now, all I have are shadows and the bitter taste of lies.

23

EVER

L ate that night, shadows cling to the walls like dark whispers as I take the stairs quietly in the dead of night, desperate for food. It seems I've been neglecting my stomach for a while now, and it is protesting vehemently.

Low, urgent murmurs greet my ears when I cross the entrance hall toward the kitchen, coming from behind a closed door that leads to a room I've never been in before. Truth be told, I didn't even notice it before now it's that well-blended into the walnut wood-panelling of the wall.

The voices inside are muffled, but each word feels heavy. My errant brain is being naughty, urging me to listen, to discover what lurks in the conversations of those who live in this house.

Glancing around to make sure no one is watching me lurk, I lean in, not close enough to touch the wood. The hush from inside makes it all feel like a ritual, something ancient and not meant for my ears. But I'm here now, and there's no turning back.

"Careful," Alistair's low, gravelly voice cuts through the silence, every syllable dripping with authority. I'm learning he's the kind of guy who never raises his voice; he doesn't need to. His presence alone commands attention, and right now, I can almost picture him in there, standing tall, blue eyes scanning the room like he owns every inch of it. Well, okay, he *does*.

"Always am," Damian's response is smooth, velvety. He's got this way of speaking that gets under your skin like he knows things about you that you haven't even figured out yourself. His words have layers, each one darker than the last, wrapping around you until you're caught up in whatever web he's weaving.

My mind races, trying to connect the dots. What are they talking about? What's so important that it has to be shrouded in whispers and shadows of midnight at the Manor?

They're talking in code almost, and it's intriguing to me, even though everything about this feels off, like a scene from one of those movies where you're screaming at the character not to open the door.

Fragments of sentences drift through the crack like smoke, curling into my consciousness, elusive and teasing. My brain is on fire, each piece of a puzzle I need to fit together.

"The sect doesn't forgive easily." Alistair's voice

cuts through, loud and clear, despite being low and dangerous.

That word *sect* sends a cold streak down my back. What sect? I chew on my lip, the taste of anxiety on my tongue. The following silence is heavy, filled with unsaid things, with hidden threats lurking just below the surface.

"Understood," comes Damian's reply, smooth as shadowed silk. "It will be dealt with swiftly and brutally." His calm sends ripples of unease, skittering across my mind. sects, secrets, and now this chill certainty in his tone?

My gut twists, a knot of fear and fascination. I'm out of my depth, swimming with sharks in dark waters. But I can't stop now. I need to know more. Whatever this is about, it's secretive and draws me in through the curiosity that is the very patchwork of my nature.

I lean away from the door, breaths shallow.

"One slip, and we're not just ruined; we're dead." Alistair's comment is casual, but strikes fear in my soul. His words are ice, and they freeze my veins. The consequences he hints at are not just scandal or disgrace—this is something else, something fatal.

"No turning back." Damien is absolute in his statement.

No turning back? My mind races. From what? What have they entangled themselves in that reeks of such darkness?

Their voices drop to a whisper again, and I strain to hear more. Nothing. Silence wraps around me like a cloak, and I'm left with the chill of their words, the gravity of secrets I'm not meant to know.

The voices fade, and I pull back from the door, my brain working overtime. There's a secret here, in the heart of the old English manor where power and tradition are etched into the very stones, and I'll find it. Because if there's one thing I've learned, it's that secrets always find a way to the surface, and when they do, I'll be ready.

I have to be.

Moving quickly to the kitchen, I flick on the light and search the cupboards for something to eat, trying to focus on the mundane task. The contents of the cupboards barely register as I automatically reach for a box of cereal and a bowl. The crunch of the dry flakes is loud in the silence, too noisy, like they're echoing the pounding in my chest.

Splashing in too much milk, I shove a spoonful into my mouth, the taste bland on my tongue. My mind isn't here; it's stuck to that door, glued to the mystery behind it. sects. Brutality. Whispers of darkness cloaked in casual conversation. This isn't just university or some rich family drama.

My hunger is overshadowed by the torrent of questions swirling in my mind. Who's part of this sect? What's at stake for Alistair and Damien? The menace in their tones was unmistakable, and it's clear they're playing a dangerous game—one where the stakes might just be life or death.

What am I going to do with this information? It's like I've stumbled upon a live wire, and now I'm holding it without knowing where to put it down safely. Do I confront them? That seems foolhardy and possibly lethal. Do I keep it to myself? The weight of such a secret might be too much for me to bear alone.

I finish eating mechanically and rinse off the bowl, placing everything back exactly as I found it.

Slipping back across the hall, I glance toward that closed door—half-tempted to listen again, half-terrified I'll be caught eavesdropping on matters that could have dire consequences. Swallowing the thick fear that clogs my throat, I creep back up the stairs to my room, each step heavy with dread and uncertainty.

KnightsGate Manor at night is a different beast; its shadows are more menacing, and its silence is more oppressive. Every creak and moan of the old building sets my nerves on edge. By the time I reach my door, my hands are shaking. I should feel safe here, in the privacy of my room, but the feeling is elusive, slipping through my fingers like sand. Even in here, I feel like I'm being watched.

"It's just the dark, Ever. You're being daft."

What game are they playing, and how did I find myself in the middle of something that feels so much bigger than any of us? The helplessness threatens to overwhelm me, but I push it down. Weakness isn't an option now.

I need to remain alert yet appear clueless.

Despite the sinister conversation I eavesdropped on, which really could be anything without context, I don't feel like this is a house of danger. The guys have protected me. Saved me, even.

It only adds another complicated layer to this mystery, and it's something that I want to solve. The feeling that I *need* to solve it swarms me, and as I climb into bed, pulling the covers up high over my head, My dreams are swept away with secrets and lies, danger and beautifully dark men.

24

EVER

I push the heavy oak door open, my hand shaky. The corridor behind me is abuzz with the office staff at KnightsGate the next afternoon, but ahead, Chancellor Aldritch's office feels like stepping into a spotlight. I loathe the spotlight. I'm not ready for this, whatever this is. The sudden and terrifying thought that he wants to see me about the report I filed on Stanley makes my mouth go dry.

Don't back down. Whatever happens, don't back down.

"Come in, Ever," Chancellor Aldritch says, his voice low and oddly soothing. He's perched behind his massive desk, stacks of papers around him like he's the king of academia. Well, I guess he is here. A prestigious job, to say the least; he is also an old friend of my dad's, so he doesn't scare me as much as he does some of the students here.

"Thanks." My words are a whisper, betraying the tremor I feel inside. I hate that. I need to be strong, unflappable Ever, not some nervous kid. "Good Afternoon, Chancellor."

"Sit down," he motions towards the chair opposite him. It's not a suggestion; it's a command. But his eyes, they're not cold. There's something like warmth there, maybe even concern.

"How are you, Ever?"

"Erm, good thanks. How are you?"

He snorts. "I'm fine. But this isn't a social call. You know your dad asked me to look out for you when you were accepted to study here. I've taken that job seriously. I've kept tabs on you from time to time. This new housing situation... it's concerning."

"Oh?"

"Hmm. Did you not think to call the Housing Office to find you something?"

"I did!" I exclaim, my cheeks going hot with the memory of being brushed off like shit on a shoe. "The after-hours guy told me to get lost. It was Friday night. I needed somewhere to stay. It's fine. They're nice."

"Are you sure? They seem a little wayward for you."

"Wayward?" This conversation is going south, but at least Stanley hasn't come up.

"The report you filed about Stanley Richford. I can only assume you were at that party because of them."

Jinxed it, you utter pillock.

"Actually, no. They came and got me out of a bad situation. They saved me."

His eyes narrow, and his lips press together as if

he's trying to suspend his belief far enough to trust me.

"Your father asked me to look out for you," he says again, folding his hands on the desk. "He's proud of you, Ever, we all are. Your academic record is impressive."

Is this what the meeting is about? A pat on the back? Relief washes over me, but it's mixed with a weird sort of embarrassment. Praise should feel good, right? But when it's related to my name, it just feels like another reminder that I'm different.

"Thank you, Chancellor."

Dad always said our name means something, but at KnightsGate, it feels like a noose around my neck. Still, knowing he's got my back, even from afar, steadies the fluttering in my chest. I've got this. Whatever 'this' turns out to be.

"I'll cut to the chase, Ever. You're on track for Summa Cum Laude," he says, his voice steady, eyes locked on mine. "You can't afford to stumble now. This is a critical time. The people you associate with and the situations you find yourself in... you need to make smart choices."

My heart skips as I ignore everything except those three glittering words.

Summa Cum Laude.

That's the dream – my dream. The reason I grind through every essay, have star attendance and bury myself in books till dawn.

But his words are a jolt; they mean I'm really doing it, not just chasing but catching.

"Focus on your studies. Be happy with your academic life." He leans back, eyeing me like he's trying to read my thoughts. "Is there anything you need? Anything at all?"

"Thank you, Chancellor," I reply, as if he had anything to do with my colossal achievement. Could-be achievement if I don't fuck this up royally. "I'm fine, really. I've got everything under control. In fact, this information is vital. I will double down. You know I want this." The personal words tumble out. We try to remain professional on campus despite him being Uncle Dave at home, but he *knows* how much this means to me.

"Those are the fighting words I love to hear." He beams at me. "As a result of this, you have been chosen as the keynote speaker for the Alumni Ball in two weeks."

The words crash into me like a wave. No. No. No. I can't.

"Me?" I can't hide the quiver in my voice, the room suddenly too tight around me. "Why?"

"Your standing as early as this to graduate Summa, and with your family's legacy... It's fitting." He nods as though it's the most natural decision in the world.

I want to tell him he's made a mistake, that I'm no orator, that standing in front of an audience turns my bones to lead. My mouth goes dry, and my stomach twists into knots so tight I could hurl. But I just nod, a robotic jerk of my head because that's what Ever the Legacy does—she keeps her shit together.

"Two weeks," he adds, oblivious to the storm raging inside me. "It's a great honour, Ever."

Great honour, my ass. My mind races with images of the grand hall, filled with expectant faces, all waiting for me to dazzle them. But all I see is their judgement, their scrutiny, picking apart every stutter and stumble.

"Oh-okay."

"Excellent. We'll need a draft by next week for review."

"Next week," I echo, feeling the walls close in further. Just breathe, Ever. Just freaking breathe.

"Any questions?" he asks, but it's like he's speaking from the other end of a long tunnel.

"What is it supposed to be on?" I feel this was vital information he had forgotten to mention. Or did he and I didn't register in my sheer panic?

"It's about legacy, about history. You're not just speaking as a student, but as a representative of KnightsGate's history."

"KnightsGate's history."

"Yes, who better than you, hmm?" His eyes lock onto mine, and I can't look away. There's no escape route here, no easy out.

"I'll get it done," I mutter, my voice steadier than I feel. The gravity of the situation anchors me to the spot.

"Good." He nods, satisfied. "Remember, we all have faith in you. And don't worry about Stanley. He's done."

I nod. Accepting that for what it is.

Faith. It's a dangerous thing to put into someone who feels like they're standing on the edge of a precipice about to plummet to a severely messy death by public speaking.

I flee his office as if chased by ghosts of ancestors past, their whispers trailing after me. The old stone corridors of KnightsGate blur as I make my way to the sanctuary of the library. It's a place of solace, where the scent of aged paper and the quiet hum of knowledge promise refuge from this horrible performance I have to put on.

Pushing the library doors open, I step in, letting the familiar environment calm my racing heart. Rows upon rows of books—each a world, a story, a piece of history—stand ready. I'm here for one purpose: to arm myself with every fact about KnightsGate I can find.

I pull down volumes of ancient texts that smell of dust and forgotten tales and spread them across a large oak table. The soft thud of each book is a call to arms. I have two weeks to craft a narrative that will grip the audience and weave the rich tapestry of KnightsGate's past into a tale fit for its present.

The Chancellor might have placed an impossible task on me, but I'll rise to meet it because Summa Cum Laude means everything to me. Even more than my fear. My fingers brush over embossed leather covers and crack open tomes that haven't been touched in decades.

Flipping through pages, eyes scanning lines of text that date back centuries. KnightsGate's history unfolds before me, not just as dates and facts, but as a legacy—a legacy that courses through my veins.

I scribble notes, quick and messy. My brain whirls with ideas, connections forming like a spider's web, intricate and deliberate. This isn't just about acing an assignment; it's personal. It's about standing tall in front of those who doubt, those who whisper behind raised glasses and smug smiles.

I lean closer to the lamplight, the shadows dancing across the pages as night draws in. The names of my ancestors stare back at me, their achievements etched in history. I won't be the one to break the chain, to falter under the gaze of expectation. Summa Cum Laude is more than a title; it's a promise I've made to myself.

I'll build something unshakable from these words, a speech that echoes through the halls and cements my place here in history, but for a different reason.

The story of KnightsGate sucks me in, the glory and the grit all woven together like a tapestry. It's not just dry facts and dates; it's lifeblood, it's birthright.

But as I dig through the archives, something else grabs my attention.

sectæ Nazarenorum.

It's mentioned a couple of times. The word 'sect' scribbled in the margin of a dusty ledger next to it. My breath hitches. That's what Alistair had mentioned, his voice low and laced with secrets. Frantically, I scour more texts, but it's like hitting a wall. Every lead turns to dust. Suddenly, there is no mention, nothing.

Frustration claws at my chest as I come up blank at every turn. Hours bleed into the night, and still nothing. It's like this so-called sect has been wiped clean like it never existed. But why? What are they hiding?

If there's a secret buried in KnightsGate, linked to some religious sect, then I need to know. It's pricking against my conscience, and it won't let go. It's a mystery. More secrets, and if KnightsGate is my legacy, what does that make this sect?

25

ALISTAIR

Darkness clings to us, thick with the scent of damp earth and old stone, as a drizzle has been coming down for the last few minutes, drenching us to the skin. Not that we give a shit. Why we are here is far more important. The library looms ahead, its grandeur lost in the cloak of night. Charlie is beside me, sitting on the back of the stone bench, his elbows on his knees, but I feel the tension rolling off him in waves. My gaze is glued to the ancient oak doors, willing them to spill Ever into the safety of the moonlight.

"Damn it," I mutter, glancing at my watch. It's nearing ten, and every second is pulling night further in. She should've called one of us if she was out this late.

Why the hell didn't she call? A chill gnaws at my spine, not from the night air, but from the void where she should be.

"Where are you, angel?" The words barely escape

as a whisper, blending with the night as if carried away by the ghosts of her prestigious ancestors. It sets my mind racing down dark paths.

I know Charlie is alert and always ready for trouble, but this situation is a thorn digging into my conscience right now. We should've been there. I should've been there to protect her to begin with.

Charlie's gaze locks on the library doors like a hawk waiting to swoop. His body is tense, coiled to spring into action the second Ever steps out into the night. I can see the worry etching lines across his face, which mirrors the unease twisting in my gut.

"We should just go in there and tell her to come home," he mutters, almost too quiet for me to catch. We've done this sort of thing enough times to know the atmosphere tilts when something unseen pollutes the air we breathe.

I'm about to agree with him when movement catches my eye—a familiar figure slinks around the corner of the library. It's Alex, his posture rigid, eyes darting around as if he expects a phantom to leap from the shadows.

"Watch him, until we know who it is," I whisper to Charlie, nudging him with my elbow. He could be a distraction for all we know.

Charlie nods, a subtle dip of his chin that's all business, and shifts his attention to Alex. He's got that look now, the hunter zeroing in on a potential threat, ready to dissect Alex's every move.

"Hey," I say as Alex shuffles closer, the moonlight

casting an eerie glow on his face. "What did your parents say about a twin?"

He's jittery, eyes flicking to mine, then away, a fidget in his step that screams he's not okay. "I'll get to that, but first, I need to know. The list, Alistair. The fucking dates—did they match up with yours?"

I nod once, short, sharp. "Yeah, they lined up. Every single one."

"Thank Christ," he breathes, pressing his hands to his face in relief. There's this moment where he looks like he might crumble right there on the grass. But he doesn't. Instead, he squares his shoulders, trying to look like the guy who has it all figured out. "Okay, good. Good."

"Now, what about the home front? What did your parents say?"

"There's a twin," he whispers.

"How do we know you aren't him?" Charlie asks, almost casually.

"Fuck you, East. This is hard enough for me as it is without you chiming in with accusations."

Charlie snickers and holds his hands up. "Gotta be cautious, man. You get it."

"Fuck," I mutter, feeling the weight of his words like a punch to the gut. "I mean, we kind of already knew, but this shit is huge."

"It's fucking messed up. I can't even think straight. I'll give you the details, but later, okay? I need time to process this shit."

"Sure," I reply, my tone edged with the kind of

understanding you can only have when you've seen too much family drama yourself.

Alex nods, his jaw set hard. We need to be sure we can trust him and that it's him next time we meet. "We will have a code word," I state. "For whenever we meet."

"Right," Alex agrees, a flicker of something like determination lighting up his haunted eyes for a second. The kid is seriously spooked. "Yeah. Let's do that." He clears his throat, steadying himself. "*In Lumine Veritas, In Aeternitate Unitas.*" He pauses, then translates our sect motto with a bitter twist to his lips, "In Light, Truth; In Eternity, Unity. I'll say, 'In Light.'"

"Works for me."

Charlie nods once, sharply. "I'll tell the others."

"I'll catch you later. I've missed three fucking days because of this bastard. I need to catch up." Alex turns on his heel without waiting for a dismissal.

I let out a breath and glance at Charlie. "Shit."

"Yeah," Charlie replies, eyes never leaving the library's grand entrance, where shadows play tricks, and every sound feels like a warning.

"Enough of this. I'm going to get her."

Movement flickers at the front door. Charlie's stance tenses, ready to spring.

"She's here," he murmurs, and we both lean closer to the dark, watching, waiting for Ever to step into our line of sight.

26

CHARLES

"Do you have someone you can call to walk you home?" the Librarian asks Ever as Alistair and I slip through the night towards her.

"We're here for her," I say, stepping into the light and making them both jump. "But thank you for looking out for our girl."

The Librarian gives me a narrow-eyed glare before shifting her gaze to Alistair. "You know these two?" she asks Ever, folding her arms. "Or am I calling campus security?"

Ever giggles, that sweet, sweet sound. "I know them. They're my housemates."

The Librarian stands down, and with a smile at Ever, she closes up and Ever gives us a searching stare.

"What are you doing here?"

"It got dark, you didn't come home, we tracked

you here and were waiting for you to come out so we could walk you home," I explain briefly.

She smiles, nodding her head so that her blonde hair fluffs around her. "I see. You're my protectors now?"

"We will never let anything happen to you again, Ever," Alistair states. "We let you down once; it won't happen again."

"You didn't let me down. You had nothing to do with Stanley and that situation."

"We should've stopped you from going," Alistair practically snarls, getting worked up, not at Ever, but at himself.

Ever raises an eyebrow. "Stopped me from going? And how you do think that would've gone down, Your Grace?"

He hisses as she uses his royal title, and I know the effect that has on him. Usually, he hates it, but tumbling from her lips, it will be a benediction.

He squints at her to her amusement as she challenges him. "You are a very frustrating creature," he growls.

"No, I'm not some damsel who needs locking up in her tower. Okay, yes, Saturday night was bad. Very bad, and if you guys hadn't shown up, I'd be a ruined mess right now and probably crying in my bed at home, having given up on all this." She waves her hand around. "But here we are, so please stop blaming yourselves." She shifts her gaze to me before looking back at Alistair. "Okay?"

"Fine, but going forward, you will not walk anywhere alone. Got it?"

"Is that an order?"

"Yeah, it is."

"Is that like a 'I live under your roof, so I'll abide by your rules' type of thing?"

"Yes," he says with a smirk. "Fuck, yes. If that's what it takes."

Snorting into my hands as she appears about to whack him around the head with that very large and dusty book she's hugging to her chest, I step in.

"It's cold and raining. Can we continue this at home, please?"

"Good idea," Ever mutters and starts walking. Then she stops. "Have either of you heard from Alex lately? I haven't seen him since that party. I don't know if he's avoiding me or what?"

"He went home for a few days. Family shit," I say, exchanging a wary glance with Alistair. We both know we should come clean about the twin, but this is not the time. She will feel extremely betrayed and worried, and it's probably better coming from Alex. With a nod, Alistair knows my thoughts and will make sure North-West has a conversation with Ever about this.

Fortunately, it's a short walk back to the Manor, and we head inside, dripping wet, and Ever is complaining about the old book being damp.

Alistair's eyes are glued to it, which catches my attention. I have zero clue what I'm looking at, though, so I fix him with a questioning glare.

"That's some heavy reading," Alistair murmurs, eyes dropping back to the tome. It's a fucking *tome*. And that's when alarm bells start to ring.

"Chancellor Aldritch gave me a horrifying assignment. He made me the keynote speaker at the Alumni Ball in a fortnight on the history of KnightsGate because who better?" Her sarcasm rains down on us heavier than that drizzle outside.

"Did he now?" I murmur. "That's interesting."

"Hmm, it is," she murmurs. "Anyway, better get back to it, and I have a test tomorrow. Thanks for walking me back, but I don't need locking away. Okay?"

Alistair nods, and we watch her head up the stairs.

"Do you think that was deliberate?"

"Yes."

There is nothing more to say on the subject right now.

"Keep your eyes on her all night," he adds.

Nodding, I take the stairs two at a time and push the door open to my room, flipping the lid up on the laptop.

I lean back in my chair as I click into the surveillance software. It's a rush, this power, like holding someone's heart in your hands and feeling the thrum of their life at your fingertips. The screen flickers, then blooms into a four-way split, each angle a different view of her sanctuary.

Ever drops her bag on the floor with a soft thud, oblivious to the invisible threads of control we've spun around her. Her hair, that cascade of wavy gold, falls over her shoulders as she sits down, just a girl and her homework. But to me, she's the pulse that drives my obsession; every move she makes is another note in the symphony only I can hear during these times when it's just me being a voyeur to her without her knowledge.

She pulls out her books, lining them up with precision on the desk, her slender fingers brushing over the pages. I watch, fixated, as she chews on the end of her pen, lost in thought, that striking green gaze scanning the words that will never reveal her secrets—not like I can. There's a sharpness to her, an edge of steel beneath the silk, and I know it's not just her mind that's brilliant, but her spirit too.

"Ever," I whisper to the screen to our girl, who doesn't even know she's become the centre of our world. "What would you do if you knew?" But she can't hear me, and part of me revels in that, in the knowledge that I am here, unseen, undetected, watching her every breath, every sigh, every stroke of her pen against paper.

My eyes don't leave her, not for a second. Ever's lost in her work, scribbling down notes with a focus that makes me lean closer to the screen as if I could somehow become part of her world just by watching. Her brow furrows in concentration, those green eyes flicking back and forth across the textbook pages spread out before her. She bites her lip, deep in thought, and a surge of something dark twists inside me.

It's driving me crazy, feeling this close to her and still worlds apart.

Time slips by, a silent thief, and then she stops. The pen drops from her hand, and she stretches, arms reaching above her head, arching her back in a way that makes my throat dry. I watch, tense, as she stands up, shuffling papers into neat piles before she turns off the desk lamp.

The room dims, but the cameras are relentless; they miss nothing, not even the subtle shift in her expression that says she's done for the night. She moves away from the desk, out of frame of one and directly into another, following her to where she pulls open a drawer and takes out fresh clothes. My pulse kicks up a notch because I know what's coming next.

Ever strips off, her movements unhurried and unaware. There's a grace to it, a quiet dignity that tells me she's never known what it is to be watched like this. She heads towards the bathroom door and steps inside as I'm caught in this web of obsession that tangles tighter with each passing day.

As the water cascades around her tight body, I groan softly, wishing my hands, my tongue, were tracing her curves.

"Fuck."

It's like a twisted solo performance, just for me, and it's sick how much I crave it. She can't see me, but I can see every inch of her.

She finishes quickly and turns the shower off, stepping out and wrapping a white towel around her.

Her hair is a wet cascade down her back as she grabs another towel and coils it into a turban.

She moves with that same ethereal grace, unaware of the eyes that follow her every motion. Every curve, every breath. I'm caught up in how normal she thinks this moment is and how far from normal I am for watching her in her intimate moments.

Watching her dry off and run a brush through her hair before giving it a quick blow dry, she gets in her pyjamas and crawls into bed with a quiet yawn.

"Sleep tight," I whisper.

My gaze doesn't waver, locked onto the form that's become my obsession, my compulsion, my nightly ritual.

I'm wrapped up in the dark reality of my own making, and even though she'll wake up to a new day, oblivious, I'll be right here—watching, waiting, lost in this dangerous game that only I know we're playing.

27

EVER

The early morning sun seeps through the bay window as I push the living room door open to find Alex perched on the edge of the couch like he's been waiting for hours.

"Alex." I don't really know what else to say. I'm confused about the way he has been behaving lately.

"Ever, we need to talk." He's straight to the point, his voice low and urgent.

My eyebrows hitch up as my brain tries to catch up with this curveball. "About what?"

He stands, and that's when I notice something's off. There's a seriousness in his stance that sets my nerves on edge. "It's about me, or rather, someone who looks exactly like me."

"Come again?" My confusion deepens and must be written all over my face because he takes a deep breath, appearing as if he is about to drop a bombshell.

"Ever, it's a long story and one I'm not prepared to

go into today, but you need to know the basics. I have a twin." His words hang in the air, heavy with implications.

Shock nails me to the spot, my brain scrambling to make sense of Alex's grenade. A twin? An entire person out there wearing Alex's face?

"Are you fucking with me?"

"Ever, I'm dead serious." His tone is flat, the gravity in his eyes anchoring the truth of his words.

"Since when?" My voice pitches high, disbelief sharpening each word. The fact that I'm only finding out now twists my stomach into knots.

"Since always, obviously. But there are complications, and I said I'm not going into it right now." He runs a hand through his hair, a gesture of frustration that's all too familiar.

"Then why spill the beans now?" I press, arms still crossed over my chest.

"Because..." He hesitates, and I can almost see him weighing his next words. "The guy who invited you to that party last week, the one who picked you up... It wasn't me, Ever. It was him."

I feel the floor tilt beneath me as if the room decides to spin just to mess with my head. I replay that night, the ease between us I took for granted, thinking it was Alex. But it wasn't.

The silence in the room stretches, thick and uncomfortable, like a rope ready to snap. My mind races back to that night, scouring through every moment for clues I missed.

"His laugh," I say suddenly, causing him to look at me sharply. "It was different to yours."

"Oh?" he croaks.

"Yeah, he was slightly colder in a way. It's hard to describe. God, I'm such an idiot." I pace the room now, every step unleashing new fragments of memory. The twin had been bolder; ditching me for a hook-up with Verity Bowden is something I should have known Alex wouldn't do. He has never wanted me as a girl-friend, but he has always been attentive and caring.

"I'm sorry. I didn't know until a couple of days ago. It's a shitshow."

"How can I trust anything now? How do I know you are you?" I demand, glaring at him with an accu-sation that hangs there.

"Ever," he pleads, and there's a crack in his usually steady attitude that tells me this is Alex. But the seed of doubt has been planted, and it's already taken root, growing fast and wild.

"Sorry," I mutter, though I'm not sure for what. For doubting him? For being so easily tricked? I don't know anymore.

"I know this is difficult, and I'm so sorry, Ever. You know I would never place you in any danger knowingly. You know that, right?"

It's like a switch flicks inside me. Despite the chaos, the fear that his twin—this mystery person with Alex's face—has woven into my life, there's this undercurrent of trust for the guy before me. Trust that's been built over late-night study sessions, shared laughs, and moments where the world seemed too heavy but lighter somehow when he was around.

"Did he have anything to do with what happened to me that night?" I ask quietly.

His face goes pale. He's obviously heard; there's no need to explain. "I don't know, Ever. If he did, I don't care who he is, he will pay."

I nod, accepting that he doesn't know.

"Do you still trust me?"

Drawing in a deep breath, I let it out and press my lips together. "I want to. But this has blindsided me, and I'm wondering why he dragged me into whatever the fuck this is. Is it because of Stanley? Were they working together? I have all these questions now."

"I know, and I wish I had answers, but I don't."

"Then I guess I need to ask Stanley," I blurt out and then jump a country mile when the door bursts open, and Alistair charges in like the devil is on his ass.

"Absolutely not. Besides. He was expelled and is facing prosecution."

"And you know that how?" I ask, pretending he didn't just eavesdrop on this conversation because I'm standing in the proverbial glass house with no stones to throw.

"I know everything." His clear blue eyes pin mine, and I gulp as if I've been caught doing something wrong.

"Noted," I growl, suddenly pissed off with all this. "You know what? You guys are fucking unbelievable." I throw my hands in the air, feeling the anger bubble up. "If you know *everything*, then spill it, Alistair. Because right now, I'm in the fucking dark, and I hate it."

Alistair looks between me and Alex, his expression hardening. "Ever, we don't want you to be tangled up in this mess."

"But I am tangled up in it!" My voice rises, the frustration at boiling point. "Because of him," I gesture at Alex with a sharp jab of my finger, "and apparently his evil fucking twin."

Alex steps forward, his face clouded with guilt. He looks like he wants to say something more, but the words seem to get lost.

Alistair shifts his weight from one foot to the other. "Look, I get it, but going to Stanley for answers isn't happening."

"You telling me what to do again, hmm?"

"In this instance, yes, because it seems you need someone to look out for you."

"Ugh! You're both maddening assholes. I need time to think," I spit out, backing towards the door.

"Ever, wait," Alex says quickly. "Text me if you need anything, okay? Even if it's three in the morning. You know I've got your back."

"Yeah, well, we'll see."

I shove the door open and scramble into the kitchen, where I'm greeted by Damien. He takes one look at me and asks, "Coffee?"

"You're a godsend. Or an asshole. I'm not sure which this morning."

"Asshole?" he asks with a raised eyebrow. "What did I do to deserve that title this early on?"

Snickering, I shake my head. "Nothing. I don't know. I just found out about Alex's so-called twin. It's thrown me."

"Yeah, it's big." He makes me a coffee and hands it to me.

Before I can stop myself, my gaze drops to his arm, and I see a fresh cut there, and it tears at me.

He sees me notice but doesn't say anything, nor does he try to cover it.

"You can talk to me; if you want," I murmur, blowing on my coffee to hide my face from him.

"What about?" he asks carefully.

"What it is that hurts you."

He throws his head back with a deep inhale. "You don't have time for that shit."

"Says who?"

"Me."

With that, he stalks out, and I curse myself for being a prying cow. I'm ruining everything, and maybe I'd be better off leaving them as they were before I landed in their laps and turned their worlds shit-side up.

28

EVER

When I step into the living room after finishing my coffee, I know something's up. Charlie lounges on the couch, a grin lighting up his face like he's got the world's biggest secret. His eyes, those hazel pools of trouble, fix on me and don't let go.

"Hey, Ever," he says, all casual like we're just two friends hanging out, not like he's about to drop some cryptic bomb on me.

"What's going on?"

"Riddle me this. I speak without a mouth and hear without ears. I have no body, but I come alive with the wind. What am I?"

"Huh?" I chew on my bottom lip, rolling his words around in my head. It's more than just a riddle; it's a challenge, a battle of wits where he's the cat and I'm the mouse. Charlie leans back, waiting, watching, and I can almost hear the tick-tock of an invisible clock counting down.

My brain kicks into gear, grateful for something to think about that isn't me having to pack my bags and find somewhere else to live so I can leave these guys in peace. The riddle hangs in the air between us, a taunting puzzle waiting to be solved. I scan Charlie's face for any hint, but there's nothing—just that smug look painting his features as if he's already won.

"Just give me a second."

Charlie's eyes are sharp, hawk-like, not missing a thing. They're fixed on me, and I can feel the weight of his gaze. It's like he's trying to peel back my layers with those piercing eyes, looking for a crack in my armour.

I push my thoughts away from him and towards the riddle, forcing my mind to cut through the fog of distraction. Charlie waits.

"Wind..." I mutter, grasping at the elusive answer, dancing just out of reach. Charlie's lips tilt upward, and I know he's enjoying this far too much.

I chew on my bottom lip, buying time. The riddle's a knot, and I'm picking at it with everything I've got. "Is it... time?" I venture, my voice less confident than I'd like.

Charlie throws his head back, a laugh bouncing off the walls of the living room. "Not even close," he says, but the twinkle in his eye doesn't dim. Damn him for enjoying this.

"Come on then, give me a clue." I cross my arms, trying to look annoyed rather than desperate.

He shakes his head, that mischievous grin not

budging an inch. "Where's the fun in that, Ever? A riddle's nothing if not a test of wits."

"An echo?"

"Hmm." He slides closer and leans in; the warmth of his breath tickles my ear as he whispers, "What asks but never answers?"

It's a different game now, his voice a low caress that sends shivers down my spine. The room feels too small, charged with a current that's both thrilling and terrifying. I blink, trying to keep my wits about me.

"An owl," I breathe out, almost without thinking. But the flutter in my chest isn't about the riddle; it's him, this space between us that's electric and alive.

"Smart girl," Charlie murmurs, approval lacing his tone. His eyes search mine, flickering with something dark and unreadable. I'm caught in their pull, drowning in a sea I've no map to navigate.

"Hit me with another," I challenge, fighting to keep my voice steady. Charlie's grin is all sharp edges, promising an abyss that might just swallow me whole if I'm not careful. But I can't help wanting to dive in, to see what's hidden in the depths of those clever riddles and that enigmatic smile.

"What dances with light but captures darkness, speaks without a voice and listens without ears?" he murmurs, every word dipped in shadows and secrets.

I swallow hard, my brain firing on all cylinders. The room is still, the only sound our breathing and the tick of the old grandfather clock. I can almost touch the tension between us; it's alive, a third presence that wraps around me, urging me to delve deeper and think harder.

Charlie's eyes hold mine, hazel depths with flecks of gold, daring me to unravel his enigma. My heart hammers against my ribs—not just from the challenge, but from him, from the heat radiating off his body and the electric charge of his stare.

"Is it a photograph?" I venture, my voice steady despite the storm raging inside me. Charlie remains silent, but his gaze never wavers, and something in the air shifts, drawing us closer in a dance neither of us knows the steps to.

Charlie tilts back, his smirk sharp as a blade. His eyes glint, eager for my next move. It's like he's thrown down a gauntlet, daring me to pick it up.

"Time's ticking," he taunts, voice smooth as silk and just as deceiving.

I exhale, slow and controlled. Can't let him see me sweat. "A shadow," I say, locking onto his gaze with all the confidence I've got.

"Spot on." He laughs.

I can't help the flush of triumph that warms my cheeks. It's not just about getting the riddle right—it's about matching wits with Charlie and coming out on top.

"All right then, genius," he says, his voice dropping to a conspiratorial whisper. "Want to know what it all means?"

My heart kicks up a notch. The game's not over yet. "Lay it on me."

Charlie's gaze is intense, holding mine captive.

"The first riddle," he starts, " was about identity, the masks we all wear. You see, I'm not just the joker, the life of the party. There's more beneath the surface."

I nod, intrigued despite myself. It's rare for Charlie to peel back his layers, even rarer for him to invite someone else to look underneath.

"The second," he continues, "that's about the roles we play, how we change depending on who's watching. Like me with you, now. I'm not acting, Ever. This is real."

A shiver runs down my spine, his words weaving around me like a spell.

"And the last one," he says, voice barely above a whisper, "shadows follow, they reflect, but they also conceal. And what I'm hiding..." He trails off, his smile turning sly. "Well, that's for another time."

"Tease," I accuse, but my tone is light and playful.

"Guilty as charged." His laughter is low, sending a wave of warmth through me.

"Why the riddles?"

He shrugs, his casual manner back in place. "Why not? Life's a game, Ever. And I intend to play it with you."

I catch my breath. Playful or not, Charlie's words have weight, and I can't ignore the edge of darkness lurking behind them. Whatever this game is, I'm already too deep in to walk away now, even if I wanted to.

DAMIEN

Hesitant, I knock once.

"Yeah?" she calls out wearily, giving me even more pause. She sounds exhausted, and I don't want to add to that.

"Hello?" she snaps, and it makes me smile.

Pushing the door open, I step in like a shadow trespassing into a realm of light. Her room is simple, a reflection of her, with books piled high and notes scattered like fallen leaves. This is the second time I've been in here, but this time feels different. As if anything is possible. But it's all in my hands.

"Hey," I murmur as I shut the door behind me. I can't look at her yet; can't face those striking green eyes that see too much. They're like scanners, always on the lookout for bullshit, and I'm a walking lie detector's nightmare. But I owe her this—my truth, raw and unpolished.

Ever sits cross-legged on her bed, the glow from her bedside lamp casting a halo around her blonde hair. It makes her look otherworldly, and for a second, I wonder if she's really there or just a figment of some hopeful delusion.

"Damien?" Her voice pulls me back, and I force myself to meet her gaze. She doesn't say anything more; she just waits. Always waiting for me to catch up.

I take a deep breath, my whole being tightening before I consciously relax. "I walked out on you today," I start, the words feeling like thorns in my throat. "That was crappy of me. You were just trying to help."

She nods, silent encouragement, and something unfurls in my soul—a coil of darkness I keep buried. I've perfected the art of concealment, but the mask starts to slip with Ever.

"It's like... there's this noise in my head, constant and loud," I confess, my voice rough with the strain of admission. "It tells me I'm never going to be enough. That the part of me that is broken will end up ruining me and everyone around me. I can't begin to explain why I'm so broken, but this thing inside me just won't shut up. It's always there, haunting every moment." I drag a hand through my hair, the familiar gesture doing nothing to ease the turmoil inside. "I didn't have an overly shitty childhood," I blurt out after a second. "It's not how I was raised that did this, I was born this way. I've always wanted to walk into the dark and never come out. It's frightening because I don't know how to fix it because I don't know why I'm so broken. But when I'm with you, it's different."

Ever leans forward, her eyes never leaving mine. "Different, how?" Her voice is soft, inviting me to reveal more, and I feel the urge to lean into that warmth.

"It quiets down." The confession feels like shedding armour I didn't know I was wearing. "It doesn't stop. It never stops, but being around you is like a moment of peace. Like you're the eye in my storm." The words hang in the air between us, heavy with something that's been building since before the day we met. Since the first day I laid eyes on her back in the first year, and we knew who she was to us.

She reaches out, her fingers brushing against mine, and it's like a jolt of life surges through me. It's so simple, but it ignites something fierce, something I'm not ready to feel, so I snatch my hand back.

She curls hers into a fist, getting it. "Damien, that noise doesn't know shit. You are enough. More than enough." Her conviction startles me because I didn't expect such a harsh response. But it's not harsh in the way that she doesn't understand; it's like she's trying to be forceful enough for both of us.

"I want to believe that. I want to believe there's something good in me that you see. But..."

"But what?" she prompts when I trail off.

"But I'm scared," the words tumble out before I can stop them. "Scared of being too much darkness or not enough light for you." My hands shake slightly, revealing more of my vulnerability than I intended.

"Damien, we've both got our baggage," she says gently. "Yours isn't going to scare me away."

I'm not used to this—someone wanting to carry some of the weight for me. It feels foreign but, at the same time, comforting.

"I don't know about that."

She sits forward suddenly, a smirk turning the corners of her mouth up wickedly. "So you think about us being together?"

The fact that this conversation went in that direction hadn't even pinged my usually carefully maintained radar. I return the half-smile and sit tentatively on the bed with her. "Yeah. Is that okay?"

"It is." Her words are hesitant and offer no insight into what she is thinking beyond her thinking it's okay for me to want her.

I'm left feeling exposed, like a raw nerve. In the quiet, Ever shifts closer. Her hand is warm as it brushes against my arm, a light touch that feels like it's searing straight through to my bones. This time, I don't jerk away. I can't move; I don't want to.

"Your demons are strong, but you're stronger, and you have me now," she says softly, and there's no pity in her eyes, just this fierce kind of understanding that knocks me breathless.

I swallow hard, struggling to maintain the walls I've painstakingly built over the years. But her fingers tracing invisible lines over my skin are dismantling them, piece by piece. There's an ache in my chest, but it's a different kind, one that spreads warmth instead of cold.

The room around us seems to retreat into shadows, leaving us in our own little world where her empathy lights up the dark corners of my soul. It's terrifying and electrifying, this closeness, this shared solitude that wraps around us, binding us in ways I've never experienced.

The air between us is alive, buzzing with something unspoken yet understood. "You make it seem possible to be less fucked up."

Our eyes lock, and the world falls away. It's just me and Ever now, every other thought pushed aside. Her hand is still on my arm, her touch a steady anchor in the storm she's stirred inside me.

"Damien," she breathes out my name, and it's like a key turning in a lock.

I lean closer, drawn by some force I can't fight. Our lips brush, hesitant at first. Then, something ignites a spark I've never felt before, spreading through me like wildfire. This isn't just a kiss; it's a fucking revelation.

Time loses meaning as we melt into each other, our bodies pressed close in silence. There's no need for words; everything is said in the pressure of her lips against mine, in the way her breath mingles with mine, in the way our tongues dance together perfectly. We're lost in this moment, two people finding a strange solace during chaos.

The intensity of our connection is like nothing I've ever known, and in this stolen second, I'm not the intense, dark, almost weird guy or the Baron of Mere, not the enigma—just Damien, raw and real.

My hands slide down to Ever's waist. I pull her closer; the touch is soft but firm, betraying a possessiveness that surprises her. She gasps into my mouth as I hold her even closer.

Desire mixes with an exposed vulnerability as we cling to each other, our kiss deepening into something that stirs the darkness into a frenzy. It's pleasure and pain all rolled into one, and I want to hurt her at the same time as soothe her. I want to drag the blade that has tasted my blood across her delicate skin and kiss the wounds better. I want to know what it feels like to make her bleed while I lick her tears away.

"Damien," Ever whispers against my lips, her voice a thread of sound in the quiet room. Her words are a spark in the dry tinder of my restraint, and something inside me snaps.

"Ever. We need to stop." The taste of her, the press of her body against mine, is all-consuming, intoxicating.

A warning bell rings too loudly in my head. The cams. The sect. My jagged soul. Everything we are trying to achieve. This is dangerous, too fast, too much—but the feel of her in my arms, the scent of her hair, and the undeniable pull that draws me deeper into the whirlwind is screaming over the top of all of it. I'm not sure I'm strong enough to resist.

"Yeah," she murmurs, breathless.

We separate; my gaze is locked on Ever's green eyes, deep pools reflecting an unspoken bond that now threads between us, tangible and fierce. I see my chaos mirrored there, understood and accepted.

"Ever," I start, the confession clawing its way up from the depths of my soul. "I've never been with anyone. I've never felt close enough to anyone to take that step." My words hang in the silence, heavy with truth. Her eyes widen slightly, not with judgment but with a kind of reverence that sends a shiver down my spine. I'm frozen, my confession out in the open like some fragile thing that might shatter any second. But Ever just looks at me with those enthralling eyes, and I swear they're not just one colour but a whole damn spectrum.

"I've never been with anyone either." Her cheeks flush a soft pink, and it's like a punch to the gut because it means something.

I want to tell her I already know, but that would be heading down an already weird path.

"Really?" The word slips out, rough around the edges.

She nods, and her hair falls over her shoulder, a golden cascade that catches the light just so. "Yeah, I've been waiting for the right person. I don't know how anyone knew to make a bet out of it. I guess it was a shot in the dark, seeing as I've never dated anyone here. All about the books. But yeah. If Stanley had..." She trails off with a gulp.

"Yeah," I mutter because it's all I have to say. I'm not good with the words when it comes to shit like this. It's like she's handed me a piece of her soul, and I'm holding it, careful not to break it.

We stay there, inches apart, and I can feel the warmth from her body like a flicker in the dark. Our breathing slows down, and it's like we sync up without even trying. The silence isn't awkward; it's full of all the things we don't need to say.

Her hand finds mine, fingers entwining, and I grip back. It's strange how a simple touch can say so much. We're both wading into something unknown, and it's scary as hell, but for once, I'm not thinking about running.

"Lie with me for a bit?" she asks shyly.

"Yes."

Crawling up next to her, lying side by side, her breath is a steady rhythm against the raging tornado of mine.

The heat from her skin seeps into me, filling the cold spaces that usually live inside my chest. It's strange, this feeling of being connected to someone else, like our pulses are beating out a new rhythm just for us.

"Are you okay with this?" Her words are soft but clear, tinged with concern, making something in me twist.

"More than okay," I admit. My fingers trail along her arm, tracing the path down to where our hands lock together, an anchor in the midst of whatever this is between us.

"Good," she says, and there's a smile in her voice that sends a jolt straight through me.

I've never craved someone's touch before, and the thoughts of hurting her twists around to her hurting me. Stifling the groan as I think about her using my blade against me makes me shiver with a longing that surpasses the usual kind of need.

"I'm not good at this whole feelings thing."

"Neither am I."

"Guess we're both screwed, then."

She giggles softly. "Maybe." She tightens her grip on me as if to say she's not going anywhere.

The thrill, the darkness, the wild pulse of desire. It all melds together, creating something that feels a lot like hope. Or maybe it's more dangerous than that—like standing on the edge of a cliff, knowing you're about to jump, and not caring about the fall.

"Just be here with me."

"Always," I reply without thinking, because I know I can promise this. She can't get rid of me now, even if she wanted to. I'm lost to her. I will crave her until the end of days, even if she wants nothing to do with me. It scares me to think that and to know the lengths I will go to ensure she never leaves me.

We stay like that, her head resting on my shoulder, our hands linked. We're two pieces that somehow fit despite—or maybe because of—the shadows that cling to both of us. The world outside fades away, leaving nothing but the sound of our breathing and the dark thrill that this obsession has just taken an unexpected and dangerous turn coursing through my veins.

30

ALISTAIR

I'm leaning against the wall, the darkness of the hallway wrapping around me like a cloak. It's late, and the shadows are my only company until I see Ever, her hair like spun gold trailing over her shoulders, tiptoeing towards the stairs like a ghost haunting these ancient halls. Damien left her a while ago while she slept. She probably wonders where he went.

"Hey," I call out softly, not wanting to startle her.

She jumps anyway, her hand over her heart and stops, green eyes catching the moonlight as she turns to me. "Alistair."

"Can we talk?"

She nods, a flicker of curiosity in her gaze. No fear, no hesitation.

"Come with me." My voice is a whisper as I lead her down the hall, away from prying eyes and closer to my world.

We reach my bedroom, the door opening to reveal

a space that's more a kingdom than a room. Rich, dark drapes frame the windows, and the king-sized four-poster bed is a sprawling sea of silk and velvet placed directly in the middle of the vast room. It screams of the wealth I was born into.

Of the wealth she *should've* been born into.

Her eyes go wide. She steps inside, taking it all in. The priceless paintings, the shelves of leather-bound books, the artefacts of a legacy too heavy to bear. I watch her and see the awe flicker across her features, which hits me hard. That look—it's how I feel about her. But there's no way to say it, no words grand enough to explain this feeling to her.

"Like it?" I ask, trying not to place too much into the outcome of that question as I close the door behind us, shutting out the rest of the world.

"It's like something out of a movie," she replies, a laugh escaping her, light and genuine.

Raking a hand through my hair, I smile. There's an itch under my skin, a need to let her see past all this, past the Duke, to the person who stands before her now, stripped bare of titles and expectations.

Or at least trying to be.

"Ever, I—" The words are on the tip of my tongue, but they're just words, and they seem so inadequate. How do you tell someone that the way they look at a room, with stars in their eyes, is nothing compared to the galaxies they've set spinning in your soul?

Biting the inside of my cheek and watching Ever's reaction turn to curiosity about me. I've got to do this; she's slipping through my fingers, getting close enough to Ben to kiss, leaning into Charlie as if they are sharing some secret no one else is privy to, and Damien... that one hurts in ways that twist my guts. I'm not good at this. I'm intense and instil fear or, at the very least, caution. I don't have an innate charm that will draw her into my web. It has to be demanded in a way that will mean opening up my closed soul to her and getting past the humiliation and vulnerability this is going to cause me.

"Ever," I start, then stop again. She waits, her green eyes steady on me. They constantly change like the sea—now they're dark, deep.

"That's my name; don't wear it out," she jokes softly as I stand here like an utter pillock, not knowing where to start.

"There's something I've never told anyone."

She tilts her head, silent encouragement without a single word. My mouth is dry, and my heart slams against my ribs like it wants to break free. I force the words out.

"When I was seven, my dad... he was more the Duke than a father. He'd swoop in, all thunder and no shelter." I pause, swallowing hard. "One night, he caught me playing on my phone past bedtime. The phone was smashed in front of me as he ranted and raved about regiment and organisation, shouting about wasted time playing games when I should be reading a book. It scared me. It was probably the first time I remember where he went off on one."

Ever's face doesn't change, but her eyes do—fierce and raging against what I've said.

"It got worse from then on. It was like being in the military. Since then, trust has been like handing someone that same phone, hoping they won't stamp on it and destroy it. He ripped through my confidence, piece by piece. Like paper."

Ever leans in, her green eyes sharp with intensity. She doesn't interrupt, doesn't try to fill the silence that screams louder than any words could.

"Every shout, every lash of the belt was like another brick in the wall I built around myself." The memories claw at my insides, raw and bleeding. "I guess part of me still hears his voice when I make decisions. Do they measure up? Would he sneer at them? It sometimes makes me seem indecisive, but it's not that. I'm waiting to get a read on the situation, so I don't fuck up. Or on the flip side of this gold coin, sometimes I'm too forceful and arrogant when I know I'm right. It's like I'm always waiting for the other shoe to drop. For people to leave, to realise I'm not worth their time. Do you know what my father's last words were on his deathbed?"

She shakes her head.

"You're not ready."

"What?" She blinks back her surprise.

"Yeah. Not I'm proud of you, or I'm sorry for being a dick all your life, or you'll do great at this Duke thing. No. It was one last stab at the confidence I was trying to rebuild by being away from the fucker, here where I was accepted, revered, even." I run a hand through my hair, frustration knotting my stomach at having to dredge all this bullshit up just to make a chink in the wall Ever has up. "I know all of this about myself. I'm not walking around with my head up my ass. But I want you to know, in part, why I am the way I am. I don't want to scare you off, but I can't seem to tone it down, either."

Ever's expression doesn't shift, but something in her posture softens. It makes me realise we are still standing in the middle of the room like two spare parts. I didn't even ask if she wanted to sit. But she's here, really here, listening to the havoc that's been festering inside me for years. But she doesn't say anything.

"Sometimes, I think if I let someone in, if they see all this fucked up shit," I gesture at myself, "they'll bolt. So, I push first. It's easier than waiting to be pushed away."

Her brows knit together; she's piecing together the puzzle of who I am, and it terrifies me because no one has ever cared to look that close before.

"I know how that goes," she murmurs.

Her hand, tentative and soft, lands on mine. Her touch sends sparks through me, a comfort I didn't know I craved. The warmth from her skin bleeds into my cold flesh, thawing the icy barriers. I look down at our intertwined fingers, then at her face, and her eyes still with a silent promise that she's here, not just physically but with every shred of her being.

"You are not this terrifying old Duke who sits on his throne of bones, shaking his fist at everyone who passes. You are amazing, Alistair. Look at everything you have come through, and you are here doing pretty fucking great if my peek at the Chancellor's list is anything to go by."

I squint at her. "How did you get eyes on that, little angel?"

She smirks. "I have my ways."

"Well, I'm surprised you aren't accusing me of paying my way." The cutting remark is out before I can stop it, and she tilts her head.

"You spoke to Damien."

"It may have come up."

She giggles. "Sorry, it was really rude, but there's talk amongst the commoners, you know."

"Oh, you are anything but common, Ever."

"Hmm."

"Thank you," I murmur, unwilling to go down that road. "For listening, for not running."

Ever's hand squeezes mine, her touch a lifeline in the darkness that has always surrounded me. "I know what it's like," she whispers, and there's a tremble in her voice that tells me she's about to let me into a part of her world that few have ever seen.

"Know what?" I ask, my voice hoarse from the truths I've spilt tonight.

"Being haunted by a name, a legacy." She takes a deep breath, her gaze steady on mine. "My great-grandparents, they were everything KnightsGate represented—noble, affluent. But they lost it all. They were disgraced. My family has lived with that shadow ever since."

I truly get it. It's more than just ambition; it's survival.

"Your walls, Alistair, are like the ones I've built around myself. To protect, to hide, to keep out pity or scorn."

"I guess we're both trying to outrun ghosts," I say, feeling the truth settle between us. "Yours are older and probably more raggedy in their sheets, though, as they rattle their chains."

She laughs, and it's the most beautiful sound I've ever had the pleasure of hearing. "That mental image is something I can't unsee. Thank you for that, Your Grace. Except we're not running anymore. We're facing them, here, now."

"If you keep calling me Your Grace, you're going to do things to my body that I won't be responsible for," I murmur darkly, unable to help the response she fires up in me.

She gasps, her eyes going wide, but I don't give her a chance to say anything out of fear of being severely rejected.

"Thank you for understanding."

"Thank you for trusting me," she replies lightly.

It's as if our confessions have chased away some of the shadows, filling the space with a fragile light.

I cup her face, knowing she will open up for me if I press my lips to hers. Stepping in closer, she tilts her head back, and I grasp the opportunity she has presented me with. Sweeping my tongue over her lips, she leans in closer, and her mouth parts with a sigh that feels like surrender. It's not just her lips that yield to me, but the walls around her heart, too.

I'm not gentle; I can't be. I don't know how to be.

Our kiss is desperate, charged with all the emotions we've been holding back. The taste of her is addictive, and I drink her in like she's my drug of choice. My hands tangle into her hair as I pull her closer, unwilling to let any space separate us.

She responds with an intensity that matches mine, her nails digging into my arms as if she's afraid I'll pull away. But I'm not going anywhere. Not when this—this connection—is what I've been searching for my entire life, and that I've found it with *her* isn't so much a revelation as it is a reality.

Picking her up and carrying her to the bed, I'm taking a great risk, but I can't stop. Not now.

When I place her down and pull back, stripping my tee over my head, her eyes fill with uncertainty.

"I'm not going to claim all of you, not yet, angel. I know the significance, and today isn't that day."

She gasps as I pull her down towards the edge of the bed and drag her soft pyjama pants off, along with her knickers.

She shivers as I part her legs. I'm not going slowly. I'm not giving her the chance to protest. I want her to feel and not think.

"Wait," she pants.

Diving between her legs, I lick her clit, and she bucks against me, a shock of desire arching through her spine. I hold her hips steady, my fingers digging into her soft skin, keeping her from writhing away as I work her pussy with my mouth, relentless in my pursuit to draw every tremble and gasp from her. She tastes like heaven wrapped in sin, and I'm the sinner willing to fall from grace just to get another hit.

"Alistair, wait, this is.,."

But I'm not pulling back now if a hoard of marauding ghosts from our pasts tried to make me.

I thrust my tongue gently inside her, feeling the tension as she let out a strangled moan of fear. She is scared stiff I'm going to take her virginity, but that's not the game. Not tonight.

I'm careful, so careful with her innocence, as I taste her wet pussy, wishing with everything that I could drive my stiff, aching cock into her.

Pressing my thumb on her clit and circling it roughly, I know she's close now; I can tell by the way her body starts to tremble and tighten around my tongue. So I double my efforts, wanting to give her this release, wanting to be the reason she falls apart. When she comes, it's a twister that I chase after, drawn into the eye by the way she cries out my name.

"Alistair! Wait!"

But it's too late for that. Her climax has ripped through her, and she is coating my tongue with her cum.

Groaning as I grip her hip tighter, trying to get my face as close to her pussy as I can, I slip my other hand into my pants and grip my cock. Pulling it out, it's aching with the need for a release.

Rising, I loom over her, cock in hand, and she scoots back, terrified. But I grab her ankles and drag her back down.

"Stay," I murmur. It's a fucking order, and she knows it.

Tugging roughly on my cock over her, I keep my eyes locked on hers, watching every flicker of emotion that passes through those depths. She's afraid, but there's something else there, too—a spark of desire, a silent plea for more.

"Don't be scared," I say in a hoarse voice with my need. "I'm not going to hurt you." But even as the words leave my lips, I know they're only partially true. Because what we're doing—it's raw and wild, and maybe it will leave a mark on both of us.

I let her see exactly what she does to me, how she unravels my control. Her breath comes out in short gasps as her eyes lock onto mine, fear and fascination warring within their depths.

"I want you to see the truth. To see how much I want you."

Her chest rises and falls rapidly, and I can tell she's caught between running and staying.

"Alistair," she whispers, her voice a blend of plea and protest.

"I need this," I say, almost grunting with the strain of holding back.

She watches quietly now, her body still trembling from the orgasm that wracked through her moments ago.

My hand moves faster now, the slick sounds filling the room. She's underneath me, but not trapped.

With each stroke, I'm closer to losing myself completely. The pressure builds in my balls until there's no holding back anymore. My groan is primal as the release hits me, the hot rush of my cum spilling over her stomach and pussy in little splats of claim, even if she doesn't realise it.

Breathless, slumped forward with my hands resting on either side of her head, I struggle to regain some semblance of control.

Ever is still as a statue, her wide eyes glued to mine, trying to understand what just happened between us. Her lips part, but no words come out, just a shaky breath that tells me she's still reeling from the intensity.

Carefully, I lift myself off her and reach for the discarded tee on the floor to clean her up. My hands are gentle now, wiping away the evidence of my lust from her skin. She doesn't flinch or pull away; she just watches me with an unreadable expression.

"Next time, I'll be taking all of you, Ever, whether you want me to or not," I murmur.

Her ragged pants are filled with fear, but there is longing there as well. I can hear it even as she tries to mask it.

I step back, giving her space, and she bolts as expected.

But I smile and let her go, even though she's run into the hallway in only her pyjama top. She will have to come asking for her clothes back. Scooping them up, feeling that this night went exactly the way I'd hoped, I dump them all in the laundry basket and then crawl onto the bed to stare at the frescoed ceiling until some form of sleep finally drags me under.

31

EVER

The plates in my hands are like a teetering tower, ready to topple with one wrong step. I weave through the sea of chairs and tables, dodging elbows and handbags, hustling the lunchtime rush from one end of the crowded restaurant to the other. The chatter is a nonstop buzz in my ears, and I can barely hear myself think over the clink of silverware and the sizzle from the open kitchen.

"Table six wants their bill, and table three's been waiting on their refills," I mutter, mentally ticking off the never-ending list of tasks. I flash a practised smile at a group of guys who whistle as I pass by, feeling the familiar sting of annoyance but not letting it show.

"Ever!" My name slices through the bustle, sharp and urgent. My manager, Terry, waves me over, his expression grim. I make a beeline for him, sidestepping a kid running underfoot with a balloon.

"Sorry to pull you from the floor," he starts,

scratching the back of his neck awkwardly. "There's been a change in the schedule."

"Change?" I echo, a knot forming in my stomach. I need every shift I can get; every hour's wages count.

"Yeah." He avoids my eyes. "You're losing your Thursday shift starting next week."

My brain scrambles for a response. "But—why?"

"New policy from the owner. We've got too many part-timers. I'm really sorry, Ever, and to be honest, you're last in, so first out, you know?"

"Great," I say, but sarcasm drips from the word like spilt soup. "Thanks for telling me," I add, keeping the bite out of my voice. Terry nods, looking as happy about this as I feel, which is not at all.

"Get back out there," he says, motioning towards the floor that hasn't stopped moving because my world has. "We'll talk more later."

"Sure." With a deep breath, I plunge back into the fray, tucking away the worry and the frustration. I have orders to take and customers to serve. But in the back of my mind, one thought lingers—how am I going to fix this?

My head spins with questions, but there's no time to chase answers—not when it is heaving in here.

I drop off the drinks and scribble out a bill, all while my brain ticks over like a broken clock. Options. I need options. Pick up another job? But when? My schedule is jam-packed with classes already. It's why I liked this job. It was a couple of shifts, but the tips make up for it.

Made up for it.

Fuck.

"Excuse me, miss, we asked for no tomato," snaps a lady at table nine, her voice like nails on a chalkboard. .

"Sorry about that; I'll get it fixed right away." My voice is sugary sweet, hiding the sour mood behind a spoonful of honey. I spin on my heel back to the kitchen.

There are ten minutes left of my shift, and every single second is taken up, making it fly by.

"Great work today, despite everything," Terry says as I despondently grab my bag to leave.

"Thanks." The word is forced, and so is my smile. I'm not great. I'm scrambling, treading water, trying not to drown in the deep end.

"See you," he says with a wave.

"See you," I echo, stepping out into the fresh air. It does nothing to soothe the heat of frustration simmering under my skin.

My phone vibrates in my jeans pocket, jarring me out of my thoughts. I fish it out, the screen lighting up with a number with my landlord's number.

"Hello?"

"Ever? It's Raj." His voice is gruff, and I instantly tense up. I've been waiting for this call.

"Hey, Raj," I reply, trying to keep my tone neutral.

"I need to talk about the house fire," he says, and I can almost hear the frown in his voice. "Can you give me your side of what happened?"

I grip the phone tighter. "Okay. I was upstairs when it started. So was Lila. The smoke alarm hadn't even gone off yet." My fingers fiddle with the hem of my tee, a nervous tick I can't shake.

Raj is silent on the other end, and my anxiety ramps up another notch. I push on. "We smelled something burning and rushed downstairs, and by the time we realised what was happening, the kitchen was like an inferno."

"Did you see how it started?" Raj's voice is abrupt, cutting through the haze of my recollections.

"No, no clue," I admit, and it kills me that I don't have more answers. "I tried to put it out, but it was impossible. We decided it was better to leave and call 999." I pause, swallowing the lump in my throat as the image of flames flashes in my mind.

"Fine," he replies, but I can't tell if he believes me or if he's just ticking boxes for his report.

I know I should be relieved to get this over with, but instead, I'm wound tight, terrified that somehow, this will all fall back on us.

"I'll call back if I need anything else." The line goes dead.

"Shit," I mutter, my hands shaking as I put my phone away. I have no idea what caused the fire, and the uncertainty is worrying, especially if I'm under suspicion. I wonder if Raj has called Lila. I try her number, but it goes straight to voicemail.

If he suspects us, if he thinks we're responsible, what then? What does that mean for us? Anxiety claws at my insides, relentless and sharp as thorns.

Shit. This isn't good. Not good at all. I lean against the wall of the restaurant, trying to steady myself.

Raj's voice still echoes in my head, his scepticism, the way he drew out his words like he was weighing them, judging us.

Did I say too much? Or not enough? Did I sound guilty? Hell, did one of us actually do something to start that fire without knowing?

I rub my face with my hands, trying to erase the worry etched into my mind. But it clings to me, heavy and unrelenting. If Raj thinks we're to blame, that could screw us over big time. Insurance might not pay out, and then there's the possibility of legal shit hitting the fan.

Fuck! Why can't one thing go right?

I kick at a stray pebble, sending it skittering down the pavement. It's not just about the money. It's the uncertainty, the feeling of teetering on a cliff edge, waiting for a gust of wind to push me over.

The weight in my chest doesn't lift as I make my way back to KnightsGate Manor. There's other things to deal with right now. I'm probably overthinking the Raj thing. Of course he was short. He's worried about his house and the insurance. But it just feels like another battle. I'm exhausted, and I'm running out of armour. First things first. I need to make this study date with the guys. I pick my pace, pushing Raj's inquiry to the back of my mind to join the other stuff, something I seem to be doing a lot of lately.

32

EVER

Rushing in from work, I smell like fried food and panic. Heading up the stairs, stripping off my uniform as I go, I leap into the shower and quickly clean up before getting dressed in casual black leggings and a long black tee to meet the guys in the living room.

I've set up a date with them for two reasons. The first being I need fucking help with this speech. Or rather, how to stand in front of hundreds of people and speak without throwing up. The second is more complicated. In the last couple of days, I've kissed Ben and pushed him away, kissed Damien and pulled him closer, but then he left me alone in the middle of the night and hasn't spoken a word to me since, the incident with Alistair has left me shaken but full of a raw desire that is clawing at my insides and screaming at me to let him take my virginity so I can see if he is as good with his cock as he is his mouth,

223

and Charlie. Sweet Charlie, who hasn't made a move but who I connect with on a deep level that makes me want him to.

What does all of this mean? I'm not the girl who dates multiple guys. I'm not even the girl who dates one guy. I couldn't get up the guts to move in on Alex, and no one seems interested in being with me unless it's for a bet.

Except these men.

Why?

All these questions are plaguing my already over-active brain, and I need answers of some kind.

As I rush into the living room, Ben is already there.

"Hey, Ever." He glances up from his laptop, eyes green and unreadable as the depths of the sea. I nod, trying to shake the memory of his lips on mine and how I wish I hadn't been scared and leaned into it a bit more. But what happened at the party has left a mark on me, despite me throwing myself out there with two out of the four guys I currently live with.

Trust?

Lust?

Insanity?

"Ready to start?" Damien's voice cuts through the haze of my thoughts.

"Sure."

"Charlie will join us shortly," Ben says, and there's something comforting about his presence, like the firm ground beneath your feet after a dizzying ride.

"Great," I mumble, forcing a smile and tucking a loose strand of hair behind my ear. I avoid looking at Damien. If I do, I'll drown in those grey eyes, lose myself in the questions I have.

We wait in silence, the kind that buzzes with things unsaid. It seems so awkward that none of them have touched me since our respective kisses. It leaves me feeling off-balance, like walking on a tightrope above an abyss.

I'm confused and trying to piece together what it all means.

Alistair strides in, his arms laden with books. He doesn't say a word; he just gives me that look. The one that screams volumes without making a sound. It's a promise, a dark whisper telling me he plans on claiming what I've never given.

Again, I wonder what it would be like and if I want him to be the one. He opened up to me last night, which is something I don't think he has ever done, judging by the way he was so awkward at it.

"Ever," he says, voice smooth as silk yet heavy with something else—intent, maybe? The way he says my name feels like a caress, one I shouldn't want but can't help responding to.

Fixing my gaze on the stack of books in his arms instead of those piercing blue eyes. "Hi, Alistair."

He watches me for a moment longer, that look still on his face, before he finally looks away.

Yeah, I'm not going to be getting any answers anytime soon.

Charlie bursts into the room with a grin that's all devil-may-care, and I return it. He's got this energy about him, like he's the star in his own movie where nothing ever brings him down.

"You look as if you're about to face a firing squad rather than an audience hanging on your every word."

"Feels much the same right now," I admit, trying to keep my voice light.

He laughs, the sound rich and easy. "Trust me, once you're up there, it's pure adrenaline. Like stepping onto a stage." He spins around as if illustrating his point, arms spread wide.

"Easy for you to say. I step on a stage, and I want to cry while throwing up and trying not to pass out at the same time. Not so fun."

Alistair clears his throat, commanding our attention with that inherent authority of his. "Speaking from experience, it's about control. Hold them with your gaze, command their attention with your words. It's not unlike navigating the intricacies of a political minefield."

"Great, no pressure then," I mutter, meeting his confident blue stare. There's steel in it, a force that both intimidates and compels.

"None whatsoever," he replies with a sly smirk. "You can do this. Picture them all naked."

Snorting into my hand as the tension breaks, I fall back into these guys just being my housemates and sort of friends. We can deal with the messy stuff later. Right now, I need to get this done.

Ben shifts in his chair. "Remember to breathe," he says simply, his voice even. "It grounds you, centres you. Don't rush through your speech even though the need will grip you to get it over with; let each word resonate."

I nod, but he can see I'm not buying it.

"Trust me. It helps."

Damien leans towards me, lowering his voice to a conspiratorial whisper that sends shivers down my spine. "Imagine yourself conquering the stage, and you will."

"Conquering," I echo, nodding. The idea seems so simple when he says it, yet profound.

"Exactly," Damien confirms, his grey eyes holding mine with an intensity that makes me believe it might be possible.

"Eye contact," Alistair says. "It's about asserting dominance, making sure they hang onto every word."

I nod, biting my lip as I jot down 'eye contact - dominance'. His eyes linger on me, a silent promise igniting a spark in my soul, remembering the heat from our last encounter. It's an inferno that seeps into my bones and sets my nerves on fire. He knows it as well as I do. He must know no one has ever gone down on me before. I was scared shitless he was going to take my virginity, but he was so careful, and afterwards, it meant the world to me.

"Right," I murmur, trying to keep my mind on the task at hand. "Eye contact."

Charlie leans back against the plush sofa, one arm draped over the back, his hazel eyes dancing with mischief. "But don't forget to let your gaze wander. Keep them guessing where you'll look next." He gives me a slow smile, and the atmosphere thickens with something unsaid, a tension that buzzes beneath my skin.

"Keep them guessing," I repeat, feeling the weight of their stares as if they are physical touches.

"Exactly."

"A speech isn't just about words," Ben adds, his voice smooth and reassuring as he flicks a glance my way. "It's about the silence between them. Let it breathe."

I write down 'silence', and for a moment, there is just that. Silence. It stretches out, laden with expectation, before Damien breaks it with a low chuckle.

"Sounds like Ben wants you to seduce the audience with pauses," he murmurs, leaning closer.

"Maybe I do," Ben retorts, an edge to his calm that wasn't there before. "There's power in stillness, in expectation."

"Power in stillness," I say, trailing off as I meet Damien's gaze. There's an unspoken challenge there, a dare to delve deeper into what we're really talking about—control, desire, the space between words where everything truly happens.

"Make them wait for it," Damien adds, his voice a whisper that sends tingles along my spine. "Make them crave the next word."

"Crave," I echo, my handwriting shaky now. The double meanings weave through the air, thick as cobwebs, and I'm caught in the middle, equal parts terrified and exhilarated.

"Anticipation is the key," Alistair asserts, leaning forward, elbows on knees, commanding the room like he was born to do nothing else. "Build it up, then deliver."

"Anticipation," I whisper, and the room hums with something dark and thrilling. The charged atmosphere clings to my skin, an almost tangible caress, and I know, without a doubt, that this study session is no longer just about public speaking. It's a dance, a game of push and pull with words as our pawns, and I'm not sure who's winning.

I feel the warmth of Ben's hand as it brushes casually against my arm, a silent communication that sets off sparks beneath my skin. His touch is light, yet laden with intent, pulling me away from the heady gaze that Damien lays on me. My breath hitches, caught in the crossfire of their attentions.

"Complexity can be captivating," Ben murmurs, his voice even and calm as ever. I nod, pretending to ponder his words about speech delivery, but my mind races with the undercurrents of our interactions.

Damien leans back in his chair, eyes locked on mine, dark and probing. He doesn't touch me, doesn't need to; his stare is enough to send shivers down my spine. The intensity of his look says he knows what's going on inside my head, maybe even enjoys stirring the whirlpool of emotions.

"Captivating."

Alistair draws my fragmented attention. He

doesn't show any sign of the turmoil that must be clear on my face. Instead, he offers a steady, grounding presence as he shifts closer, a small space away from the charged air between Damien and Ben.

"When you stand up there, remember, we're behind you. Every word, every pause—you'll own it."

His assurance wraps around me like a cloak, offering comfort amidst the chaos of my scrambled thoughts. For a moment, I'm grateful for his solid certainty, the way he presents an anchor in the unpredictable storm that has become my life at KnightsGate.

"You don't need to be there," I murmur.

"Invited anyway," he whispers back with a sexy smile.

"Of course." My cheeks go warm as I remember who these guys really are outside of the Academy. They are *somebodies*. Their vast wealth funds this place, and it's high time I remembered that.

"Do you have the speech all laid out?" Ben asks.

"Yes," I breathe. "The Chancellor wants it this weekend to go over."

I glance at each of them—Alistair, with his commanding presence; Ben, calm and reassuring; Charlie, with a smile that could disarm anyone; and Damien, whose stare seems to see right through me. They're all different but seemingly here for me. It's a heady feeling, knowing I've somehow become the centre of their world, even if it's only for today.

"Thanks, guys," I say, and I mean it. For the first

time in a long while, the fear that usually grips me feels distant, like a storm on the horizon that might never reach shore. "I feel a bit more confident. We are down to crying and throwing up."

"Good," Ben replies, his tone soft but firm. "Because you're going to be fantastic."

But the study session isn't over. Something significant has shifted between us. I'm part of their circle now, woven into the fabric of their lives whether I intended to be or not, and as the darkness outside wraps around KnightsGate Manor, I can't deny the thrill—or the terror—of what lies ahead.

I want to ask them, to demand answers, but it doesn't seem the right time. They're all on a different page to me, yet the same to each other by the feel of it. Not that I'm an expert. Do they know that most of them have kissed me, and Alistair kissed other parts of me that make me blush? If I had any of the confidence they have, I'd ask, but as it is, I leave it. Part of me thinks I might not like the answers, which definitely hurts me more than I'd like.

My phone buzzes next to me, and it's a text from Crystal.

Finally.

She's been dodging my calls for days now.

Opening it, I freeze, all the blood draining from my face.

Gulping back the sudden sob that catches in my throat, I excuse myself quickly, blinking back the tears that one of my so-called best friends could be so mean and for no reason.

Hurrying up the stairs, I push open the door to my room and slam it closed, reading the text again to make sure I didn't misunderstand it. But there is no misunderstanding the words I see before me: Hope you die, bitch.

33

EVER

Crystal's words burn on my phone screen, a toxic promise etched in pixels. I can't shake it off. My thumb hovers, trembling as I punch in Lila's number and wait for her to answer. It takes longer than normal.

"Heeey," she murmurs.

"Hey, do you have any idea what's going on with Crystal?"

Lila's words are clipped and cool when she answers. "Nope, haven't got a clue. Sorry, Ever." The line goes dead quicker than I expected.

"What?" I stare at the phone in disbelief. What is this?

Sending a text back to Crystal, the letters blurring into a plea for some clarity, my hands are shaking. Crystal has always played it cool, but she was my friend. We *are* friends. None of this makes any sense.

The house is silent as a grave, shadows draped over every corner like funeral shrouds. I'm alone, except for the echo of my footsteps as I wander downstairs. Wondering where all the guys disappeared, I amble blindly towards the kitchen, hoping for something stronger than water to dull this ache of anxiety in my chest that Crystal hates me, and Lila is acting weird. A sliver of light beckons me, sneaking out from under a door tucked under the grand staircase—a door I'd always dismissed as a cupboard for mops and forgotten dustpans.

Squinting at it, I wonder why the light was left on. Reaching for the brass handle, the metal cold against my palm, it turns easily in the stillness of the night. The door swings open, revealing not brooms or buckets but a space bigger than expected, cluttered with boxes and old furniture that line the walls. Seeing an old portrait of a man who looks just like Alistair, I chew my lip and look over my shoulder as I step inside.

His dad.

The late Duke of KnightsGate

Peering at him with a scowl as he was clearly not a nice man, my curiosity gets the better of me despite feeling so awful about the situation with my friends. Checking my phone again, there are no messages, and it hits me again, making me choke back the sob.

Turning my head as I wipe the tears from my eyes, I draw a deep breath and then frown. The area is clear, save for a few chairs stacked up a few feet away from each other. It seems odd why there is a gap, so I cross over to it and notice another door with surprise. It has no handle, but I can see the outline of it.

Curiosity claws at me, stronger than the unease that's taken root in my chest. This is an old house built on the even older university grounds. It wouldn't surprise me in the least if it has a crypt or something equally as eerie down there. But do I really want to go looking?

The history buff in me screams that I do want to open the door and see where it leads. I mean, it's just there, daring me. My gut twists, the rational part of my brain screaming that some doors are meant to stay shut, but the other part, the part that's hurt and curious, needs something—anything—to drag me away from the mess of my thoughts.

Reaching out to where the handle should be, I push down and hear a click. Pressing my lips together, I feel a spike in my blood and ease the door open. A dark tunnel stretches out before me, lit by sporadic glimmers that dance just at the edge of my vision.

I should turn back, but here I am, stepping into the unknown because the known is too much to bear right now.

The air shifts as I move forward, thick with a musty scent that clings to the back of my throat. Dust motes float lazily in the shafts of light, revealing little about what lies ahead. It's like the tunnel wants to keep its secrets, and honestly, I can respect that.

With each step, a low hum that vibrates through the walls. Voices? My heart stutters, but I creep closer, drawn by the same force that pushes people to poke at bruises to see if they still hurt. Yeah, they usually do.

The darkness isn't pure; there's enough light to make out the rough-hewn stone and the moisture seeping through cracks, giving the whole place an eerie sort of beauty—if you're into the whole 'abandoned crypt' aesthetic, which, for the record, I'm not. It's creeping me out on a scale that hasn't been reached before.

But I keep going, sloping down further into the bowels of the earth.

The voices grow clearer, a reminder that I'm not alone down here. That thought should comfort me, but it doesn't. Not one bit.

The tunnel ends, or at least feels like it should. I edge closer to the source of the murmuring voices, my slippers silent on the cold stone floor. The air is much cooler, sending a shiver not entirely from the temperature.

My fingers trail along the damp wall, guiding me as the light dims further until it's just the ghostly glow from an unseen source. Maybe it's my overactive imagination, but it feels like every shadow holds a whisper of the past, each one urging me forward.

I reach the end, my heart thrumming in my chest like it's trying to break free. There's a corner, sharp and beckoning. I press my back against the cool stone, take a slow breath that does fuck all to calm me down, then I peek around it.

Holy shit.

The sight slams into me, knocking any semblance

of sense right out. Four men stripped to the waist and on their knees—Alistair, Damien, Charlie, and Ben—in a circle around a golden compass, large and ominous.

My hand flies to my mouth, pressing tight against my lips to stifle the gasp clawing its way up my throat. They're moving in a rhythm, a synchronised dance of pain, arms drawing back and then lashing with a violence that echoes against the stone.

It's twisted, fucked up on a level I can't even begin to fathom. They whip themselves, each strike making me jump, a thud that feels like it lands on my own skin. These guys, with their polished looks and smooth talk, are here beating themselves like they're penitents in some medieval cult.

I can't tear my eyes away, even as my brain screams at me to run, to unsee what's unfolding before me. There's something dark and serious going down, and I've unwittingly stumbled right into it.

Or have I?

The light was left on. They know I live here. Did they want me to see this?

No, Ever. Slow your brain down. No one in their right mind would want you to see this.

Every thwack sends a jolt through me like I'm the one feeling the bite of the leather. Shit, I can't even blink. The air in this hidden chamber is thick with something darker than dust, and it's choking me, but my feet are rooted to the grimy floor like I've grown there.

Alistair's back arches with each hit.

God, why?

His face, always so controlled, is twisted in a smile that speaks of pleasure rather than pain and something fierce burning in his soul.

Damien, too, has shed his usual calm. His pale skin is marred with red streaks, the stark black of his hair a shadow against the dim light as he punishes himself. It's silent and terrifying.

Charlie's eyes are shut, his body tense as he strikes himself again and again. He is facing me, so it's good he can't see me, but what happens when he opens his eyes?

Whatever demons they're all facing in this fucked-up ceremony are bad. Big and bad and if this is the type of demon Damien has inside him, I'm no match for it.

This is madness. A nightmare. I am witnessing something that feels ancient and secret and way too deep for me to understand. My mind races, trying to piece together this horror show, but my thoughts scatter, unable to stick to anything that makes sense.

I need to leave, to unsee this, to forget their backs rising and falling with the weight of each stroke. To forget the sight of the whip hitting Ben's back. But my legs won't obey; they're not mine anymore. They're frozen, and I'm just the soul trapped inside, screaming to break free.

Suddenly, the lashes cease, and a heavy silence falls like a shroud over the room. Alistair raises his head, and as he speaks, his voice is commanding and eerily calm.

"Our resolve must not falter. The blood we spill today fortifies our bond for the trials to come."

I press my back against the icy wall of the tunnel, my heart hammering in my chest. Panic claws at me that they'll find me here spying on them, but I'm rooted in place, compelled to understand this macabre scene.

Are they some sort of cult? Is this what power looks like behind closed doors?

The questions swirl in my mind, a maddening whirlpool that refuses to spit out any answers.

Alistair continues, "The pain we endure cleanses us, strengthens us."

I've stumbled upon a secret so vast and insidious that it might swallow me whole. My brain begs me to move, to leave, but my body disobeys, transfixed by the chilling ritual.

sect.

My breath comes in short gasps as I turn on my heels, the word 'sect' echoing in my head like some sinister mantra. Alistair's voice when he dropped that term casually during that eavesdropped conversation flashes through my mind. That same word leapt out from the pages of a dusty tome I poured over for the speech, a speech that now seems trivial in comparison.

Move.

My flimsy footwear slips slightly on the stone beneath me as I scramble back up the tunnel. The voices fade behind me, their low hum replaced by the thundering of my heart in my ears. God, what have I stumbled into? These men, with their secret pains and hidden marks, they're not who I thought they were.

But who did I think they were? I don't really know them.

"Shit, shit, shit..." I mutter under my breath, each step a desperate bid for distance. The damp air of the tunnel feels thick and cloying, wrapping around me like a shroud. I should've stayed out, locked away in my room, safe from whatever madness this is.

But would I be safe not knowing? Or more in danger?

The faint light at the end of the tunnel calls to me. But it's not just the dark that I'm running from—it's the realisation that these men, the ones I've studied with, laughed with, *kissed* and other things, might just be monsters cloaked in human skin.

I burst out of the tunnel door and press it closed, panting. They're a sect of some kind, something old and dangerous, and right now, they're just floors away. How can I look at them the same way after this?

"Fuck," I whisper, glancing over my shoulder as I hurry out of the understairs cupboard and shut the door as quietly as I can, feeling the weight of a thousand questions pressing down on me—questions I'm too scared to answer. I lean against the wall, trying to calm the tremor in my hands and the dread in my gut.

There is a grave darkness that lurks beneath the elite, glossy, polished KnightsGate University surface.

Something tells me that this runs a lot deeper than this house. But *how* deep? Do I have the guts to find out, or am I better off sticking my head in the sand?

34

CHARLES

I blink, and the shadows in the corner of the underground chamber shift. My gaze is locked on the place where I saw Ever peeking out from behind the corner as we engaged in the act of self-flagellation.

She's seen it—the ritual, our secret. The thing we keep locked up tight, away from prying eyes, and now, she's standing on the inside, her world about to tilt off its axis. Her presence here is like a live wire, sizzling through the thick air that reeks of candle wax and something darker.

I know what this means for her, for us. She's in deep now, whether she likes it or not.

"Friday is the day we exact justice for True North. The Elder knows his role."

Hearing Alistair's words, but not really taking them in. It's done. We finish the meeting, but the echo of the final word doesn't fade—it hangs there, waiting for Ever to uncover the secrets we bury in the dark.

As I slip out of the chamber, my mind's a mess, but Ever has stepped into a nightmare, and I can't wake her up. Not yet.

"Shit," I hiss as I make my way back up the tunnel. Do I call it out?

No. Telling now would be lighting a fuse to dynamite. Alistair would go ballistic; his cool façade would crack, revealing the tornado underneath. Ben might look like he's lost in thought, but he'd snap to attention, sharp as a blade. Damien would drag her back in here as quickly as he could.

My head's spinning faster than a carnival ride. If I blurt it out, drag her secret into the light, Ever is thrown into the deep end without a life vest. She's tougher than she looks, but this is another beast altogether. It's not just secrets; it's a legacy of shadows we're all shackled to.

"Damn it," I mutter, every nerve ending in my body screaming that this is wrong. But if I keep my mouth shut, maybe I can shield her a bit longer.

Ever doesn't belong here, not among these ancient stones that have witnessed too much. Her name carries weight, but the darkness we dabble in? It's poison, and she's not built for our brand of chaos.

Not yet.

There is supposed to be more time.

Always more time.

There will be hell to pay when the truth spills out, but for now, I'll let the lie protect her. Just for a little longer.

She's seen too much, and now she's in the game

without even knowing the rules. I rake a hand through my hair, thinking about how she's tied to us now. She's got no idea how deep this pit goes, and I've just let her fall right in without catching her.

I shuffle away from the underbelly of KnightsGate Manor. The shadows seem to reach for me, as if to snatch the secret right out of my chest. I don't let them. With each step, the floor throws my heavy footfalls back at me—a mocking reminder that I'm walking this tightrope alone.

"Fuck." The word barely cuts through the haunting silence. The secret burns in my throat, itching to break free. Ever's green eyes flash in my memory, wide with shock, fear, and *disgust*. She shouldn't have seen what she did.

Waiting's a bloody game, but I'll play it. I'll wait for the perfect moment to spill everything, even though every second weighs a ton. Because when the storm comes—and it will come—I need to make damn sure Ever isn't swept away by it.

35

EVER

A chill worms through my jacket and raises goosebumps on my skin. I keep my head down, books clutched to my chest like a shield as I navigate the sea of students spilling across the KnightsGate University campus. I left home early, so I didn't see any of the guys before I slipped out. The whispers from last night echo in my mind, dark rituals and chants that I can't shake off, making me feel like I'm still trapped in that eerie moment, drenched in a cold sweat.

I can sense the stares; the sideways glances shot my way. I realise my mistake instantly. I'm alone and fair game. Despite his shittiness towards me and many others, Stanley was popular. The resentment that I got him expelled and worse is being aimed in my direction even though I did nothing wrong. I've always been an outsider, but now I'm on the inside of a very hostile situation.

Looking over my shoulder as I stumble over the

grass, when I face forward again, Eric and Robbie are lurking by the old oak tree, sneers plastered on their faces like they're the kings of this place. Gulping, I want nothing more than to turn around and blend into the crowd going the other way. But it's too late; they've seen me.

"Hey, Ever!" Eric calls out, his voice sickly sweet with malice. "Where the fuck are you off to in such a hurry?"

Robbie steps in front of me, blocking my path. "You're not going anywhere, little bitch," he hisses.

"Snitches get stitches."

Gasping, I turn at the poisonous comment of a second-year girl I've seen hanging out with Stanley. They're all around me now, circling me like hyenas.

I try to sidestep them, but Robbie shoves me back. Hard.

A bubble of terror swells in my chest, threatening to burst. These guys have been quiet since the night Stanley drugged me, but now here they are, all fired up and ready to tear into me.

I know it's because I'm alone. Easy prey.

"Leave me alone," I say, my voice steadier than I feel.

"Aw, what's wrong?" Eric taunts, moving closer. "Can't handle being called out for what you are? A whore and a low-class bitch who thinks she's better than everyone."

"Shut it," I growl, anger flaring in my gut.

"Hit a nerve, did we?" Robbie laughs. His laughter is sharp, cruel. Other students start to circle around us, drawn by the commotion, hungry for some drama to begin their day.

"Look at her," someone shouts from the crowd. "Thinks she's all pure and innocent, but we all know she turned on her friends."

"Betrayal suits you," another voice jeers.

I'm surrounded, each insult a slap to my face, a strike to my heart. They don't know a damn thing about me or what happened; I'm the fucking victim, but they're making it out like I was out to get Stanley. All I wanted was to be left alone.

Their words cut deep, opening wounds I thought I'd managed to hide. I stand there, clutching my books, fighting the urge to scream, to lash out, to do anything but feel so fucking helpless.

"Little bitch whore," the girl taunts. "Couldn't get her own guy, so she had to take mine."

"What?"

Staring into her cruel brown eyes, she spits at me. I stumble back, shocked at the abrasive action.

They close in. I have nowhere to turn.

But like a break in the clouds, Ben steps into the circle. Silence falls heavy around us, the taunts dying on lips that suddenly seem unsure. The bullies' faces turn pale, and I can almost smell the fear rolling off them as they step back, giving space to the guy who commands it without saying a word.

"Problem here?" Ben's voice is low and calm, but something underneath it makes my skin prickle.

"No problem, Ben," Eric mutters, and the crowd parts quickly as he and Robbie disappear into it. The others follow suit, leaving me standing there, shaking.

Without thinking, I lunge at Ben, wrapping one arm around him as I smash my books against his chest. Relief floods through me, so intense it's nearly painful. I hear more whispers, hushed and cruel.

"Fucking the Four Cardinals, probably. Who knew she was such a slut?"

Laughter follows, and I bite back the tears, not even knowing what they're talking about.

"Thanks," I manage to say into Ben's shirt, my voice muffled. He doesn't hug me back right away, but then his arms come around me, and it feels like a piece of the chaos inside me settles.

Pulling away quickly when I remember the ritual in the cellar, I trip over my feet and, shaking my head, I hurry away, needing space. Needing to get away from everyone and everything. It's all overwhelming me and as I race into the old KG building and push my way into the ladies' room, I stumble into a stall and let out the choked sob that was thick in my throat.

'The Four Cardinals.' The name buzzes in my head. Have I heard that term before? I can't remember. My head is focused on academics, not people.

Shaking my head to clear it, knowing I have to move or be late when I open the stall door, I come face-to-face with the second-year girl who had mouthed off the loudest, now alone, fixing her lipstick in the mirror. Her eyes dart up, meeting mine in the reflection, and she gives me a cruel smirk.

"Well, if it isn't little, slutty bitch."

It lights a fire under my ass like nothing ever has before. Why do these bullies think it's okay to talk to people like this?

"Hey," I snap, slamming my books down on the countertop beside her, making her jump. "You need to shut your fucking face and listen."

Her eyes widen in surprise at my force. She clearly wasn't expecting it, and quite frankly, neither was I.

"Ever, I—"

"Don't even think about using my name *now*."

She starts to back away, her hands up, and I smirk. She's got a vicious mouth when she's got friends at her back, but here, alone in the bathroom, she's just another cowardly bully.

Good to fucking know.

My glare pins her to the spot. "Who are 'The Four Cardinals'?"

She frowns as if having expected something else from me. "You mean you don't know?"

"Cut the crap." I lean in closer, and she shrinks back. "Who are they?"

Her words tumble out in a rush, her bravado from before completely evaporated. "It's the guys you're living with. How do you not know this? They run everything. People say they can make or break anyone here."

"So if you know I'm living with them, why are you hounding me like a pack of wolves?" I snarl, quite enjoying this shift in power for a change. I will never stoop to her level, but I want answers; I want her to know she can never come at me again with her bullshit.

She straightens up and fixes me with a glare. "We didn't know you were *living* with them, but duly noted. Thanks for the info." Her smirk doesn't reach her eyes as she flees, leaving me alone and shaking with the anxiety of the confrontation, but also this news.

My head hasn't just been in a book all this time, it's been up my ass. Am I the only one who doesn't know this?

In a way, it makes sense. All the times the guys have come to my aid, people have backed off. But they keep coming, so clearly, they don't think I'm involved with any of them, only a poor housemate getting into trouble with bullies and not worth their time.

Until now.

The way the girl said *living* with them has alarm bells ringing.

Picking up my books, I stride out of the bathroom and through campus, my mind a whirlwind of whispered rumours and uneasy glances, that have shifted exponentially. Now, it's fear, not scorn.

The Four Cardinals.

Apparently, they wield power here that I can't even begin to fathom.

I push open the door to the lecture hall, the murmur of students already deep in discussion. But as I slip into a seat, everything erupts into chaos.

"Cheating? That's bullshit!" Nick Henderson's

voice booms across the room, heavy with anger and disbelief. Two campus security guards are flanking him, primed and ready for him to lose his shit. Which is close. Papers fly around him like a snowstorm as he flings the essay into the air. "I have never cheated. You've got this all wrong."

Professor Noblett gives him a disgusted glare and waves his hand at the security guards, who escort Nick out of the lecture hall. My mouth agape, I glance around as all eyes land on me.

My eyes land on Ben, who gives me a slow, sexy as fuck smile and then goes back to reading the textbook in front of him.

Nick Henderson had my phone and taunted me with it a few days ago. And now this?

Done. Just like that. Fear coils in my stomach. Is this the work of the Four Cardinals? Are they really pulling strings behind the scenes?

As the lecture settles into work mode, my hands are shaking. Two students behind me are talking in hushed voices, and one of the girls is crying.

I look over, my pulse hammering, when I see it is a girl who was taunting me when Nick had my phone.

"Shit, man. They're reviewing your scholarship?"

"Out of nowhere! They said there might be discrepancies with my financial information."

"Discrepancies, my ass. You're one of the top students!"

"Guess that doesn't matter now."

Slowly facing forward again, my mouth has gone dry.

What is this?

My mind is a battlefield suspicion warring with the trust I've placed in these guys. Living with the Four Cardinals isn't just a matter of cohabitation; it's a twisted game of chess where I'm unsure if I'm the queen or a pawn.

Leaving English Lit, for once not having a clue what happened, my heart hammers as I navigate the crowded pathways, feeling eyes on me, judging, assessing. It's like walking through a minefield; one wrong step, and everything could blow up in my face. So I keep my head down, trying to be invisible.

Rushing, I don't even see the girls in front of me before it's too late. I slam into one of them, apologies on my lips, which dies off when I see who it is.

Crystal.

"Crystal," I murmur.

Her glare could shatter glass. "Didn't think you'd have the guts to show your face around us again." Crystal's arms are crossed, her posture rigid with anger.

"Can we clear this up, please? Can you tell me what I did wrong?" I plead. "I don't even know why you're being so mean to me."

"Clear what up? That you're a backstabber?" Crystal spits out, her voice rising. A few heads turn in our direction, hungry for the latest drama that's unfolding starring me. Again.

"Backstabber? Crystal, what are you—"

"Save it! We all know about the fire and that *somehow*, you're the one who ends up at KnightsGate

Manor while the rest of us scramble for a place to crash." Her accusation hits like a punch to the gut. Does she believe I started the fire? The idea is ludicrous, insane.

"Crystal, what are you accusing me of, exactly?"

"Oh, cut the crap, Ever. You've always wanted more, haven't you? To stand out from your family's shadow? Well, congratulations. You got your wish at everyone else's expense." Crystal's eyes are blazing, and it's clear there's no reasoning with her.

Lila joins in, her eyes mirroring the same cold judgment. "We know you did this so you could position yourself in that house," she spits out, jealousy laced through her tone like poison.

"What?" I start, my voice desperate for them to understand. "How could I have done that? I was in class. We walked home together and went upstairs."

"Must be nice, huh, Ever?" Crystal crosses her arms, her gaze cutting through me. "While we're all stuck on sofas and floors, you've got your own room in a mansion. That fucking fire cost me this semester, you fucking bitch. My project was in that kitchen!" Tears spring to her eyes, and I want to console her, but she is being unreasonable.

"Crystal, listen to me—" I plead, but it's like talking to a brick wall.

"Save it," Cass interjects, her first words to me sharp as knives. "We're not blind. You played us all."

"Played you? No, that's not what happened—"

"Whatever," Crystal interrupts with a dismissive

wave of her hand. "Just fuck off and never speak to any of us again."

"Wait!"

They turn their backs on me then, leaving me standing there, alone and gutted. The whispers around campus become roars in my ears, everyone watching this humiliation unfold before them. Harsh laughter echoes in the distance, but it doesn't reach my numb heart.

The pain of betrayal is fierce, twisting deep in my heart. How can they think I'd do such a thing? But the doubt and scorn in their eyes are clear—they believe this lie about me completely.

Who would do such a thing?

36

EVER

Back at the house, my hands shaking from all that has transpired today, it's a battle of wills, and I'm losing.

Alistair's azure gaze is like ice, Ben's green eyes calculating, Charlie's hazel spark with an intensity that scares me, and Damien's grey ones are as unreadable as ever. I'm sick of the games, the whispers, the shadows trailing my every step.

I'm being stalked on campus by every fucker who attends the Royal Academy of KnightsGate, and I've had enough.

"This is bullshit," I snap, slamming my palms down on the antique table. "I know you're pulling strings around here; just give it to me straight. Are these things happening because of me?"

Alistair leans back in his chair, the very picture of arrogance. "We haven't the faintest idea what you're talking about."

"Cut the crap, Alistair." My voice is a blade, sharp

and ready to cut through his lies. "You think because of who you are, you can just mess with people's lives?"

Ben arches an eyebrow, his voice calm but irritatingly patronising. "We assure you, Ever, our influence isn't used so trivially."

"Trivial?" I scoff, feeling the heat rise in my cheeks. "You call this trivial?"

Charlie chuckles, but there's no humour in his eyes. "Come on, love. You give us too much credit."

"Or not enough," Damien adds quietly, his expression impassive yet intense at the same time, further confusing me.

Their non-answers twist in my gut, igniting a fire I can't contain. But as I glare at them, determined to break through their united front, I know they won't budge, they won't crack—not here, not now.

Not until I have evidence.

Fine.

I will get it, and we will try this again.

"Fuck you all," I snarl and walk out, wishing to God I'd never kissed any of them or let Alistair get his hands on me.

They probably think they've won this, but hell, no. I will dig until there is nothing left but molten lava lapping at my feet.

Heading out and straight for the library, the scent of old books is like a punch of determination to my senses. I'm going to dig up whatever dirt they're buried in, even if it means poring over every cursed page in this place.

"Come out, come out, wherever you are," I mutter, heading straight for the history of KnightsGate section and grabbing a book at random. If these books hold the secrets to taking back my life, I'll find them. I've lost my house, my friends, my dignity, nearly my virginity, all since I got involved with these Four Cardinals.

It ends now.

Hunching over the ancient text sprawled in front of me, where I first saw mention of a religious sect, my eyes dart from symbol to cryptic letter. Each word is a puzzle piece, and I'm slamming them together, forcing them to make sense. Sweat beads on my forehead, but I barely notice, too caught up in the urgency that's got my heart racing.

"Damn it," I grumble as another dead end mocks me from the parchment. This isn't just some casual reading; this is a full-blown siege of their secrets. *All* their secrets.

I shuffle through the pages, my mind piecing together snippets of legends and half-whispered lore that cling to the edges of each line. There's something here, something they're desperate to keep hidden, and I can almost taste it.

A chill runs down my spine when a fragment jumps out at me—a seal, sinister in its simplicity, etched into the bottom corner of a page. My pulse quickens.

Tracing the outline with my finger, I frown. It's the same emblem I've seen branded above the front door at KnightsGate Manor. The Duke of KnightsGate coat of arms. The pieces click together in my head, a picture forming that's as clear as it is chilling.

This sect—they're not just a campus legend, not just royal boys playing at secret societies. They're older, darker, and woven into the fabric of Knights-Gate and the university itself. If these books are correct, then their influence stretches way beyond ivy-covered walls and hushed hallways.

"Shit," I hiss under my breath, sitting back in my chair. My brain is firing on all cylinders now, fear and adrenaline mixing into a dangerous cocktail that has me both terrified and thrilled. I'm onto something big —bigger than I ever imagined. "Who are you people?"

I flip another page, my eyes devouring the text in Latin. It's difficult and clumsy, but I'm not a book nerd for nothing. I get the gist of most of it. This sect, going by the wholly different title of 'group' to be nice and bland to blend in when you aren't desperately searching for answers, isn't playing at power; they are power. Centuries of manipulation and control threaded through history like a toxic vein. Knights-Gate University was *founded* to be the beating black heart of this Order. My ancestors created this sect along with Alistair's. "What does that mean?" The words come out louder than I'd intended, catching the attention of the student at the next table. I smile lamely and hunch down further.

The library's silence is suffocating, the weight of what I've uncovered presses down on me with an almost physical force. These guys, these students who walk the same halls as I do—they're part of something vast. Something dangerous. But is it just them, or are there others? If so, how many? The Four Cardinals are the leaders? So where are all the followers?

Casting a sideways glance at the student next to me, he watches me intently until he sees me notice him and drops his eyes.

Is he one of them?

As it grows darker, the library lamp casts long shadows across the pages, making the ancient symbols dance before my eyes. I should stop, shouldn't I? This is way over my head, but I need to know where, *if,* I fit into this somewhere.

"Fuck." If I dig deeper, if I poke the beast, there's no telling what might happen. They've already shown they can reach into every corner of campus. Every direction, every... *cardinal point*.

"The Four Cardinals... North, South, East, West. Is that what it means?"

With shaking hands, I pick up another old book, fingers stained with dust and the guilt of knowing too much. The fear is there, gnawing at my insides, but so is the anger. Anger that my autonomy is being stripped away, piece by piece, by these men and their games.

You're playing with fire, Ever.

But the fire is already lit, and I'm the one holding the match. That thought alone makes my decision for me. I can't unsee what I've seen, can't unknow what I know.

Fire.

I take a deep breath, letting the chill of the room fill my lungs. It steadies me and sharpens my intention to get answers. I'll confront them, I have to. With each secret I uncover, their hold tightens, and mine loosens. It's time to tighten my grip.

"Let's see how far this rabbit hole goes," I murmur as I turn back to the texts. My voice is steady now that I know what I'm looking for. Groups, not sects. Groups. "You can't hide from me, assholes." The fear is pushed aside by a sense of purpose. I need answers, and I'll be damned if I don't get them.

These men who walk around with their secrets cloaked in charm—they're not just influential; they're guardians. Guardians of a legacy so dark, so twisted, it seeps into the very foundation of KnightsGate University.

"KnightsGate." I pause, squinting at the text. "KnightsGate. Knights Templar?" I pull my face. "Bit of a reach."

But maybe not. All religious sects start somewhere, and ones as ancient as this one appear to be... fuck. The dots are there, I just need to connect them.

I suck in a sharp breath, the revelation like ice water down my back. They're not just protecting their status or their wealth; they're keepers of an ancient agenda, one that involves bloodlines and power, rituals, and sacrifices. It makes sense now—their obsession, their intensity. They're bound to an oath older than the cobblestones of this fucking place.

"Shit," I curse, the word slicing through the silence of the library. Every whispered word, every lingering touch—it wasn't just some sick game. They've been grooming me, shaping me to fit into their world, whether I want to or not.

A cold wave of dread washes over me, threatening to drag me under. I'm in too deep, drowning in their world of shadows and lies. This knowledge is frightening—I am entwined in their web, and there's no clawing my way out.

There's no ignorance to hide behind anymore, no bliss in not knowing. I'm a pawn in their game, but I'm also the only one who knows enough to bring it all crashing down.

"And they will *never* let that happen."

I close the book with a thump, the sound echoing off the walls. I stand up, my legs shaky but resolute. Fear laces through my veins, but it's edged with something fiercer—a determination to fight back, to reclaim my life from the shadows that seek to consume it.

I slip out of the library, the door closing with a finality that rattles me to my core. "Time to end this."

37

EVER

My feet pound against the cobblestones. The chill evening air bites my cheeks as I make my way towards KnightsGate Manor. It's a fortress of secrets, and I'm about to storm the gate.

Gaight. Gate. However you spell it, it means something here.

"Brave or stupid?" I mutter under my breath, but it doesn't matter now. The darkness inside me stirs, fed by anger and a remorseless need for answers. I can't turn away from this, not after what I've learned.

I reach the towering doors of the Manor and hesitate, my hand hovering over the ancient brass knocker as I look up at the coat of arms.

It swings open, making me jump and clutch my heart with a loud squeak, revealing Alistair's imposing figure, backlit by the low light of the entrance hall. His blue eyes meet mine, assessing, calculating. "Find what you were looking for?"

Stepping past him, I give him a withering glare, which seems to only amuse him. My heart hammers —not with fear, but with the adrenaline of confrontation.

"Join us," he says, and there's a thrill in his voice that matches the dangerous glint in his eye.

He slams the door, and we walk into the living room.

"Ever," Ben greets me as we enter.

"Benedict." My reply is curt, a verbal shield against his calm possessiveness. He knows I'm pissed as I've used his full name, and he arches an eyebrow in acknowledgement that friendship time is over.

Charlie sits beside him, his laughter absent, replaced by a seriousness that sits oddly on his usually cheerful features. "Ever."

"Charles."

He snorts. "Is that the way it's going to be?"

"Yeah."

Damien emerges from the shadows like a spectre. His light grey eyes lock onto mine, reading me as easily as a children's book. "Determined to play your part?" he asks, a challenge woven into the simplicity of his words.

"More than you know," I reply, meeting his stare head-on.

He reaches for my hand and grasps it firmly.

His touch sends a shiver through me, not of fear, but of defiance. His grip is tight, like a shackle, but I don't pull away. "I'm done being a puppet."

Damien's lips quirk up in that half-smile that drew

me into his web of lies. "Puppets have strings, Ever. We're all bound by something far stronger." He releases my hand with a faint squeeze that feels like both a warning and a welcome.

I step back, reclaiming the space between us. "Then consider this me severing the bonds."

A murmur of amusement ripples through the room, starting with Charlie's throaty chuckle and ending with Alistair's bitter laugh. Beneath their amusement lies something darker—recognition, perhaps? They're not used to resistance, especially not from someone who's supposed to be under their control.

Ben stands up; his movements are controlled and precise. "Ever, you've always been part of this, whether you chose it or not."

"And therein lies the problem. I didn't choose any of this. You made those choices for me." My eyes hold each of theirs in turn. "But now I'm rewriting the script."

There's an edge to my voice that slices through the tension in the room.

Alistair steps closer to me, his gaze sharpening. "You think you can simply walk away? That you can expose us without consequence?"

The threat in his voice is as clear as the moon that hangs high outside the window, a chilling reminder that these men aren't just university hotties—they're predators in a game that's been played for centuries.

"I'm not walking away. I'm tearing this down. People are not pieces you can move around the board to your liking. You, this *sect*, it's all elitist bullshit, and it ends. Tonight." My words are empty bluster. I have no clue what I'm even doing except trying to dance out of their reach. They don't know what I know. Hell, *I* don't even know what I know. I'm trying to box them in, to say something, anything that will make all of this make sense.

Alistair's eyes narrow, sensing my conviction, and for a moment, there's silence—a duel of wills where words are weapons and stares cut deep.

Charlie shifts uncomfortably, disrupting the stand-off. "Ever, you don't understand the forces you're meddling with."

I snort at his attempt to intimidate me. "Nice try."

Damien folds his arms across his chest, analysing my every move as if calculating a chess match. "This isn't a battle you can win."

I raise my chin defiantly. "Says who?" It's a bluff, but one I'm willing to play to its last card.

Ben's expression darkens. "This isn't a game."

"Oh, but it is. One that you've been playing at my expense. But I'm changing the rules."

Alistair exhales sharply through his nose, his control slipping for a moment before it snaps back into place like a vice. "Consider your next move very carefully, Ever. Our reach extends far beyond these walls."

The threat hangs heavy, coating the room in an ominous shroud.

Damien once again reaches out to grip my fingers

tightly. He tilts his head and pulls on my arm, forcing me to walk with him.

Pushing down my fear, I lift my chin higher. Whatever they're planning, I won't go down without a fight.

That much, I can guarantee.

The rest, well, I guess we'll find out.

38

DAMIEN

As I lead Ever into the darkness that will latch onto her soul and never let go, I pause as Ben opens the door to the understairs cupboard. The darkness swallows us when we step inside, and I lead Ever over to the secret door. Reaching out, I push the hidden button, and the door swings open to reveal our path—a tunnel that leads to places no one dares speak about. Ever's hand is a cold whisper against mine as we enter the shadows. Her trust has turned to curiosity, and I'm not sure if we will ever get the trust back after this. We knew as soon as she confronted us about the incidents on campus that things were coming to a head. She is too smart, too curious, too pissed off with her legacy not to delve deeper. A couple of phone calls were all it took to ensure Ever veered onto the path we chose for her and ended up here in this moment.

The space feels tighter with her beside me, every step echoing along the stone walls and into the void of my mind where twisted fantasies play out like a macabre dance.

I picture it vividly—Ever, bound and at our mercy, her green eyes wide with fear and something darker, something like desire. The thought alone sends a jolt through me, a thrilling blend of power and hunger that hardens my cock. This is what I crave, this dangerous edge where pain and pleasure meet.

But tonight, I want to watch.

Her aura wraps around me, innocence and steel, and I imagine the ways I could make her gasp and then soothe the ache with my touch. My hands itch to feel her skin, to leave marks that remind her she's ours. But then, I'd chase each crimson line with my lips, a bittersweet apology for the hurt I dream of inflicting.

Tightening my grip on her hand, I ground myself in the present. I want to hurt her, yes, but God, I want to protect her, too. It's a war in my black soul and one I'm not sure I want to win.

The tunnel spills us into a cavernous darkness, where secrets slither through the shadows like serpents. She shivers, her hand in mine, an icy contrast to the heat that simmers in my veins. Ahead, the chamber waits, our playground for tonight's twisted festivities.

There is complete silence.

I expected Ever to ask questions, to be nervous and to ramble as she does when she feels anxious. But she is stoic and rigid. The anticipation coils inside me, tighter and sharper with every step. A gift for her, a secret wrapped in silence and tied with dread. It's something she'll never forget, something that will mark her, change her. My lips twitch into a smirk at the thought of her seeing it all unfold.

As we cross the threshold, the chill of the underground chamber envelops us, swallowing the warmth from our bodies. I tighten my grip on her even more, not just to reassure her but to claim her with the pressure of my possession.

"Watch your step," I murmur, guiding her across the uneven, cold stone floor. The scant light from the entrance fades, leaving us in near-total darkness. I relish the power I have over her, the control. It's intoxicating.

The ritual awaits, and with it, the unveiling of her gift. The moment that will strip her bare, expose her fears, her desires. I can almost taste her shock, her awe. It's delicious.

We stop before a wall carved with ancient symbols, the history of this place etched into the very stone.

Ever twists her head, looking around. Her blonde hair caresses my cheek—an angel about to fall. And we, the devils, are ready to catch her.

Black candles flicker to life as Alistair strikes a match, the flame's brief sizzle cutting through the silence. It's a slight sound, but it echoes in my ears like a starting gun. This is really happening. Charlie follows, his match sparking up another wick. The candlelight throws their faces into sharp relief—grim, resolute.

Ben is almost reverent as he lights the last of the candles. Their soft glow doesn't reach far, but it's enough to make the shadows dance, to give this whole thing a nightmarish edge.

My pulse hammers with a need that's dark and urgent, beating through my veins like a drug.

Ever stumbles slightly, her body close to mine, so fucking close, but this isn't my time. That will come. I can feel the heat of her, smell the faint floral scent of her shampoo. It's intoxicating. She looks up at me, those striking green eyes wide with uncertainty, a silent question hanging between us. She's scared now —I can taste it in the air, see it in the slight tremor of her lips. But there's something else, too, a flicker of defiance that makes me want her even more.

We're at the centre of the chamber now, the red velvet-covered altar looming before us like an accusation. It's ancient, the stone cold and unyielding, and I walk her past it, my fingers digging into her skin. She gasps, the sound loud in the silence.

Alistair nods at me, approval etched into the lines of his face. Ben and Charlie move with a purpose that's been drilled into them; their part in this ritual is as vital as the blood in their veins. Everything hinges on this, on her.

"Good girl," I whisper, almost tenderly, as I press her back onto the cold stone. I let my fingers trail down her arm, a mock caress that has my insides coiling tight with anticipation. Her breath hitches, and I know she feels it too—the pull of the darkness that's about to swallow all of us.

Her eyes catch the candlelight, flickering with fear and confusion. For a second, I'm caught in their depths, drowning in the what-ifs. But then the shadows shift, and the moment's gone. The darkness of this place feeds the hunger inside me.

Ever's chest rises and falls sharply, and I can almost feel her fear. It's potent, the power I have over her in this space where light and shadow merge. My gaze stays locked on hers.

This is our world, a place of control and darkness, and we're about to show Ever just how deep it goes.

Ever's body stiffens against mine, her breath hitching.

Alistair, Ben, and Charlie are like one machine. Each step they take is precise, and each movement is calculated. They finish setting up the last of the black candles and laying out the necessary tools.

"Damien," Alistair's voice cuts through the tension, "It's time."

I nod, feeling Ever's gaze on me, searching for an answer I don't dare give. My fingers wrap around her slender wrist, and I lift it without hesitation. Guided by my hand, the cold metal of the cuff above her head clinks open and then shuts with a finality that echoes in the chamber. She tries to pull away, but my grip is iron.

"Don't fight it," I murmur, close to her ear. Even as the words leave my lips, a part of me thrills at the defiance in her eyes. This is the game we're playing—cat and mouse, predator and prey, and tonight, we're the monsters she fears most.

Her body jerks in a futile attempt to escape as I catch her other wrist, my fingers encircling it with a ruthless grip. The cold links of the chain rattle ominously before I snap them closed around her, anchoring her arms above her head against the unforgiving stone wall.

"Damien, please," she gasps, but her plea is brushed aside. My name, even spoken with such desperation, is a siren call to the darkness inside me.

The candles flicker like the whispers of those long gone, casting a spectral light over us. Their glow bathes the chamber in otherworldly hues, shadows dancing across Ever's face, accentuating the fear and defiance in her eyes. It's like watching an angel trapped in hell—a sight that stirs something twisted in my core.

The chains rattle softly as Ever shudders against them, her vulnerability stark in the dimness. A chill runs down my spine—not from the cold, but from the sheer intensity of what is about to unfold.

I can't tear my gaze from Ever's face; her terror is a blade twisting in my gut. But the thrill surges through me, a dark wave I ride with a sick kind of joy.

"Damien..." Her voice breaks, that one word heavy with an unspoken plea.

"Shh," I mutter.

My fingers fumble with the hem of my shirt, and I yank the fabric over my head in one swift motion. It's a symbolic shedding of civility, of any pretence at decency. The chamber's chill bites at my bare skin, but it's nothing compared to the heat roiling inside me.

Alistair, Ben and Charlie move around us. Their faces are all focus and dark intent, a grim picture against the flickering light. We're all players in this twisted game, bound by desires and traditions darker than the chamber we stand in.

"Ready?" North Cardinal's voice cuts through the thick silence, his tone devoid of any warmth.

The ritual will start, and when it's done, nothing will ever be the same. Ever's life—as she knows it—is about to shatter.

39

BENEDICT

The moment stops my breath. Ever, chained to the wall like some medieval captive, is a sight I can't shake off. She's never looked more out of place than in the dim, cavernous room, her eyes green pools of shock. Around us, the sounds of leather against skin ring out—a chorus of pain we inflict upon ourselves.

I whip myself harder, the sting sharper with each crack, but it's nothing compared to the torment in Ever's gaze. Her tears, silver trails on her cheeks, are like gasoline to my fire. The arousal comes fierce and wild, a storm that rages in my soul, uncontrollable and forbidden.

"Please stop," she whispers, but her plea only tightens the coil inside me. I'm lost in this dark craving, sinking deeper as I watch her break.

When the ritual ends, the whips fall silent, heavy with our sins. I drop mine, the leather slick in my grip, my skin burning underneath. There's a pulse in my head, loud and demanding, as I turn toward her.

Crossing over to the altar, its red velvet catches stray flickers of candlelight as my fingers close around the knife, cool and solid, a promise of what's to come. Each step back to Ever echoes off the stone walls, a drumbeat to my quickening heart. I can feel the weight of every eye in the chamber, but they're just shadows now, blurred at the edges of my vision as I play my part in this ancient game.

Chained and breaking, yet still so goddamn beautiful it hurts, I get closer, and the reality of her terror hits me—hard. Her eyes are wide, fixed on the knife, that sea green losing its fire to something colder, something like the first frost biting into late autumn leaves. It's fear, raw and unfiltered, and it etches itself across her delicate features.

"Ben, please," she chokes out, her voice a shard of glass in the stillness. But there's no going back. Not now.

Her body shakes, small quivers that ripple through her like she's a leaf in a storm. I hate myself for what I'm about to do, for the part of me that craves the sight of her laid bare. Desire is a dark beast, and it's got its claws deep in my soul.

"It's time."

My breaths come in soft pants as I hold the knife, cold and certain in my grip. Ever's eyes are clouded with fear. It cuts deeper than the blade ever could. It almost makes me hesitate.

Almost.

274

The ache to protect her, to tear down these walls and whisk her away from all this madness, is overwhelming. But it is fleeting. There is no place for mercy here. My role is clear, scripted by twisted tradition and expectations I can't escape even if I wanted to.

I press the blade steadily against the fabric of her t-shirt. Her sharp intake of breath only serves to arouse me further. Slicing through the material, slowly and methodically, to my surprise, she doesn't fight, doesn't scream, just watches me with those damn eyes that seem to see right through me. There's a plea in them, silent and desperate, but I can't afford to understand it. Not if I want to keep my own sanity intact.

The knife hisses, a whisper of steel against cloth. Each tear of fabric is a note in a deadly song that has been sung for centuries.

"Please," Ever's voice is a shattered murmur. Her body stiffens, the tremble in her limbs betraying the cold and fear that seizes her.

Peeling her clothes away, bit by bit, I eventually slide the knife under the fragile fabric of her bra, the only barrier left between her bare chest and my burning gaze. Her skin is a canvas of candlelight, each cut freeing more of her from the confines of her clothes. The delicate material gives way with a last gasp, falling to the floor like a broken wing.

Her breasts tumble free, and I stifle the gasp at seeing their luscious beauty, her pink nipples pebbled as if eager for me to bite down on them.

The knife slips beneath the waistband of her underwear, and I pause, looking up at her. Ever's face is etched with terror and humiliation. With a quick snap, her underwear falls away, and I drop to my knees to remove her shoes and socks. In this moment of unwanted intimacy, my lips graze against her pussy. It's not part of the ritual, but I can't stop it. A raw need has taken hold of me, one that I've pushed back for too long now.

Ever flinches, a sharp intake of breath that slices through the thick atmosphere. Tears streak down her cheeks, and it makes my cock go stiffer. She's so vulnerable, so real in her distress, and for a second, I hate myself for being part of what's brought her to this breaking point.

The chamber is dead silent now, like we're the only two left in the world. Just our breathing – hers fast and scared, mine all fucked up with want. We're teetering on some dark edge, about to tumble into something wild and dangerous. Something that will change the game for good.

Time freezes. My hand lingers on her skin, the silence swallowing us whole. Ever's eyes lock onto mine, and I'm drowning in green sea storms.

Rising, I take a step back, my hands falling to my sides, my body aching with a lust I can't put into words. She stands naked, her beauty raw and haunting in the flickering candlelight. Intertwining with the uncertainty hanging thick in the air, I wonder how far we'll fall before the dawn finds us.

40

EVER

Chills claw at my skin, the stone wall icy against my bare back. The shackles dig into my wrists, the metallic taste of fear thick in my mouth. My breaths come out in ragged puffs, visible in the cold air of the underground room.

Witnessing the ritual with them, knowing I was watching, was horrifying. It made it more real, somehow. But now I'm waiting to see if they'll whip me before they do other things that I can't bear thinking about. Not now. Not yet.

We aren't there. Yet.

I'm already bound and naked, and the fear coursing through my veins is terrifying in its simplicity.

Movement near the far right side of the chamber draws my attention away from the men in the circle around the golden compass, my insides withering as the realisation that more people are about to join us.

My eyes widen in shock as the Chancellor of

KnightsGate University, Dave Aldritch, my dad's old friend, strides in dragging someone behind him.

My heart skips a beat. What the hell is he doing here?

Stanley, the asshole who thought he could bully me, drug me and take what wasn't his, eyes are wide with terror, stumbles in behind the Chancellor surrounded by four other men. Stanley's frightened gaze meets mine, and for a split second, I feel a twisted satisfaction seeing him so scared before I remember my current situation, and the fear slices through me again, as cold and steely as the knife Ben used to cut my clothes away.

The Chancellor, it's hard to think of him as Uncle Dave right now, shoves Stanley to the ground, and it hits me like a punch to the gut. The Chancellor is one of them. One of these sect members.

The blood drains from my face as I wonder if my dad is as well.

The Four Cardinals—that's the only way I can differentiate between all the men in this chamber—circle Stanley, like wolves closing in on prey.

I'm shivering. Every muscle in my body tense as Alistair steps forward, his presence commanding the space. The cold of the chamber seeps into my bones, but it's nothing compared to the chill that runs down my spine when he lifts a knife that looks like it belongs in a twisted fairy tale. Its blade catches the candlelight, glinting in a way that makes my stomach clench.

My gaze latches on to his, trying to find an anchor

in this twister that has whipped me up and is throwing me out of control. But there's no warmth in those blue depths, just a dark promise.

He moves behind Stanley, who's whimpering on the ground now, a pathetic mess of fear and tears, and drags him up by his upper arm.

"Please," Stanley chokes out, but his plea is cut short.

It happens in one fluid motion—the blade slashes across Stanley's throat. I gasp and stifle a retch of disgust as his blood spurts out, painting the stone floor. It's unreal, the life leaving Stanley's eyes so fast.

My breath sticks in my throat as my chest tightens. I want to scream, to rage, to cry, but I'm frozen. All I can do is watch as Stanley collapses, his life seeping away into the cracks of the cold floor, and with each drop of blood that falls, I know I'm sinking deeper into this nightmare.

My skin crawls as Alex, the man I thought I knew so well, steps forward with a bowl as much a part of this as the Cardinals. My stomach churns as the silver glints like a warning sign, but there's no turning back, no escape. I struggle in the chains, in fear for my life, my virginity, my whole being.

He holds the bowl against the wounds in Stanley's neck, the crimson liquid dripping into the container. My stomach heaves, bile rising in my throat.

"Ever, don't look away," Alistair's voice cuts through my horror. Obedience isn't a choice; it's survival. So I watch, horrified, as Alex turns to me, the bowl in his hands an offering to some twisted god.

"Pure and untouched," Alistair murmurs, almost reverently. The words are like ice against my fevered skin. "She will be our sanctity."

The Cardinals close in on me, their naked chests a reminder of the welts on their backs from the lashings. Their faces are masks of solemn duty, their eyes devoid of any humanity.

I have never been more scared in my entire life.

Each takes a turn dipping fingers into the bowl, smearing Stanley's blood across my body. It's warm, alive, a contrast so vile against my cold, exposed skin.

"Fuck, stop," I whisper, but they're relentless. Blood marks my forehead, a macabre crown befitting this nightmare coronation. I'm shaking, my flesh crawling under each touch, under the weight of their gaze.

A young man, a freshman, it seems, by his baby face, is the last in the line. He dips his fingers in the bowl, and with a heated stare, he places his fingers between my breasts and slides them all the way down to the top of my pussy.

Alistair's hands clamp down on his wrist before he can dip any lower, and I almost weep with gratitude.

I want to vomit, to scrub my skin raw until every trace of red is gone. But I can't move, chained and painted in Stanley's lifeblood, a canvas for their perverted ritual.

Knees buckling beneath me, I'm forced to my feet

by the wrenching in my shoulders. I cry out with agonised pain and slip on the slimy, cold, blood-soaked stone under my feet. The Cardinals' eyes burn into me, awe swirling in their depths. They kneel before me, the chill of the chamber's air forgotten in the heat of their devoutness.

"Guide us, True North," Alistair says. "Lead us down the righteous path."

"Your light will pierce the shadows of our souls," Ben murmurs, the sound cutting through the fog of my fear.

"Redemption through her purity," Charlie whispers, his hands clasped as if in prayer.

"Salvation in the sacrifice," Damien states, head bowed low.

I stagger, my limbs aching with cold and panic. Their words are poison, a sick liturgy for a ritual I never asked to be part of. My name, my body, they're going to claim it all for their twisted cause.

"No!" I choke out, the word a shard of glass in the silence. "I'm not your fucking messiah."

They look up, startled, as if seeing me clearly for the first time. But there's no understanding in those eyes, only a deep, unsettling hunger.

Alistair stands. "You are light and eternity."

"In Light, Truth; In Eternity, Unity." Ben rises as well and fixes me with a solemn stare.

"Ever, your defiance changes nothing," Alistair adds in a more normal tone now. "There is no refusal. You belong to us."

With a flick of his wrist, he dismisses the Chancellor and the other four men who drag Stanley's dead body into the shadows of the chamber back the way they came, leaving behind an oppressive silence.

Ben and Charlie move toward me. I'm shaking so hard my teeth chatter. They unhook the chains from the wall, but the cuffs stay around my wrists.

I'm naked and vulnerable, and my legs can barely hold me up as they lead me across the chamber.

"Easy," Charlie murmurs, his grip on my arm both restraining and steady as I slip in more of Stanley's blood.

The only thing holding back the urge to purge my stomach of its contents is the thought that if I'm locked down here for an indeterminate amount of time, I'll have to live with the stink of it, and there's enough horror down here already with Stanley's blood everywhere.

The altar looms, huge and covered in a soft red velvet. A red satin pillow rests at the top, The men help me up, positioning me where they want me.

"Please..." My plea dies in my throat as they lift my arms and fasten them to a hook above the altar. The chains rattle, echoing off the walls, a sinister symphony to my entrapment.

"Stop struggling, It will hurt less," Ben murmurs gently, but his voice is distant, lost in the rush of blood in my ears. I can't stop, though; every fibre of my being screams to fight, to flee.

"Shh," Charlie soothes as if calming a spooked horse, but his hands join Ben's as they push back on my shoulders, pinning me down with surprising strength. "Just relax."

I buck against their hold, my skin sliding against the velvet. But the more I fight, the tighter their grip becomes. Frantically glancing around, I see Damien standing off to one side, his gaze unwavering as he takes in the sight of me laid out on this altar. It can mean only one thing.

"Damn you all," I gasp, the words tearing from my lips. But they're empty curses, lost in the vastness of the chamber and the madness that fills it.

Alistair moves closer, too close, his shadow falling over me like a shroud.

"Ever," he murmurs, and I flinch, not from the chill but from the darkness laced in his tone. His voice doesn't have to rise above a whisper to fill the chamber, to wrap around my mind like chains. "This pain and suffering is only a prelude to the pleasure I'll give you."

My skin crawls as if his words are living things scuttling across my flesh—fear knots in my throat, tight and suffocating.

"Fight or yield," he continues, his tone velvet over steel, "it makes no difference. Either way, you'll be mine tonight."

"Stop," I whisper, hating how my voice breaks. But they don't listen. Ben's mouth closes over my nipple, drawing a gasp from my lips at the warmth. Charlie's fingers are cruel in their gentleness, circling my clit, stirring a response I'm powerless to quell.

"Fuck," I hiss as unwanted pleasure spirals within

me. Their touches weave a confusing tapestry of fear and arousal, leaving me trembling beneath them.

Ben reaches out to tweak my other nipple, rolling the tender peak between his fingers with a knowing pressure that sends an involuntary jolt of sensation straight to my core. Charlie's strokes become more insistent, coaxing moans from my lips despite my resolve to remain silent as my pussy betrays me and goes damp from their attention.

I can't look away from Alistair; his eyes are dark pools, holding promises and threats in equal measure. He spreads my legs, naked and triumphant as Ben and Charlie push down on the tops of my thighs to stop me from struggling. The head of Alistair's cock nudges at my entrance, and I brace for the pain.

"There's nowhere to hide from this," Alistair tells me in a voice that rumbles like distant thunder. He holds his hand out, and Damien steps forward, placing something on his palm. Alistair squeezes the tube of lube and rubs it all over his cock before he presses his fingers to my pussy.

I gasp at the chill from his fingers.

"This will ease your pain, angel," he murmurs, working his fingers over my entrance.

"Please," I whimper, tears pricking my eyes as I can't stop the inevitable. I twist my body away from his touch, but the other two guys and the chains make it impossible to escape him.

He removes his fingers and looms over me, gripping his cock in his fist. He guides it to my pussy, and

I brace myself for him ripping away the one thing I had left that was mine.

The first push is excruciating—a searing stretch as he breaks through the barrier I've guarded for so long. My breath hitches, a sharp cry breaking free as I feel myself tearing, opening up for him in a way that is invasive and shocking.

"That's it, angel," he purrs. "Claim my body as your first. Coat my cock in your innocence, stain me with this claiming of my soul."

Gasping as his words send a bolt of unexpected lust driving through me, I go still as the darkness drags me under the surface, and I can't fight it anymore.

41

ALISTAIR

"**E**mbrace this, Ever."

With careful precision, I claim what has been promised, watching the myriad of emotions flicker across Ever's face. Her ethereal beauty is stark in the candlelight, the green of her eyes darkening with every second that slips by.

"Mine," I breathe out, marking her with words unspoken but understood. She's a prize unlike any other, a conquest that will echo through the halls of KnightsGate University, a secret etched into the history of our families.

Victory tastes sweet as I savour the surrender, the power of this moment wrapping around us both like a cloak.

Heat floods my veins, raw and urgent. Ever's breath hitches, a fragile sound against the backdrop of shadows dancing on ancient stone. I'm relentless, driven by an all-consuming hunger.

Her struggles, once fierce and determined, melt into whimpers that are music to my ears. The fight leaves her in waves, each one crashing into surrender. I leverage my body over hers as I sink my cock deeper into her pussy.

"Please," she moans, the sweetest plea I've ever heard.

"Ever," I rasp, her name on my lips driving me further.

Her body opens up like a secret, her resistance crumbling under the onslaught of sensation.

With each thrust, I'm etching myself into her very soul. My balls are aching to explode inside her, filling that sweet, innocent pussy with as much cum as I can.

I watch her beneath me, every tremor that ripples through her body tells me she has accepted her fate. She is mine. I've claimed her, and there is no turning back now.

"Fuck, Ever," I groan as I feel her pussy encase me completely as I thrust deeper. She whimpers as the feeling is too much for her. Pulling back, I drive into her again, her pussy soaks me, surprising me. She is closing in on an orgasm, and it's more than I could hope for. She is lost to the darkness, to the men surrounding her. To me.

"Let go, angel," I murmur through gritted teeth, feeling my own climax building at my base.

My cock slides in and out of her easily now. The lube is easing the way of her tight little pussy.

"Fuck, so tight," I rasp, the words tumbling from

my lips. "So fucking tight. You're perfect, angel. Fuck, you're perfect."

She gasps, her eyes locking onto mine.

"Help her," I murmur to Charlie, who immediately slips his fingers over her clit as I pull back slightly to allow him access.

She bucks beneath me, the added touch driving her closer to the edge. Charlie's fingers work her with expert attention, his dark gaze never leaving her face as he looks for every sign of her unravelling.

"Ours," I murmur, my voice a low growl as I feel Ever's inner muscles flutter around my cock.

Her cries grow louder as the other men, even Damien, move in closer to witness this pleasure. We are all entrapped in this dark rite, this claiming that seals her to me. To us.

It's too much for me to bear. I'm relentless now; there's no holding back. My hips jerk forward with a brutality that matches the dark craving inside me.

"Fuck," she moans. "Fuck."

Charlie groans softly as he speeds up his attention to her clit. I feel her dampen my cock further. She's close, so fucking close.

Ever shatters, her orgasm ripping through her body like a fierce storm as her back arches, the chains rattling above her as her arms pull against them. Her pussy clenches tightly around me, milking me for all I'm worth. It's ecstasy and agony wrapped in one, the intensity nearly blinding me as I ride out her climax.

The wave of my release crashes over me. "Fuck! Ever!" The words tear from my throat as I spill my cum into her, every pulse of my cock marking her deeper with my essence.

Sated and needing the next step more than I need to drag air into my lungs, I pull out of her gently.

Damien emerges from the shadows, his grip tight on the knife, blade gleaming an ominous silver. My pulse quickens; this is the plan, our pact made flesh.

"Ready?" Damien's voice slices through the quiet.

A nod is all I give him, the signal to proceed with what must be done.

With careful hands, Ben lifts Ever to a seating position as her eyes dart around, her pleasure still clouding her mind, her back exposed like a canvas awaiting the artist's final stroke as I move around her.

"Shh..." I murmur, a seductive poison meant to soothe as Ben holds her steady.

Damien hands me the knife. It's cold in my hand, a familiar weight, a responsibility I bear as their leader.

The tip of the blade touches the skin at the top of her spine, and a sharp breath escapes her lips.

I carve meticulously and slowly, needing her to feel every second of what I'm doing to her. Marking her, Scarring her for life.

Her response is a cry muffled against Ben's arm, yet it carries the weight of her surrender. Each letter carved binds her closer to our world, a world where light and dark play the same treacherous game. Her struggles wane, her body yielding to the inevitable as the letters take shape—each one a mark of possession, each one a scar that tells a story of dark love and darker desires.

In Light.

The irony of the words isn't lost on me. In this chamber of shadows, where power is our doctrine and lust our prayer, the light has no place save for the one we brand upon her.

We have marked Ever, claimed her in every way that counts in our world. And as I watch the crimson lines form the words that now define her, I know we have crossed a threshold from which there is no return.

I step back, and my chest heaves with heavy breaths, not from exertion but from a dark satisfaction that coils in my gut. Charlie laughs, a sound that bounces off the stone walls and fills the space with a haunting echo. Ben releases his hold on Ever gently, his eyes never leaving the crimson-stained words that mar her skin.

"Beautiful," Damien murmurs, his grey eyes reflecting the flicker of the candles that light the room. He means the cruel artwork on her back, the way it declares her ours, but I see the twisted beauty in all of it—the power, the possession, the pain.

We're all silent for a moment, taking in the sight of Ever, sobbing and curving her back against the pain as she hangs her head, wanting to wrap her arms around herself but unable to. She is marked and broken, yet undeniably part of something greater than herself. She's no longer just a scholarship girl, an outsider among the elite. She's bound to us by blood and by darkness. It's fucked up, but it's the truth.

This is our world—a place where desires are law, and consent is a blurred line. We stand around her, kings in a kingdom of darkness, watching as Ever bears the physical manifestation of our dark love for her. She is ours in every sense of the word.

42

EVER

Shivers race through every inch of my body, clenching every muscle until they ache. The red velvet of the altar scratches against my bare skin, a harsh reminder of what has just been taken from me. My soul aches and feels sick from the brutal murder I witnessed. My wrists are raw from the chains that dangle overhead, echoing the throbbing pain carved into my back by Alistair's blade. I don't even know what he did to me, what he carved into my flesh.

"Beautiful," Ben murmurs, and there's a rustle of fabric as he strips off his pants. His movements are deliberate, almost reverent. The air shifts and grows heavy with his intent. His eyes never leave mine, dark pools of desire that seem to reach inside me, stoking embers of fear and something else—something dangerous and forbidden.

"Wait," I murmur, knowing what's coming and

I'm not ready. My pussy is raw and aching, and I can't. I just can't.

Panic grips me as Ben closes in, the shadows of the chamber clinging to his skin. I'm frozen, a deer caught in the blinding headlights of his lust. He's over me now, his breath hot against my cheek, and there's no room for doubt. It's real, raw, and it's happening.

"Ever," he whispers, and that single word is like a match struck in the darkness, igniting a fire that I don't want but can't snuff out. His hands are on me as he pushes me back, the fire from the wounds on my back making me gasp loudly in the stillness of the chamber. Firm and demanding, he pries my thighs apart with an ease that belies the storm in his gaze. My mind screams, pushing against the helplessness that shackles me tighter than these chains. But there is no stopping it.

He pushes his cock inside me, and a gasp rips from my throat that mingles with his groan of sheer longing. Each thrust is a declaration, a forceful claim that marks me just as surely as the knife did. But there is a fucked-up undeniable surge of pleasure that makes me want to sink into the depths of this dark ocean, even as I fight to stay afloat. It's a twisted dance, pain mingled with pleasure, and I'm lost in the rhythm of Ben's controlled movements.

His thrusts are steady, even. His eyes are fixed on mine, and a hint of a smile curves his lips up. "I love you," he murmurs.

I blink back my surprise as he thrusts deeper. My

pussy is so fucking sore, but I can't move, I can't even breathe.

He pounds into me with a ferocity that wrenches my shoulders caught up in the shackles above me. I know that there is no way I can give into the pleasure. It's too soon, too painful, too overwhelming. Moments ago, I was a virgin, now I've claimed two lovers and who knows how many more to come. My mind starts to close down as that thought is dark and frightening.

With a low growl, he thrusts deep and then freezes as he shoots his load into me.

He pulls away, leaving me in shock. But there's no time to process, no moment to catch my breath because Charlie is already stepping forward.

"Shh, love," he soothes. There's a tenderness in his touch that differs from Ben's intensity. Gentle fingers brush against my skin, tracing invisible lines only he can see.

I whimper and shake my head. "Please. No more."

But it's like my voice is lost in a sea of desire.

Charlie's hands, steady and warm, dip into a bowl of water beside the altar. When he wrings out the sponge, it drips, clear droplets falling onto my skin, cooling the burning that throbs between my thighs. His fingers are gentle as they cleanse me, wiping away the remnants of Alistair's and Ben's possession. I flinch when the sponge brushes too close to the rawness.

His care is a paradox, kindling a fire in the pit of my stomach despite the icy dread coiling around my heart. It's a cruel game, this pretence of tenderness, and yet my body betrays me, responding to his touch with an eagerness that tastes like shame.

As he discards the sponge, his hand replaces it, cupping me with an intimacy that has tears spilling down my cheeks. The sound of my sobs fills the chamber, echoing back at me like a chorus of ghosts. He looms over me and pushes his cock inside, slow at first, a careful exploration that belies the hunger in his eyes. My back arches against the onslaught, seeking more even as my mind screams in protest.

His pace quickens, each thrust igniting sparks that race along my nerves. The pleasure mounts, a rising tide threatening to wash away reason, dignity, self. I cling to the edge of sanity with my fingertips, teetering on the brink as Charlie drives me closer to oblivion.

In an unfathomable act of betrayal to my mind, my pussy convulses around his cock in a climax that rips a strangled cry from my throat. It's a brief respite, a momentary lapse in the relentless assault on my senses, leaving me hollowed out and gasping for air as he unloads into me with a satisfied grunt that echoes around the chamber.

But there's no time to recover, no peace to be found, as the chamber erupts into chaos. Voices clash against the stony silence, sharp and jarring. Robbie and Eric are dragged in, their protests a noise that grates against my raw edges.

"No," I whimper, shaking my head as my terrified gaze catches Charlie's. "Please, no!"

"Don't worry, love," he murmurs. "They won't touch you."

Eyes wide, I stare at Robbie and Eric and the other four men who anointed me in Stanley's blood. The remainder of that earlier horror churns my stomach, my nakedness a glaring declaration of what's been taken from me, what's been done to me. There's horror etched into every line of their faces, reflecting my own inner turmoil. They're seeing me broken, desecrated on an altar that was never meant to bear witness to such acts.

I'm stripped bare all over again, exposed in ways that go beyond the physical.

Shock ripples over my bullies' features, eyes wide and mouths agape. They're trying to make sense of the scene, but it's clear—their brains can't process the nightmare in front of them fast enough.

Charlie's hands are warm on my skin as he unlocks the shackles that confine my wrists. The clink of metal is loud in the hushed room, and when the last chain falls away, my arms follow, heavy and life- less. His fingers gently rub where the cold iron bit into my flesh, soothing the raw, angry marks as Ben rubs my arms to get the blood to flow again. The dull ache is no match for the burning between my legs, the wounds on my back, or the gaping maw in my soul.

"Good girl," Charlie whispers, but his tenderness feels like a lie. It's a softness that doesn't erase the harshness of everything that has happened since I set foot in this chamber, this house. The gentleness does nothing to mend the brokenness inside me.

I'm shivering, but not only from the cold. It's the aftermath, the vulnerability, the lingering echo of all the events rolled into one that has me quaking.

"Eric spread rumours about you," Ben murmurs into my ear, his breath warm against my skin as he continues to caress my arms. The words slither through my mind, cold and nasty.

"Robbie lit the match that torched your place," Charlie adds, his tone dripping with disdain. It's all a twisted chorus, their accusations gnawing at my thoughts.

"Liars," Robbie spits out, his voice edged with desperation as Alex kicks him in the back, and he falls to his knees. Eric stands beside him, shaking his head vehemently, eyes wide with disbelief.

"What is this fucked up shit?"

"Think of what they've done to you, Ever," Alistair presses, his stare unyielding. "They tore your friends away from you. Burned your house down. Isolated you."

"Fuck," I mutter under my breath, my gaze darting between Robbie and Eric. My chest heaves with each breath, my mind racing with images of flames, betrayal, loss.

"They placed a bet to see who could drug and rape you first," Damien murmurs.

Shaking my head, I try to swallow, but my mouth has gone dry. What is this? What are they doing?

"They've fucked you over," Ben says, his voice low and coaxing. "Bullied you, hurt you, made your friends hate you."

"How..." I trail off as words are impossible right now.

"Think about your home, charred and broken because of him," Charlie adds, nodding toward Robbie with a sneer.

The room is silent except for my breathing, harsh and ragged against the stillness. The tension hangs heavy, like a storm cloud ready to burst.

Alistair's hand is steady as he offers me the knife, the blade catching flickers of candlelight. His eyes lock onto mine, blue ice burning with expectation. "You have a choice to make, Ever Knight," he murmurs, his voice a dark melody that pulls at the strings of my will. "And make no mistake that you *will* choose. Which one will you kill first?"

Read on immediately with Burn Me, Book 2
Burn Me
The Second KnightsGate Duet which will feature Alex in Year 3 can be pre ordered: https://geni.us/RAKG2

Join my Facebook Reader Group for more info on my latest books and backlist: Eve Newton's/SE Traynor's Books & Readers

Join my newsletter for exclusive news, giveaways and competitions: Eve Newton's News

ALSO BY SE TRAYNOR

https://evenewton.com/se-traynor

.

Made in the USA
Middletown, DE
20 March 2024

51825055R00170